DARK GENESIS

The Darkling Trilogy

Book 1

A. D. Koboah

Twenty Four fantasy
PUBLISHING

www.adkoboah.co.uk

Copyright © 2012 A. Addo

Cover design: http://ronnelldporter.wix.com/design

ISBN: 978-0-9573003-0-9

To Jan and Jonesy. Thank you for your support.

Atlanta 2011

I don't know why I got such a sharp presentiment of danger from the woman – no, girl – leaning against the lamppost ahead of me, but I did and it was strong.

I've had warnings like that before. For example, I knew my grandmother was going to die months beforehand, even down to the exact time and date. And when I first laid eyes on my ex Carl, I'd had a warning which I ignored, something I bitterly regretted months later when I found out what a lying, cheating dog he was.

The strongest one by far happened a few years ago when I left my parents' apartment on New York's Upper East Side and heard a voice, or something I perceived as a voice, in my head saying gently but insistently: *Not that way*.

It stopped me cold in my tracks and I stood on the sidewalk taking in quick startled breaths as snow, light and ethereal, fell all around me. Realising that the doorman was looking at me quizzically, I began walking away, treading carefully through the snow, having to stop and turn around when I realised I was going the wrong way. That was when I heard a loud screech of tyres, what sounded like an explosion and the awful gut-wrenching sound of twisting metal.

Knowing somehow that I needed to see whatever had made that noise, I hurried down the street and around the corner where the sight of a green car wrapped around a lamppost met my horrified gaze. I don't know if that car would have hit me if I hadn't been spooked by the warning and gone the other way, but it scared me nonetheless and feeling like a criminal, I ran away from the awful sight to slip and stumble my way back home.

This one was a lot more intense than the one I'd had that day in the snow. It was like a vibration in my mind, getting stronger with every step I took toward the girl and had my whole body tingling in response to the perceived danger. She may as well have had a neon sign above her head flashing 'Warning!! Danger!!' and I couldn't understand why because the woman – no, girl – leaning against the lamppost didn't appear to be much older than sixteen and couldn't possibly be of any threat to me.

It was dark, yes. But there were lampposts casting little oases of light along the street and I was only a couple of doors away from my aunt's home. The street was deserted, yes. But I was in a nice middle-class area of Atlanta and there were plenty of lights on in the two- and three-storey townhouses on either side of us. And she was tiny, no more than five foot tall and very slight, making me feel like a giant at five foot eight. I couldn't see her expression as her long braids had been parted down the middle and hung like a curtain over her face, but I'm sure I wouldn't have seen anything sinister even if I could. She looked like a normal teenager in her spaghetti strap yellow summer dress and sandals.

Yet the scent of danger was strong, like thick smoke in the air and as I got closer, I knew somehow that she was waiting for someone to prey on. She may have appeared completely oblivious to my presence, but I knew, I just *knew* that her thoughts, along with her heightened senses, were attuned to my every movement as she waited with an air of heavy anticipation.

When I was a few feet away from her she looked up and smiled.

6

"Hey. You got a light?" she asked.

Her voice was soft and breezy. She was still smiling but there was something sly and furtive around her eyes and in the curve of her lips.

"Sorry, no," I said, not breaking my stride.

"Sure you do," she said, falling into place beside me.

It seemed she wasn't going to take no for an answer, which wasn't a surprise as there seemed to be something about me that gave most people the impression that I was a bit of a pushover. It must have been something about my small delicate face, soft sleepy-looking brown eyes and generous mouth that had them fooled. Perhaps that was why this girl was following me, smiling slyly as if she knew something I didn't. Well, she was about to find out that Dallas Marshall was no pushover. So I faced her, ready to deliver a cutting remark, but then stopped and simply stared.

I was looking at her but I was no longer seeing a young girl. Instead I saw a much older woman of around forty-five. What I was seeing was bizarre and yet I knew that this was the same person. I was seeing her as she really was or as she would have been. This made absolutely no sense but it was exactly what my sixth sense was trying to show me.

I blinked and the impression was gone. All I saw now was the same young girl, but instead of that sly smile she now wore the same shocked expression that was no doubt on my face and I had the horrifying sense that she could read my thoughts and had seen what I saw a moment ago. I also knew that she was angry and frightened by the fact that I somehow knew she wasn't what she appeared to be. Her eyes narrowed to thin slits and that is when I knew with one hundred per cent certainty that the warning had been right. She was dangerous. Very dangerous and she had no intention of letting me live to see another day.

"What...?" she began and then went rigid and her head slowly veered to the right to look down the dark street from which I had just come.

Her face contorted with fear and she started to tremble. I followed her gaze and thought I saw something in the dark for a moment, someone standing in the shadows watching us. But it must have been my imagination because there was no one there. And yet she was terrified. She still looked like a cat that had cornered something but now her expression betrayed the fact that the defenceless mouse she had been toying with earlier had turned into something much deadlier.

"Okay, cool. S-sorry I bothered you."

She walked away and quickly crossed the road before I had time to respond, looking back over her shoulder at me and then down the street as if she expected something to pounce on her at any second. I turned in that direction but there was no one there.

I felt silly now for thinking she meant me harm. She was just a kid and she had only been asking for a light.

I was about to call her back and offer her the lighter I had in my purse but when I turned around, she was gone and I could only stand there wondering where she had disappeared to so quickly.

I continued on my way and tried to forget that girl but there was something about the whole thing that had left me deeply uneasy. Worse, I still couldn't shake the feeling that I was lucky to be alive.

***

Later that night, I wandered into the garden at the back of my aunt's small but homely two-storey town house with a glass of rum and Coke. It was past midnight but insomnia, my faithful friend, was once more keeping sleep at a distance, so I sat down on the back step hoping that the balmy night air would help draw it near.

As I sipped my drink, the scent of the gardenias drifted by on a light breeze and I felt loneliness clamp down on me like a tight fist. My grandmother had loved gardenias so we had planted them in her memory when my aunt bought this house two years ago. God, how I missed my grandmother. She had been a refined, stately woman with a beautiful rosewood complexion and had been more of a mother to me than my own distant, superficial mother would ever want to be. With Grandma gone, I felt desperately alone and found no respite from the emptiness that had been with me for as long as I could remember. It also meant that there was no one to act as a buffer between me and my parents and the arguments at home had gotten worse, reaching a new level of viciousness when I dropped out of college at the beginning of the year and spent the following months partying.

I hated my parents at times. The rest of the family were no better. They were a haughty, driven bunch who seemed to care only about increasing their millions. Aunt Rose, a humble, caring artist was the only one who was any different. She had chosen to make her own way in the world on her small income as a sculptor. But then again she didn't want anything to do with the Marshall family millions as she thought the money was cursed. And I suppose she had good reason for thinking that.

For as long as I can remember, my relatives have joked about the Marshall family luck or our guardian angel. And from the stories I've heard over the years, it would seem that we have been very lucky. Even during slavery our family had been fortunate enough to escape some of the hardships that blacks suffered during that particular point in history, and in some cases, we'd even managed to prosper. There were also stories of ancestors who had ended up in some dire life-threatening situations only to somehow come away unscathed. The one told most often was the story of Jonas, a free black living in the eighteen hundreds whose life almost came to a premature end when he fell down a well. He spent most of the night in that well treading water and was sure he would die there. He eventually lost consciousness and awoke to find himself lying at his front door with no knowledge of how he had escaped the well.

Another such story was about Lina, Jonas's mother. Her parents and siblings had been runaways living in the north who were captured by their Master and were about to be taken back to the south when a mysterious benefactor had bought their freedom. Despite their attempts, the family had never been able to find out who this man or woman was or how they had been able to persuade their Master, who had said many a time that he would rather die than let any of his slaves taste freedom, to sell them.

There were many stories like that right up to the present day and I thought they were all just that, stories. Tall tales that my relatives had invented to keep from thinking about the proverbial pink elephant in the room. And that pink elephant was why so many family members had met gruesome deaths under mysterious and often bizarre circumstances. Sometimes it was suicide but most of the time it was murder, the details of which were horrific enough to make the hairs on the back of your neck stand on end. And the really odd thing was that in each and every circumstance, the assailants were never found. The police could expend large amounts of resources trying to find the murderers but they never ever found so much as a stray hair to help them in their investigations.

At least three such deaths occurred in every generation and that sure as hell wasn't the norm for the average family.

Even so, I didn't share my aunt's view about the money being cursed. Every family had their demons, ours just happened to be a little bit stranger than others. To me, the family millions were a blessing and when I received my inheritance on my twenty-first birthday in a few months' time, I would enjoy spending every last penny. And if the money did turn out to be cursed then I would make sure that when I met my end, it would be at a bar with one hand on a fine-looking man and a tequila in the other. Yep, there was nothing like endless nights of drinking and dancing to keep the yawning emptiness that was forever snapping at my heels in check.

Knowing that this would be one of those nights when sleep would fail to arrive, I thought about bringing my sketchpad down so I could spend the next few hours drawing. But in the end, the memories of my grandmother were so hard to bear that I left the balmy warmth of the night air and stepped inside, making my way to the basement where I knew my aunt kept some of my grandmother's things.

Interestingly, the basement was the only room in the house that was kept in order and I made straight for a large wooden trunk, grandma's trunk, and opened it. It contained books, photo albums and the quilt I had come in search of. As I scooped up the quilt, my fingers brushed against something at the bottom of the trunk, and as sometimes happened whenever I touched an object, I received a vibe or a psychic impression.

I jerked my hand back in alarm, as whenever something like that had happened in the past, the impression I received was usually vague and indistinctive like a hazy dream. Besides, alcohol had the effect of dulling these psychic vibes down to nothing, and yet what I got this time was so strong it took my breath away. Letting my curiosity get the better of me, I carefully reached under the quilt and picked up a battered leather-bound notebook.

And there it was again. It wasn't so much an image but a strong emotional vibe of a woman in love. A fierce – *if I can't have him I'll die* – kind of love.

It was starting to fade, which was a relief because the force of the emotion was debilitating, and I felt a little bit disturbed by the intensity of it.

Had this belonged to Grandma? Was this how she had felt about my grandfather?

I would have liked to believe it was, but I had been

around them long enough to know that it wasn't. Theirs had been a slowly unfolding kind of love, like a warm languid sunlit afternoon filled with joy and laughter. This was something else altogether and I couldn't imagine how someone could function with that degree of emotional attachment to another human being. How did it not drive her insane?

I was one hundred per cent sure that this journal wasn't written by Grandma. But I felt a familiarity, or a connection with the unknown woman who had written it so there was no way I was going to put it back inside the trunk and just walk away. So, completely forgetting about the quilt, I closed the trunk and left the basement with the journal held to my chest.

As I mounted the steps to the spare bedroom, I could feel excitement building and by the time I finally settled into bed and opened the journal, my hands were shaking.

I didn't need my sixth sense to tell me that this book was important. But what I didn't know was that it would end up being the single most exciting discovery of my life and that everything was about to change.

Chapter One

My name is Luna and my tale begins on a dry summer evening in 1807.

I was walking quickly along a dusty country road, my shoes stirring up a small cloud of dust that turned the hem of my faded violet dress a muddy brown. The trail of dust I left in my wake soon settled. But the pressing need that had me make this two-hour journey in beaten shoes and a broken spirit, in the midst of a particularly merciless Mississippi summer, would not be settled as easily. Wiping the sweat from my brow and waving away the flying insects that droned lazily near my face, I wished for some respite from the relentless heat but found none. Although the sun hung low in the topaz blue sky, it felt as if I were walking through warm soup and it was likely to stay like this long after the sun went down.

I would have found some relief from the pitiless sun if I had chosen to walk through the woods that rose up on either side of the road like a green and brown wall. But green woody spaces such as those have been a deep source of fear for me since I was a child and I imagined that they would continue to be so long past what I guessed was my twenty-second or twenty-third year on this earth. So I clutched my lantern and small cloth bundle and walked on in the heat, listening to the birdcalls punctuate the otherwise still air.

I was lucky to be able to make this journey during the summer months as the previous two trips had been made in the dead of winter when night gathered up the day long before I could finish serving the family's supper and slip away, leaving the other house slaves to do my share of work and conceal my absence. That small mercy meant that I didn't have to walk alone in the dark, afraid to light my lamp in case the solitary glow brought unwanted attention my way, or have to dive into the trees every time the sound of a horse's hooves disturbed the sweet melody of the crickets. It also meant that when I turned the corner and saw the woodland give way to cotton fields, marking the beginning of the Marshall plantation, there was still roughly two hours of daylight left, which meant I would be able to finish my business and be back before dark, hopefully before I was missed by my hawk-eyed mistress.

I stopped for a second to gaze at the rows of cotton up ahead. I have always thought that there was something heavenly about cotton fields, which looked like row upon row of fleecy white clouds caught up in brown nets. But I'm sure that the brown-skinned figures bent double between those rows would have disagreed. For them, there was nothing even remotely celestial about the cotton fields in which they had been toiling since sunrise. And they were likely to still be working in them when the sun set. Even from this distance I could see that most of them were wretchedly thin, their few flimsy items of clothing in tatters. And although I wasn't close enough to see their faces, I was sure that they all wore uniform expressions of misery and fatigue.

I left that unhappy sight and ducked into the trees on my left, a necessary shortcut to the slave quarters. Although many slaves have used this shortcut on their way to see the African woman, I'm sure I'm the only one who ran all the way through the trees looking back over my shoulder even though I knew I wasn't being followed. Only when I saw a flash of white through the trees did I slow down so my breathing could return to normal by the time I exited the screen of trees.

The slave quarters were little white cabins made of wood, which lay in two long rows some distance from the Master's mansion. Only a few children were around at this hour, some of whom recognised me and stopped what they were doing to stare with a quiet reverence that made me uncomfortable. It was the same reverence I had received from the grownups the last two times I had come here under the cover of darkness and they had not only stopped what they were doing to watch me pass by, but nodded or offered some sort of greeting, which I returned before hurrying on by. I didn't have to endure that kind of scrutiny today, but I still hurried down to the lone cabin at the back of the clearing, which was nestled under the shadow of the trees some distance away from the rest of the slave quarters.

Many slaves came to visit Mama Akosua for her medicines, and her skills were known far and wide. It was also rumoured that she dealt in more than just herbs and was actually a witch. Whether that was true or not, she was feared by many, even some of the whites, and few dared incur her wrath.

As I got nearer to the cabin, I saw that the door had been left open and a light was burning inside even though the sun had yet to go down. I approached gingerly. Already feeling the unease that always possessed me in the presence of the African woman, I walked up to the door, and stopped.

"Mama Akosua."

There was a short spell of silence and then her voice floated out to me.

"I have been expecting you." The voice was low and dry like the sound of rustling leaves.

She probably said that every time someone came to her door, no doubt to help foster the belief that she was a powerful all-seeing, all-knowing witch. But the words still sent icy fingers trailing down my spine and I swallowed before taking her words as permission to enter.

The cabin, which consisted of only one room, was rich with the slightly bitter, but not unpleasant, smell of dried herbs. Most of the room was taken up by a long wooden table, which held bottles, bowls and an assortment of other instruments that were used to prepare her concoctions. Every wall in the room was lined with shelves holding bottles, jars and baskets of fresh and dried herbs. The only evidence that someone lived in the cabin was the pallet in the corner. This was the most furniture I had seen in any slave cabin, but as her Master profited from the sale of her herbs, it was in his interest to make sure she had everything she needed. There was another smaller table in the centre of the room and that is where she sat, peering at me by the light of an oil lamp.

She was a small lithe woman with delicate features like mine. Her head was cleanly shaven and she would have been considered beautiful were it not for the scars, rows of lines about an inch long, marking her forehead and cheeks. It was rumoured that those scars had been self-inflicted when she was first brought to America as a slave. Some people whispered that she had done it to honour the customs of her people, others, that the journey, the horrors of the middle passage, had driven her to scar her face in madness and despair. Although I would never dare to ask her, I didn't believe she had been driven insane. The shrewd dark eyes that met mine belonged to a strong, sharp mind and I doubted that anything could, or ever would, be able to break it.

"Evening, Mama Akosua," I said as I walked into the circle of light.

There was still daylight outside but it didn't seem to reach the small window in Mama Akosua's cabin and so it was always dark in here no matter what the time of day.

She gestured to the chair opposite hers, her eyes never leaving my face. I moved to the chair and when I sat down, she pushed a small cup toward me.

"Drink," she said.

I picked up the cup and sipped the cool concoction, which tasted vaguely of mint leaves. Whatever it was, it seemed to have an immediate effect because I no longer felt as hot and the fatigue, which had been pulling on me like lead weights, seemed to evaporate.

Feeling slightly better, I was able to meet the force of her gaze fully. She seemed to have aged a great deal since I last saw her, nearly four years ago. The lines around her eyes and the ones running from her nose to the corners of her mouth had deepened and although she was not yet forty years old, she looked much older.

She studied me for a few moments and a soft sigh escaped her when she finally shifted her gaze away from my face.

"It is as I feared," she said and stood up, wincing from the small movement.

"You hurt?"

"It is a small price to pay," she mumbled, more to herself it seemed.

She reached into a basket on one of the shelves and pulled out a small black cloth bundle. Moving back to the table she placed the bundle before her and when she sat down again she closed her eyes for a few seconds. She was clearly in a lot of pain.

"I have prepared what you need," she said pulling open the cloth bundle to reveal six paper sachets of herbs.

There was no need for her to ask me why I was here. I would only risk making this dangerous journey for one reason.

"Take this tonight." She pointed to the larger of the bundles. "The rest is to be taken for five nights after, to stop the bleeding."

She tied up the bundle and pushed it across the table toward me.

"Thank you, Mama Akosua."

"Is it the son this time?"

I looked up and met her intimidating gaze, but on this occasion, I couldn't hold it. She knew how much these things shamed me yet it didn't stop her from asking about them. When I answered, my voice was barely a whisper.

"Yes."

"How long?"

"He... he be at my cabin near about three times a week now since Easter."

"He is worse than his father, no?" It wasn't a question; it was a statement.

"Yes."

I fought back tears as an image came to me from a few weeks before. I was standing in my tiny cabin and Master John was behind me gazing at our reflections in a small handheld mirror. I don't know if making me look at myself was one of the many ways he had of tormenting me or if he really was oblivious to the fact that I despised my face. Either way, he would make me stare at my piercing dark brown eyes framed by long sooty eyelashes, deep mahogany skin, small delicate features and large sensuous lips. My springy, unruly hair was pulled away from my face, something he insisted on, as my hair was the one thing a man like him could find no beauty in. It was always the same ordeal with the mirror whenever he came to my cabin. And I honestly don't know which face I hated more, that of the blond-haired, blue-eyed man I had come to despise even more than his old, decrepit father, or my own. The face he was enamoured with. He eventually pulled the mirror out of my hand, and placing it on the window sill, held his arms out.

"Dance with me," he had said in a soft, silky voice.

I remained where I was, my face a blank mask but rage no doubt burning behind my eyes. I may not have had a say over his nocturnal visits, but I would not play these little games or pretend that I wanted him in my wretched little cabin.

Fast, so fast that I didn't have time to protect myself, he raised his hand and slapped me, sending me crashing to the floor. Pain bloomed along my temple and the left side of my face. I had also bitten my lip when I hit my head. His foot came down on my neck and I felt the dirt on the sole of his boot rubbing into my skin as he pressed down, cutting off my air supply. I struggled in vain to breathe and was close to losing consciousness when he slowly removed his foot and hauled me back onto my feet as if he were picking up a sack of potatoes. Then he held out his arms again, that smile, which never seemed to leave his face, swimming before my eyes as I struggled to clear my vision.

I was bristling with anger and yet fear won out because he could do anything he wanted to me and there was nothing I would be able to do to stop him. No one I could go to for protection. I had been born and bred purely for men like him, not only to do with as they pleased, but to increase their riches by breeding more slaves for them to own.

"Dance with me," he said again.

Tasting blood in my mouth, I did as I was ordered to do.

"Massa Henry used to please hisself and leave," I told Mama Akosua. "But Massa John... he like to play."

I sensed rather than saw her rage.

I had led a relatively painless existence, for a slave, up until around the age of eight or nine when Master Henry had sent me on an errand to one of the neighbouring farms, an errand which would take me through the woods. I had run eagerly out of the house, hardly believing the good fortune that meant I could spend most of the morning walking through the woods instead of working. And it was the perfect day for a long walk, a beautiful spring day. The air was crisp and cool and the sun filtering through the fresh green leaves created patches of golden haze for me to walk through. I skipped along carefree and untouched at that time by the burdens of a female slave, deviating from my path only once to chase a squirrel, losing it moments later when it darted up a tree and out of sight.

It wasn't long before I came to a stream winding its way through the trees directly in my path and saw Master Henry on his horse. I froze straight away but wasn't immediately frightened as it seemed his face lit up with the kind of excitement you would expect to see on the face of a man on a long quest for buried treasure at the moment he finally finds it.

"Massa Henry!" I cried, dropping the parcel he had given me to deliver. I stooped to pick it up and when I straightened, he had already dismounted and was walking quickly toward me.

Master Henry, who was in his fifties, was tall and thin, had brown hair that was peppered with grey, a beak of a nose and thin, pink lips. I felt immediately uneasy about being on my own with him so far from the house, especially since it seemed as if he had gone to the trouble of saddling up his horse and riding out of the plantation with the sole intention of overtaking me.

But I tried to allay my fears by telling myself that he had never actually given me reason to fear him. The only unnerving thing about him was that he had a habit of turning up wherever I was working and would watch me intently for far too long as if he were looking to find fault with my work. He had never actually reprimanded me for anything, but something about his manner, his long wrinkled neck, bony elbows and knees, reminded me of a vulture waiting patiently. Mary, the cook, seemed uneasy about his apparent interest in my work. Perhaps she was worried that if he found fault with anything I did it would be blamed on her. So whenever Master Henry was at home she was always beside me, helping me with my chores even though I was more than capable of doing them on my own, a light sheen of anger marking her every action, the quick furtive glances she cast in Master Henry's direction always fearful. Sometimes she would find an excuse to call me away if Master Henry made his way into whatever room I was in. I noticed that the other house slaves did the same.

I was too young at that time to know why his greedy eyes had become my shadow or why he showed such an overt interest in everything I did. I was also too young to understand the acid rage I saw in his young wife Mistress Emily's eyes whenever she saw him watching me, or why she had tried on more than one occasion to send me to work in the fields. And the other slaves obviously thought it was kinder not to explain it to me.

So when I saw him waiting for me that day, I knew I was in a lot of trouble but I didn't know what I had done.

When he got to me I saw a feverish light in his eyes as they moved over my tiny body. It was as if he couldn't see or hear anything but me. Then his hand shot out abruptly and he pushed me to the ground. When he began to wrestle with his belt I tried to crawl away, knowing now that something awful was about to happen. But he was already on top of me, ripping my dress off whilst he moaned and reached for my chest to paw at what had not yet begun to form there. The pain had been horrific and my screams seemed to heighten his pleasure as he rode me as if I were the stallion he had obviously ridden furiously in order to catch me here alone in the woods. I lost consciousness at some point, and when I came to it was to the sight of him pulling up his trousers. He had mounted his horse and then turned to look at me with what I now know to be lust and it was clear that he was considering getting off his horse to repeat what he had done. Thankfully he gently urged his horse on through the trees to make his way back to the road.

Once he was gone I rolled onto my side and sobbed. I didn't fully understand what had happened, but I knew it was something to be ashamed of and that I couldn't go back to the house and face Mary. There was a faintly

21

metallic smell mingling with that of the cold dry earth and I realised that it was the smell of my own blood, which was seeping through my legs. I tried to cover myself but my dress was torn in two so I wrapped my arms around what was left of the garment and lay there crying.

After a while, when the sun had reached the highest point in the sky, the sound of a twig snapping under the weight of a person's foot told me I was no longer alone.

I sat up with a start to see one of the slaves, Jupiter, standing about three metres away from me. He was a tall, handsome African of around eighteen years old and had coal black skin and big beautiful brown eyes. I used to find excuses to go to the fields along with some of the other slave girls so that we could catch a glimpse of him toiling under the relentless heat of the Mississippi sun and we would run away giggling whenever he saw us watching him. Those days seemed like a lifetime away from where we were now, watching each other under the emerald leaves. And I noticed that the haunting quality that had been in his eyes since he had arrived at the plantation a few months ago had been replaced with a mixture of rage and despair.

He abruptly lowered his eyes and removed his shirt as he strode toward me. Fear shot through me. I screamed in terror and made a feeble attempt to try and scurry away, thinking that he meant to do what Master Henry had done. My reaction made him jump and he looked at me in bewilderment before taking in his own naked chest. Making the connection between his actions and my apparent fear, he shook his head in alarm and then threw the shirt on the ground before taking a few steps back.

Breathing harshly, I watched him point to his shirt, then to me, and he mimicked wrapping something around himself.

He hadn't spoken a word since arriving at the plantation and all efforts to teach him English had failed. Master Henry had come to the conclusion that he was

22

dumb, but some of the other slaves thought it was only an act.

I tried to rise, and when the pain between my legs reared up, I froze and remained on my knees crying until Jupiter slowly moved toward me. I eyed him warily through my tears as he picked up his shirt. When it became apparent to him that I was in too much pain to try and move away, he gently laid the shirt over my shoulders and pulled me to my feet, grimacing at my cry of pain. I let him button the large shirt around me, and when it was done, he took a few steps forward and gestured for me to follow.

I ground my teeth together and tried to walk without letting a scream escape my lips and he let me take a few steps like that before he abruptly closed the space between us and swiftly picked me up.

"Naw!" I screamed. "Naw!"

I tried to slap at his chest and face as he began to run through the trees with me in his arms.

"Please. Please. We hurry," he panted in a gruff, heavily accented voice as he tried to dodge my tiny hands. "Your pain. Please."

I stopped my feeble attempts, surprised to hear that the other slaves had been right. He could speak. He carried me back to the plantation, his coal black skin glistening with my blood by the time we got there to the quiet anger and dismay of the other slaves.

What I will never forget about that day was Mistress Emily walking into Mary's quarters where I lay sobbing whilst a distraught Mary tried to clean me and tend to the damage that had been done. A small, pale redhead, she stood over me, her eyes gleaming with unshed tears and her anger so pure and intense that I was sure she would find a way to make Master Henry pay for what he had done. But I saw my error with the next words she spoke.

"I want you back in the kitchen now!" she said to Mary.

"But... but Mistress..." Mary had stuttered but she was soon silenced.

"I said I want you back in the kitchen, and if dinner is even one minute late, I'll whip you myself."

Mary had gotten to her feet slowly, her hands balled into fists at her side and her hazel brown eyes a cauldron of barely concealed hatred. For a moment, unease passed over Mistress Emily's face and it seemed like an unbearably long moment before Mary spoke again.

"Y... yes, Miss Emily," she mumbled.

Shaking with anger, she quickly wiped away her tears and glancing helplessly at me, bowed her head and left the cabin.

Left alone with Mistress Emily, I lay as still as I could, trying to ignore the pain down below as I choked back my tears. The look she gave me in those few seconds before she left the cabin was one of such hatred that I was chilled to the bone. I will never forget it.

Jupiter never spoke to me or even looked me in the eye again after that day. Whenever I saw him he would drop his gaze and nod politely but he never stayed in my presence for long. Of all the things I had to endure during the years that followed, having Jupiter never look me in the eye was no doubt the worst. I never forgot his kindness that day, but I knew that seeing me soiled had changed his view of me in a fundamental way, and even though it was painful for me to accept, I understood it and so kept my distance from him. He was sold a few years later and although I missed his presence on the plantation, it was a relief not to have him avert his gaze or find a reason to get away from me whenever our paths crossed.

The wounds I sustained that day healed, but the mental scars never left me alone.

Neither did Master Henry.

He found every opportunity to accost me again and again. Three years passed and his weekly visits only stopped when my breasts and stomach began to grow. I hadn't known why I was sometimes sick in the morning and why my appetite had increased, until Mary, who was the closest thing that I had to a mother, explained that I would soon have a child of my own.

The child came on a devilishly cold winter night under the fury of a raging storm, the worst that anyone could remember ever being unleashed on Mississippi. I screamed out in pain as a contraction rippled through my stomach with almost as much force as the wind and rain lashing against my tiny cabin. It was a Sunday so my mind was still crowded with the sermon I had heard at church during the day, the story of Noah and the Great Flood taking on greater meaning in my panic-stricken mind. It felt like the end of days for me, and as hour after hour passed, the pain and the storm began to take on biblical proportions until I was sure that morning would never come.

Mary was equally anxious. She had come to my cabin thinking that this was another false labour, the third one that week. But it soon became clear, not only that this was the real thing, but that there was something seriously wrong. She was about to leave to go and get help when Mama Akosua, knowing somehow that she was needed, entered the cabin. Mama Akosua had been sold when I was about three, so I only recognised her because of the scars on her face. I had been screaming at the time as another contraction ripped through me and yet in the midst of the pain, the panic and sense of doom left me the moment I laid eyes on her. When she came closer, I stifled another cry when I saw the look of black thunder on her face.

"I will kill him," she had spat and I guessed that she was talking about Master Henry. "I will cut out his heart with my bare hands. I will kill him."

Her face hadn't lost that rage even as she set to work, ordering Mary to boil water or get more rags. It was an extremely difficult birth, complicated by the fact that my womb had only dilated a few centimetres. If Mama

25

Akosua hadn't been there with her herbal medicines to help me fully dilate, both I and the child she delivered a few hours later would be dead.

When I first heard the baby scream, a sound not unlike the squeal of a pig being slaughtered, I immediately turned my head away, repulsed by this thing that would always remind me of that day in the woods and the years of torment that followed.

For a few moments there was only the sound of the rain lashing the cabin and the awful sound of the baby's screams. Then at last Mary spoke, the relief and excitement in her voice unable to completely mask the clenching sorrow I could hear flitting around her words.

"You a mama now, Luna. You got you a baby girl." Her voice wavered on the word "girl".

"Take it away," I heard myself say.

"Hush now, Luna. You..." Mary began but I didn't let her finish.

"Take it away! I don't care what you does with it. Just take it away!"

I secretly hoped that she would kill that thing and for a moment I thought Mama Akosua had heard my thoughts because she was glaring at me. As frightened as I was by her expression, I kept my eyes on her and pleaded silently with her to take the baby away. The cold fury left her after a few moments and I knew then that she would do as I asked.

I never saw the child again and I don't know what became of it. It was often on the tip of my tongue to ask Mama Akosua and I'm sure she expected to hear the question every time I saw her. But I couldn't bring myself to ask because I still hated that thing and I didn't want to know whether it lived or had died.

I was whipped when they discovered the baby was gone, the first time Master Henry ever took a whip to me. I accepted each stroke of the lash with dead eyes and barely a murmur, feeling far removed from the shocking pain and

26

the warm rivers of blood running from the open wounds on my back and down my legs to lie in a glistening red pool on the ground. The weeks that followed were a pain-tinged blur in which I repeatedly begged death to wrap its tender arms around me. During those weeks I walked a tightrope between life and death, but two faces kept drawing me back toward the barb-tipped snare of life: Mary's during the day, and Mama Akosua's at night. She was there every night forcing me to drink some foul-tasting mixture or rubbing something into the open wounds on my back. I would often wake from a restless sleep to hear her singing to me softly in her native tongue. I didn't understand the words but there was so much sorrow in her voice that it was hard for me to turn my back on life and slip into the arms of death. The anger I had seen the night I gave birth was slowly smoothed down by exhaustion but it was still there as, night after night, she made the long walk from the Marshall plantation to nurse me back to health. I also recall the frequent but fleeting spectre of Master Henry's tall, stooping figure as he stood in the doorway of my cabin blotting out the sunlight. If it had been any other slave, they would have paid with their life. But Master Henry wanted me too much to ever consider killing me and he fretted that he had perhaps been too hasty in taking the whip to me so soon after I had given birth. But I recovered and nothing was the same after that.

I told everyone that I couldn't remember what had happened during the birth. I told them that I went to sleep alone and the next thing I remembered was waking up in the morning to the sight of blood everywhere and the knowledge that I had somehow delivered the baby during the night but had no idea what had happened to it.

Nobody believed my story, especially since I kept referring to the child as "it" and didn't bother to hide my hatred and revulsion every time she was mentioned. From that moment on, the other slaves began to keep their distance from me, probably believing that I had killed the child with my bare hands. I can't say that I cared either way what they believed as I knew that if I hadn't been given another option, that is exactly what I would have done rather than let Master Henry have her.

Only Mary knew the truth and she couldn't tell anyone because if Master Henry ever found out that she was involved in any way, he wouldn't have hesitated to kill her. So she kept quiet, even though I saw how painful it was for her to hear what was said about me and not be able to defend me with the truth. She also refused to let me push her away. No matter what I said or did, she kept finding ways past the wall I erected until I eventually stopped trying to shut her out. And I believe that even if she hadn't known what had really happened that night, she would never have forsaken me, because Mary was loyal and the closest thing that I had to a mother.

The visits from Master Henry continued for years until he suffered a stroke. Then they became less frequent until another stroke put an end to them altogether. I was left alone for a year until Master John, Master Henry's son from a previous marriage, came to take over the daily running of the plantation. That's when the nightmare began all over again.

Chapter Two

Mama Akosua's voice brought me back to the present.

"Forgive me."

"Forgive *you*?" I asked harshly, forgetting that I was frightened of the woman seated before me. "You ain't the cause of my troubles."

She opened her mouth as if to speak and her bottom lip quivered for a fraction of a second before she looked down at the table. I saw weariness in her face that frightened me more than her usual fierce gaze and this in turn infuriated me.

"Don't you feel sorry for me, now!" I hissed. "I's lucky compared to most niggers."

I laughed harshly, not only at the absurdity of the statement, but at the bitter knowledge that what I had said was true. I was luckier than most that I worked in the house and didn't have to suffer the back-breaking work in the fields. I was lucky that the flesh on my back had been shredded by the whip on only one occasion and not countless times like so many others. Yes, I was lucky compared to most but it didn't mean that my life wasn't one of fear and degradation. Those midnight visits, one pregnancy, and now three trips to Mama Akosua for herbs to kill my unborn children, had taken its toll. Yes, I was fortunate that Master Henry and his son wanted to keep me in the house so that their greedy eyes and filthy thoughts could follow me around and that their desires meant they didn't treat me as harshly as some of the other slaves, but at times I wished I wasn't so fortunate.

"Here," I said and laid the bundle of apples wrapped in cloth on the table.

When her eyes fell on the bundle, some of the weariness left her and a small smile passed briefly across her lips.

"Ah, apples." She nodded once to show her appreciation.

The slaves that came to see Mama Akosua paid her with whatever they had. Sometimes it was information, other times money or food. I knew she didn't expect me to bring anything but I always brought her apples from the apple tree behind an abandoned chapel on the plantation that no one else seemed to know about. That tree yielded the sweetest apples and whenever one of our slaves was sent on an errand to the Marshall plantation, I always asked them to take some to her. It was a small thing but I liked to see that little smile, as though she were glimpsing some forgotten pleasure, even though it was always gone as quickly as it was now when she peered past me toward the door of the cabin.

"Hey! What are you doing there?" she said sharply.

I turned to see a small brown face peering around the open door. The little boy stepped out from behind the door with a sheepish smile on his face. He was dressed in an oversized white shirt and torn brown trousers that were too short for him.

"They says your daughter's here, Mama, and I wants to see her." He moved forward quickly to stand by my chair. "She sure is pretty," he said when he saw me fully in the light of the lamp.

"Go away, Ebe!" Mama Akosua replied with a glare that looked as if it could shake the very foundation of her Master's mansion and bring it crumbling to the ground.

But Ebe didn't seem to even notice and smiled at her

before he returned his gaze to mine. I found myself smiling back at him. He was a beautiful little boy who had wide innocent eyes, long eyelashes, an impish smile, and dimples.

"She sure looks like you, Mama," he said, still beaming at me. "But she don't look as mean or as old. Why you so *old* looking. And why it be so dark in here all the time?"

He looked around the cabin, his brow creasing as he pondered the answer to his question.

I held my breath, wondering how he could dare say such a thing in her presence. He seemed like such a sweet little boy but he clearly didn't have much growing between his ears for him to speak to Mama Akosua like that. He also didn't seem to have a healthy sense of fear for he was still standing there grinning.

"I am going to count to ten – no, five," Mama Akosua said. "If you are still here by the time I finish, I will turn you into that dog of Massa's. The one that looks like you."

Her face was deadly serious and although I knew she couldn't possibly have the power to turn him into anything, her tone made me apprehensive and I tried to catch the boy's eye so that I could try and signal to him to do as she said.

"I's gonna go if you let me has one of them apples."

"No."

"But you don't likes apples."

She didn't like apples?

I turned to her but her attention was still on the fearless little boy.

"Ebenezer!" She slammed her hand down on the table. "If you don't..."

At last he seemed to gain a healthy sense of fear for he looked alarmed for the first time since entering the cabin. Then he turned and fled. A few seconds later we heard the sound of his laughter, a deep throaty sound that sounded too big for such a small child, fading away as he ran off and I realised he hadn't been afraid at all.

"Foolish boy," Mama Akosua said looking as if she too were trying to hold back a smile. "Forever trying to test my patience. Hm. It amazes me that the children can still be happy, even here."

"You don't likes apples?"

"No," she said, calmly meeting my reproachful gaze without any hint of an apology.

"Why pretend to likes them when you don't? You know the trouble I goes to to get them for you?" I exploded.

It seemed some of Ebenezer's empty-headedness had rubbed off on me, for I hadn't even tried to check my tone. I felt stupid and embarrassed by the small measure of pride I had felt only moments ago at bringing these to her and it was infuriating to see another small smile touch her lips.

"I do not pretend. I cherish anything my daughter brings me. And yes, I do know the trouble you take. Trouble that had you fall from that apple tree not so long ago and land with your pretty behind exposed to the sky. Yes, my dear. I know the trouble you go to."

I opened my mouth to speak but nothing came out. That fall she was talking about had happened nearly a year ago. I remembered being hot and flustered as I hurried down the apple tree, missed my footing, and fell. I also remember that there had been no one else around.

"How...?"

"I know many things. Some things I hear about from others. Some, like knowledge of herbs and healing, I learn from my mother. Some things come to me in dreams. That one had me laughing in my sleep."

I felt the corners of my mouth twitch and I began to laugh. The fall *had* been funny when I looked back on it. Mama Akosua was laughing too now, a soft rustling sound, and a very rare sight for me.

"You laugh now but you did not find it funny then, did you?" she asked.

"No. But you ain't seen it in no dream. Somebody seen

32

me and done told you."

"You have given yourself to the white man's God so you do not believe in my powers, the powers of our ancestors. But it is there. It is within you as well. It binds us together and it is how I know things you do not wish me to know."

She sighed and lowered her eyes, the smile completely gone. "Yes, my dear. I know many things. As I know that after this time, you can take these herbs no more."

It seemed the brief moment of light-heartedness was over.

"What you mean?" I asked, my voice barely above a whisper.

It felt as if all the air had been sucked out of the room.

She met my gaze again. "The herbs should only be used once, twice at the most. This is the third time. I cannot give it to you a fourth."

I felt my shoulders straighten and my eyes turn to slits.

"You *can*, and you *will*."

"I may be willing to help you kill the babies that have been made through force. But I will not do it if it means I kill you too."

I made to say more but she reached over and put her hand on mine. I wasn't exactly comfortable with this unexpected show of affection, but I didn't pull away.

"My child, motherhood does not have to be the curse you see it as. I was a mother for only three years before I was sold away from you. But I would not give away those years for anything on this earth. Not even my freedom."

"I ain't gonna give them a child of mine. I ain't bringing a child of mine into this... this..."

She leaned back in the chair, removing her hand from mine. It seemed as if my words had shamed her because she looked down at the table and the weariness I saw, not only on her face but her whole body, frightened me for a moment. The rising panic I could feel fluttering around in my chest at the thought that I wouldn't have the option to remove the thing growing inside me in the future made my breath come out in harsh gasps.

We didn't speak for a few moments whilst I rubbed away the moisture from my eyes and managed to calm myself down.

There was no point in carrying on this conversation now. When the time came again she would either help me or I would find some other way.

"What you gonna do with them apples if you ain't eating them?" I said when I could trust myself to speak.

"I will walk with them. Everywhere I go, I will carry them with me."

I allowed myself a smile. "You gonna carry this big old sack around with you till them apples turn bad?"

"Yes, until I am forced to throw them away. Even then I find it hard to do it."

Her words had an unexpected effect on me. One of intense sorrow. I had never associated the word "mother" with this woman because she had been taken away when I was so young. There were other women on the plantation that fit the word better in my head. I had never even considered the fact that the word "daughter" would always be me to her regardless of whether she was far or near. And it never even occurred to me that she thought of me often and maybe even missed me.

I looked down at the apples with a bittersweet smile, picked one up and placed it in her hand.

"Here. Let the boy have the rest."

I let my hand rest there, our fingers wrapped around the apple between our palms. "Next time Massa sends somebody on over here, I's gonna send you something. I's gonna send something different each time till I finds out what you *do* like."

She smiled again and nodded.

I let go of the apple and stood up. "I gots to get back."

I hadn't meant to stay here so long. It was sure to be dark long before I got back to the plantation.

Mama Akosua stood up as well, doing a good job of concealing the pain the movement caused her, but not completely. It was there in the tightening of the muscles around her mouth.

"Do not worry so," she said as she moved around the table to come and join me. "One of the farmers who comes to me for medicine has waited for you. He can only take you part of the way but it means you will be back before dark."

I turned to her, startled. So she *had* known I was coming. But how?

"I see you still doubt my powers, Luna. But I assure you, they are real. You also have the gift. Don't you remember when you were a child? You always knew when I was coming home. Even those times I used to sneak away during the day to be with you, I would find you by the trees waiting for me and when I would ask how you knew I was coming you told me that my spirit – yes, you said the word spirit and I would wonder who taught you that word. You said that my spirit came through the door and said hello and that is how you knew I was coming. Can you imagine my happiness at such a display of your gift? If I had been able to teach you, you would be a powerful witch by now. Maybe not as powerful as me, but powerful, yes."

She must have seen the disdain on my face. "Ah, but I forget you have embraced their white God so mine are of no use to you."

There was a trace of mockery in her voice.

"No. Them heathen gods ain't no good to nobody," I said, the fire in my eyes more in response to her tone than her words.

When she smiled this time, it revealed a flash of small white teeth.

"It is good to see your anger, Luna. The women in our family have always been strong. Strong like stone boulders. I was beginning to think that life as a slave had

35

crushed that strength. But no. It is still there and that makes me happy. Here." She picked up the apples and placed them in my arms. "That troublesome boy is never far from my quarters. I am sure these will taste sweeter if you give them to him yourself."

"Yes, Mama," I said, the first time that I had allowed myself to call her that.

***

Mama Akosua was right. Ebenezer was not far from the cabin and seemed to have gathered a small band of other boys of various ages, all of them looking eagerly in my direction as I emerged blinking into the sunlight. I gestured to him and he came bounding to my side wearing that wide smile of his.

"Here," I said. "For you and your friends." He took the bundle eagerly but then his face fell.

"Do I *has* to give them some?" I couldn't help but laugh and his smile instantly returned.

"Yes, you do. Now go!" Mama Akosua replied, her expression so fierce it was a wonder that he was able to smile up at her before he scampered away, holding up the apples like a trophy as he rejoined the little army of raggedy boys.

"There is a place you go to often," Mama Akosua began as she led me away from her cabin. "I cannot see it clearly but you are always alone when you go there."

I tried to think of what she meant and where this line of conversation was headed but came up blank.

"It is an old building that has been eaten by fire," she continued.

"The old chapel?" I said.

I didn't bother to ask how she knew this time. It seemed as if there wasn't much that she didn't know about what I did.

"Yes. You must stay away from that place."

36

"Why?"

She led me past the last of the slave quarters toward the front of the plantation. I noticed that she didn't take the shortcut through the trees.

"I sense something. A...a... shadow. Something very powerful and not of this world is making its way there so it is no longer safe for you to be there."

Her demeanour had changed and she walked faster as if trying to escape whatever it was that she sensed.

"Great evil was done there a long time ago. The fire was started to put an end to it but whenever that much evil is done in a place, some of that energy lingers. Perhaps that is what keeps drawing this other... I do not know what to call it, but I have felt it a few times over the years. And I know that if you cross its path it can take you away from me completely. So stay away from that place."

We reached the long road leading up to the house and I saw two men on a horse-drawn wagon. Well, one of them was a man; the other was no more than a boy. They were both dressed in simple farmers' clothing.

"They are good people," Mama Akosua said, no doubt seeing the fear that sprung into my eyes at the thought that I would be making this journey alone with two white men. "They are farmers and do not own slaves, so their hearts and minds have not become diseased by the evil of slavery. Even though Massa Marshall takes payment from them for my herbs, they always try and give me something too, no matter how small. They are good people. I would not trust them with you if I believed there was even the smallest chance they would harm you in any way. Besides, they know what I can do. As Massa Henry should have known that no matter how far he sent me, I would find my way back here to have my vengeance."

We had reached them now so she wasn't able to say anymore, but my curiosity had been awakened by her words. What could she possibly mean by that?

"Mama Akosua." I was surprised to hear the older

farmer call her by that name and not Alice, her slave name. "So this is your daughter. I can see that the slaves didn't lie about how pretty she is."

I felt my stomach lurch at the compliment and fear cinched my heart. Thankfully I managed not to let that unease show.

"But of course, she isn't anywhere near as pretty as you," he continued.

Mama Akosua accepted the flattery with a raised eyebrow. "Hm. Your lies grow longer every time I see you, Mr Walker."

They all laughed good-naturedly at the joke.

"I know your mother gets tired of me telling people this," Mr Walker said, addressing me. "But her herbs saved my wife's life nine Christmases ago. I've been coming to her ever since, and if it weren't for the potion she gives me for my bad knee, I wouldn't be able to work my fields and we would have starved years ago."

"You are too generous with your praise. And too generous with your gifts. But thank you. Maybe one day I will repay your kindness by telling you what is in my herbs."

"When that day comes I will happily sell you everything I own in return." They laughed again and I smiled weakly. "Help her up, Matthew, so we can get going."

I accepted the work-roughened hand that the boy offered me and climbed up to sit beside him on the wagon.

"Don't worry, Mama Akosua," Mr Walker said once I was sitting comfortably beside them. "We'll take good care of her."

"I would trust her with no one but you, Mr Walker," she said warmly and he nodded humbly in return.

We said our goodbyes and as the wagon pulled away, I noticed that Ebenezer had followed us and was hiding behind one of the trees. When Mama Akosua turned around and headed in his direction, he left his hiding place and ran toward her with his arms outstretched. I felt myself tense as he neared her, as I knew that when they collided, the jolt would no doubt be painful for her. But he slowed down before he reached her and wrapped his arms very carefully around her waist as if she were made of glass. She tenderly patted him on the cheek and as they walked away I noticed that she appeared to lean on him quite heavily and that he seemed to expect her to.

How much pain was she in and how long had it been going on?

I felt a rush of anxiety.

As much as I didn't want to care about that woman, or anyone else for that matter, I did care. And it hurt to care because I was helpless to protect the people I loved. So I held my bundle of herbs even tighter as the farmer urged the horse into a brisk canter.

I was doing the right thing, the only thing I could do about the life growing inside me. But as I looked back over my shoulder and caught sight of Ebenezer and Mama Akosua disappearing into the trees, I felt a deep sorrow settle over my heart.

Back at Mama Akosua's cabin I had wondered at the boy's fearlessness. But he had shown Mama Akosua no fear because unlike me, he had been around her for a long time and knew he had no need to fear her. That knowledge twisted painfully in my chest. There was so much that I had already lost, even the child I had hated on sight had been a loss. And I was about to lose the one that was fruitlessly trying to survive in the warm darkness of my womb.

Chapter Three

The journey back passed relatively quickly and without incident. Perhaps sensing my unease at being left alone with them, Mr Walker spent most of the ride talking about anything that came to his mind: the weather, his crops, his children, his wife's cooking, and of course, Mama Akosua's miracle herbs and potions. His son, who sat between us, spent the journey staring at me whilst I pretended not to notice his apparent interest. It was only when his father gave him a sharp jab in the ribs with his elbow when he thought I wasn't looking that the boy finally tore his gaze away from me. A pink flush crept up his neck to bloom on his cheeks and he kept his head down for the remainder of the journey.

Mr Walker did more than take me part of the way home. He took me all the way to the plantation and dropped me off at the edge of the woods as the sun began to set, casting blood red streaks across the sky.

"Thank you kindly, Mr Walker," I said when my feet were on the ground again and the anxiety that had stolen over me during the journey had lifted.

"My farm is just yonder," he said pointing into the distance. "By old man Reynolds's place. You know it?"

I nodded, although I wasn't sure that I did.

"Well, if you ever need anything, come on by or send word to me. We ain't rich folks like some of those plantation owners, but even if we can't help, we can at least try. I've said the same to your mother and I know she'll hold me to that promise. I hope you will too."

His words were unexpected and I had to concentrate to keep back the tears that had started burning behind my eyes.

"Thank you, sir. God bless you."

He nodded, seemingly satisfied with my answer, then turned the wagon around and waved me goodbye. I headed for the trees and before I entered them I glanced back and saw that his son was looking over his shoulder at me. His father glanced at him and then cuffed him lightly around the head. He laughed when his son finally tore his gaze away from me and ruffled his hair playfully.

I dipped into the trees, and as always, broke into a run. The woods seemed to hold an extra degree of menace today with the green canopy above broken by splashes of red from the setting sun. My thoughts kept returning to images of Mama Akosua with Ebenezer and my last glimpse of Mr Walker and his son. I felt an intense loneliness course through me and without even thinking about where I was headed, I found myself running away from the main house and toward the abandoned chapel.

As I ran I fancied that I heard Mama Akosua's voice in my head saying, *Turn back. Turn back!*

Upset even more by my silly imaginings, I pushed that voice away and ran faster. It was no wonder I thought I could hear her. Mama Akosua and Ebenezer. Mr Walker and his son. They were all I could think about. Their close bonds and all the things I was missing out on sat heavily on my heart as I raced through the woods.

I hadn't wanted to acknowledge the fact that although she was virtually a stranger to me, I cared deeply about Mama Akosua, my mother, a woman I had seen only a handful of times since she'd been taken from me. I cared about her. But what good did this do me? What good did it do her? I was jealous of the closeness I saw between her

41

and Ebenezer but I had no right to that jealousy because she didn't belong to me. She didn't even belong to herself. She belonged to Master Marshall. So I ran on.

The chapel was a hulking, brooding structure set in a clearing at the farthest reaches of the plantation. Its exterior was a yellowed white and large sections of the stucco had fallen away to reveal the brick beneath. The windows on either side of the wooden door were broken and looked like empty eye sockets staring blindly out on the clearing. A large black cross above the front door gazed down upon me as I entered.

The damage caused by the fire couldn't be seen from the front of the building but inside were the charred remains of pews and a large hole in the roof at the back of the building where the flames had eaten through to the sky. No one ever came to this place as most people thought it was haunted, but I liked it here as it was the only place I could be completely alone.

I inhaled the familiar smell of burnt wood that still hung in the air as I walked up to the remains of the altar and knelt down. It was the only area of the building that had been swept away and cleaned, something I had done years ago when I'd first found my little hiding place. Pulling up a loose floorboard, I retrieved a small, green bible that was worn with age. It was one of Mistress Emily's bibles. I had stolen it a few years ago. She had never used it and I'm sure that she didn't even know it was missing, but if I were ever caught with it I would be whipped within an inch of my life.

This bible was my most treasured possession but every time I held it in my hands I was filled with pain because I had never been taught how to read, and so would never have the pleasure of reading the Lord's words with my own eyes.

I opened the bible anyway and stared at the rows of printed words that were locked to me and instead said the bits of prayer I had memorised from the church sermons

42

we had to attend every Sunday.

Then I prayed out loud. I poured out all my grief. I told God that I loved Him and that although I couldn't read the words in the bible I held, I cherished it anyway. I told Him that although I hadn't been able to hold onto my virtue, my body still belonged to Him and that I was pure in my heart. I prayed for forgiveness for the sin I was about to commit in killing the life that was growing within me and told Him that although it was a sin I would never be able to forgive myself for, it would be a greater sin to bring an innocent being into the hell of slavery.

I prayed with tears streaming down my face, letting them fall on the charred floor until words left me.

Then I placed the bible back in its hiding place, left the chapel, and walked to the stream at the back of the building. It was nearly dark now and the sky was a dark red blotted by smoky grey clouds. Kneeling on the ground, I splashed water from the stream onto my face and then gazed at the water. There was enough light to see my reflection in the shallow stream and it filled me with rage and hopelessness.

There were rare moments when the full horror of a female slave's life fell on me and I felt that now when I glanced up at the woods and the path I would take back to the house. An all-encompassing despair rocked me from head to toe. I didn't want to go back to a life of bondage. I didn't want to go back to my quarters and drink the evil concoction which would hunt down and kill the innocent in my womb. I didn't want to go back to a life where I saw evil practiced with ease and nonchalance, a life in which even my body was not mine to own.

Master John had been away for the past week but when I got back to my cabin tonight and fell asleep, would I find myself jolted awake by him, his form looming over me in the pale light of the moon streaming through the open window, his male tool already awake and straining against the cotton of his trousers?

The mere thought caused me to double over with my arms wrapped around my waist, my face close to the water and the rocks beneath its surface.

The cause of most of my problems lay in the face that was almost lost in the watery surface now that the light was gone. I reached my hand into the stream and pulled out a large black rock. It looked as if it had split in two and the split end was as sharp as the blade of a knife. I held that rock up above my face and thought about Mama Akosua being brought to a strange land against her will at the age of fifteen. I thought about how lost and frightened she must have felt being so far from everything she knew and loved, and the strength and fearlessness she displayed when she took a blade to her own face and cut those marks into her skin. In doing so, she had honoured and held onto the customs of her people, people she would never see again. Those scars that I had previously been repulsed by and seen as part of the savage ways of her past, had given her strength. They had been a way to take ownership of at least one part of her body and keep it forever hers.

I would do the same thing. I would take control of at least one aspect of my life and destroy the face that drew men like Master John to me like predators to the scent of fresh blood. I would use this rock to take away the pleasure he found in looking at this face and keep him out of my bed forever.

I brought the sharpest point of the rock down to rest in the middle of my forehead and closed my eyes. I began to apply pressure until I felt it break the skin, a point no bigger than the tip of my fingernail, and felt a warm release of blood. Strangely, I felt no pain, only exhilaration that I could finally do something to stop the terror inflicted on me by my Master.

I was about to bring the rock down my forehead, across my nose and down my cheek, when something, some force, stayed my hand. All at once I grew cold and it felt as if the air around my wrist was alive and humming softly in tune to some sinister beat, making goose bumps spring up along my forearm.

I pushed down with all my might but miraculously this force increased and when I felt my hand begin to move away from my face, I opened my eyes.

I was still facing the woods and for a moment I thought I saw something amongst the trees, a sliver of something that was an almost translucent white. At the same moment I experienced a wave of dizziness that made me feel as if my mind and body had turned to water. I quickly shut my eyes but the dizziness increased and I felt myself swaying, my thoughts and emotions a confusing melee, and I heard a voice in my head. Or was it my *own* voice?

That will not stop him, it said.

My eyes snapped open when I heard a sharp crack to my right. I whirled around to trace the sound, a sharp streak of fear leaping and twisting within me. It was only when I noticed that my hand was now empty and clenched into a fist that I realised that what I had heard was the sound of the rock I had just been holding hitting one of the trees on my right. The distance to that tree was a good seven or eight metres away. Had I really thrown it that far?

I got to my feet uneasily, knowing that I needed to get away from the chapel immediately. Something was very wrong here. The light was nearly gone now and there was something here with me. I could feel it now, an immense power unfolding and drawing strength as the last of the light seeped out of the sky.

Terror beat furiously within me, radiating to my very core. Mama Akosua had been right. I shouldn't have come here. I was in danger, I...

Intoxicating dizziness washed over me again and although I tried to fight against its pull it drew me in, causing me to close my eyes and sway in time to its suffocating rhythm...

And then I was standing at the kitchen door of the main house, having walked through the woods from the chapel and back to the house with no memory of the journey.

But no. That is not what happened. *I didn't go to the chapel today*, my mind insisted. *Mr Walker dropped me off and I walked back to the house through the woods.*

Except...

I never *walked* through the woods. I always ran, and when I parted company with the farmer the sky had blazed red as the sun set but it was dark now. The sun couldn't have fully set within the five minutes it would have taken me to reach the house. But that is what had happened, wasn't it?

I tried to probe deeper and remember but my mind resisted and, almost as if someone had pushed me forward, I found myself stumbling toward the kitchen door. I opened it and stepped inside.

Mary the cook, a short, thin copper-coloured woman with hazel eyes and a kind-looking face, had been cleaning the last of the dishes from the evening meal. When she turned and saw me standing in the doorway she smiled and relief melted over her features.

"Luna! Thank the Lord. Mistress Emily was just asking 'bout you." She frowned. "What happened to your head?"

I reached up and touched my forehead. When my hand came away, my fingertips were sticky with blood.

"Well?" she demanded.

The image of a sleek black rock glistening with water came to mind and was swiftly pushed aside.

"I's running and I guess I... I..."

I stopped because I couldn't remember what had happened to my forehead, and although I reached for the memory, there was something about it that made my insides curl and twist in horror.

Mary's frown deepened.

She had been looking after me since I was about three. She used to tell me that when Mama Akosua was sold I had been inconsolable and used to stand outside the slave quarters at sunset calling for her. When it slowly dawned on me that she wasn't amongst those returning to their cabins and I grew more and more distressed, thirteen-year-old Mary was the only one able to stop me from trying to go out into the night to find her. Even then I spent most of the night crying and Mary would stay with me in what used to be my and Mama's cabin so that my wails did not keep the rest of her family awake. She did this every night and would go off to work exhausted, only to return and spend the next night trying to comfort me as I stood at the window crying whilst I watched and waited for my lost mother to return to me.

After about two weeks I resigned myself to the fact that Mama Akosua was not coming back and I started to scream and cry every time Mary tried to leave me in the mornings. So she had no choice but to take me with her whenever she went to work in the house, warning me that if I got her into trouble she would give me the biggest beating of my life, something I doubt the soft-hearted Mary would have done. I didn't remember any of this. But I could imagine the wide-eyed, sullen child I was as I followed Mary around. And I suppose Mary would always see me as that inconsolable three-year-old clinging to her skirts because she had never stopped mothering me.

"You gots to be careful now, Luna." Zila, one of the other house slaves, had come into the kitchen.

She was a reed-thin, high yellow mulatto who had birdlike features and a smattering of freckles across her nose and cheeks. She regarded me icily, looking over every inch of me, and finding nothing wanting, there was undisguised agony in her eyes when they met mine. "You don't wants nothing to ruin that pretty face of yours."

It occurred to me that she would have been delirious with joy if I had come back with my face ripped to shreds by that rock.

I frowned. Face ripped apart by a rock? What rock? What an odd thing to think.

"Why you acting so strange? And what that be on your

dress?" Mary asked, pulling me from my thoughts.

I looked down at my dress and brushed away bits of earth from around my waist. How had that gotten there?

"There be some on your face too." Mary was nothing if not relentless. "What is wrong with you, girl?"

"I's fine," I mumbled. But the truth is I wasn't fine. I felt sort of dazed. "You go on upstairs. I's gonna finish up down here," I said, taking a large tray out of her hands.

She gave me one last questioning look then shook her head and left the kitchen.

I finished off the rest of my work and went back to my quarters, a small soulless one-room cabin with only a bed, a wooden barrel that held a lonely beeswax candle, a basket for my few items of clothing, and some bowls for water.

I mixed up the herbs Mama Akosua had given me, drank the bitter mixture and lay down on my pallet. I closed my eyes, expecting the pain to start biting as it always did almost immediately after I drank it. But tonight, the moment I felt the first stabbing pains in my womb, I felt everything waver and then the pain disappeared and a warm mellow joy filled me. I drifted toward sleep with a smile, and before I succumbed to its blissful depths, I thought I heard a voice whisper in my mind.

Goodnight... Luna.

"Good..."

I was asleep before I could finish saying the words.

The following day would turn out to be the strangest day of my life.

Chapter Four

I woke up the following morning in my airless little cabin suppressing a scream. For a moment I was convinced there was something prowling out there in the predatory predawn darkness and that this "something" was watching and waiting.

But the next moment the feeling had gone and a low giggle escaped my lips. I clamped my hand over my mouth, bewildered by this sudden onslaught of unexplained mirth but the laughter continued like air bubbles rising to the surface of a lake, and before I knew it, I was completely lost to it. When it finally began to subside, I felt an odd sense of joy begin to flow through me like cool water. For some reason I thought of the chapel and the feeling intensified until I felt almost delirious with the force of the emotion.

But somewhere beneath all of that elation, deep down within, I felt profoundly uneasy. The sensation was small and weak, however, like a seed trying to push its way up through packed earth and the happiness soon trampled it out of sight.

So after my usual breakfast of fried fat pork and cornbread, I began my day and floated through the morning in a heady state of happiness, a soft distant smile never leaving my lips. Nothing could disrupt the feeling of wellbeing; not the puzzled glances I received from those I encountered, not even Mistress Emily's acid tongue. When she sent me into the blazing heat to collect water from the well on the other side of the plantation (even though we always used the one at the back of the house), I had obeyed without grumbling. I actually didn't mind the extra work as, for some strange reason, I felt strong and energised. Normally Mama's potions left me weak and bleeding profusely, but today I felt alive like I'd never felt before, and apart from a few clots of blood, there was no sign of the heavy flow that normally accompanied these abortions.

The only thing that came close to disrupting my quiet joy that day was Master John's return from his trip. I saw him in the distance with his brother Master Peter and he had dismounted to speak to Lola, one of the young field slaves. I felt disgust when I noticed that, as young as she was, Master John's eyes stayed firmly on her chest and the small bosom, which had only just began to blossom, whilst he spoke to her. She wasn't where she was supposed to be and I knew he would automatically assume she was trying to cheat him out of a day's work, so I wasn't surprised when he gestured for her to get to her knees. When she was on all fours like a dog, he ignored her desperate wide-eyed, pleas and began beating her across the back with his rawhide riding whip.

I was close to the three of them now, although out of their sightline, and could see the sweat on Master John's brow and that his face had turned a fierce shade of pink from the exertion of the beating. Holding onto his horse with one hand, he used the other to steady himself as he lustily brought the riding whip down on her back repeatedly. He also had a hard smile on his face as he put all of his strength into the blows he delivered. The low, monotonous tone of Lola's voice drifted to me on the still air as the whip came down.

"Please, Massa, please! Oh, Massa!"

I caught a glimpse of Master Peter's expression as he

sat on his horse watching his older brother and for a moment I thought I saw disapproval in the set of his features. But I was no doubt mistaken. He was probably bored and impatient for them to be on their way.

Beatings like that, and worse, were a daily occurrence on the plantation, but they still had the power to leave me shaken and feeling sick to my stomach. But today I remained strangely unaffected by what I was seeing, even when Master John told Lola to pull up her clothes and lie face down on the ground with her skirts bunched up under her arms. He began hitting her across her bare legs and back and the sounds she made grew a lot more distressing to listen to.

"Oh, oh, please, Massa! Please, no more! Oh God, Massa! Please stop, Massa!" she screamed as the whip came down again and again. The sound of the blows eventually stopped but the sobbing and groaning continued until they were swallowed up by the distance my slow easy steps placed between us.

I filled the pails with water, my thoughts drawn back to the chapel, and began to make my way back to the house, stopping half-way to rest my aching arms and wipe the sweat from my brow. I was about to pick up the pails of water and resume my journey when I heard a soft, silky voice behind me.

"My dear Luna."

I straightened immediately. The smile that had been glued to my face all day wavered and then disappeared.

I turned to face the man with the shoulder-length blond hair, blue eyes and smooth boyish features, and was immediately filled with repugnance. Everyone thought he was handsome, even the slaves grudgingly admitted as much. But he would always be repulsive to me.

"Massa," I mumbled.

The anxiety that always arose in me whenever he was near was strangely absent today. I felt calm and regarded him with coolness instead of the fear and loathing that I

51

had never managed to hide from him. He noticed the difference in me immediately and I could tell he didn't like it because his smile faded.

"How I've missed you, Luna," he said.

Instead of answering, I bent to pick up the heavy pails of water. His riding whip came crashing down on one of the handles, missing my fingers purely by luck. I froze as he brought his hand up again and the whip came down sharply on my shoulder.

"Up!"

I did as he commanded, the flesh on my shoulder smarting even though the blow had not been anywhere near as hard as those Lola had endured. When I met his gaze, mine was steady and calm.

"I said I've missed you," he said, tracing the tip of his riding whip along my cheek and down my neck. I stayed silent even though I knew he expected me to say I had missed him too, something I normally would have said to avoid his anger. But not today.

When the reply he wanted didn't come, he grabbed my chin and searched my face with those cruel, icy blue eyes other women seemed to find so appealing.

"You're different somehow," he said. "I could see that from across the field." He waited. "Well, say something."

When I didn't answer he roughly pushed my face away and smiled derisively.

"No matter. I'll find out all I need to find out tonight, won't I?"

Again he expected my usual reaction of poorly concealed fear and hatred, but I merely stood with my hands in front of me and regarded him coolly. His smile quickly disappeared and his face turned a livid shade of red.

He made as if to move away, then spun round and shoved me. I struggled in vain to stay on my feet but fell onto my knees as he kicked over the pails of water it had taken me so long to carry up the hill. With a satisfied smirk, he walked away, only to stop again.

"I'm sorry, Luna. I shouldn't have done that. I don't intend on letting you get much sleep tonight so you'll need to conserve your strength."

He waited for a response but didn't get one, so he carried on talking.

"I can see I'm going to enjoy getting to know the new you. I think I'll bring this with me," he said looking at his rawhide whip. "It will make things that much more fun."

He laughed and walked away for good this time.

As I watched him stride off, a small part of me screamed in anger and dread at what was likely to happen come nightfall. But the dominant part of me didn't feel any of those negative emotions, only the clear certainty that Master John would soon be dead.

The image of the chapel came to me again and it was like hearing a particularly sweet melody from a distance and wanting to follow that sound to its source. I wanted to be there now, in fact every part of me ached to forget my work for the afternoon and run to the chapel.

Reluctantly, I picked up the two empty pails and when I started back the way I had come, it was as if I hadn't run into Master John, even though I could still see him walking away, his fury as palpable as the shimmering heat every time he glanced back over his shoulder at me.

All I wanted was to be at my chapel, but I had to be patient. If I worked hard I could be there at sunset. The thought made me almost giddy with anticipation and I found myself singing softly as I walked back down to the well.

There was one other thing I knew with that peculiar certainty and it was that Zila was standing behind one of the trees watching me. I knew Mary had told her to go and help me carry the water back to the house and that she had seen Master John jump off his horse and hurry down the hill toward me, something that had filled her with rage. I didn't know where this knowledge came from, but I knew she had lain with him many times in the past, and that she loved him. That was why she hated me as much as she did. She blamed me for the fact that Master John took absolutely no notice of her nowadays.

Poor Zila. How she could love a brute like him was beyond my comprehension, but she did, and deeply. That sad, sweet lullaby came to me again and I walked faster.

Soon. I would be there around the time the sun began to set.

***

The moment I had spent most of the day pining for had come, but as I walked through the trees toward the chapel, I could feel a growing apprehension. I walked quickly, driven forward by a need that bordered on pain. But that deepening dread was fighting its way up through the melody that had kept me in thrall all day, and when I stepped through the trees and into the clearing, that feeling intensified to the point that I almost turned and fled.

Something propelled me onward and I ran across the clearing to the chapel door and threw myself through it. I knew something waited for me at the altar even before I was through the door and as I raced up the aisle, the fear that had been pushing to get through had all but consumed me.

What I found on the altar made no sense at all. I saw books. Brand new books. I also saw a beautiful jade green dress of the finest cloth I had ever seen in my life. There were also a few items of jewellery lying there: a gold chain with a large ruby hanging like a giant drop of blood from its centre, and diamond earrings. All of this was carefully laid out on the altar. For me.

As I looked at the bewildering sight before my eyes, I felt something loosen and fall away from me, leaving my mind unbound for the first time that day. Images began to flood me then. Images of being at the chapel the day before and kneeling by the stream with the jagged black rock held above my head.

Oh my God!

My stomach curled sickeningly when I thought about what I had come close to doing and I brought my fingertips up to my forehead, but there was no sign of the cut. I began to tremble as an overwhelming sense of danger as sharp and clear as the chiming of bells filled my mind.

I told you to stay away from that place.

That was Mama Akosua's voice, faint but clear in my head, and with my senses and mind in such a heightened state of awareness, I knew it was really her I was hearing. Just as it had been the night before when I ran through the trees.

"Yes. You sure did," I whispered, not knowing if she could somehow hear me.

I took a step away from the objects that had been placed on the altar for me.

Run.

I whirled around and began walking swiftly down the aisle. I didn't doubt the fact that I was in danger but I knew it was already too late to run. So I walked out of the chapel into the burnt gold of the setting sun, hoping that if I appeared unaware of its presence it would let me go.

I was halfway toward the trees when the atmosphere in the clearing, the very air seemed to change and I came to an abrupt stop, frozen by a presence, the shadow Mama Akosua had referred to.

It felt as if there was a powerful force emanating from behind me. It swept through the clearing causing a powerful shiver to ripple through me. It was so strong that it was almost like a throbbing heartbeat saturating everything from the aged bricks of the chapel to every single blade of grass beneath my feet. Yet nothing had actually changed physically around me. It was only what my now "open" mind could detect.

55

I tried to stay calm but my heart was racing and my breathing came out hard and fast as I pondered what to do next.

Knowing I could do nothing but face this thing, this evil, head-on, I turned around.

My vision told me there was a white man standing at the chapel door. But my sixth sense, which was sending a million pinpricks of fear along my skin, told me that the figure standing at the chapel door was something that merely wore the guise of a man. It wore nothing but a pair of black trousers and an old blue gentleman's coat over its bare chest. It was also barefoot. Its skin was a pale, almost translucent white, and gleamed softly in the light of the setting sun. From this distance, I could see it had long, tangled brown hair almost to its waist, and that it was tall with broad shoulders, a muscular well-formed chest, a narrow waist, and long powerful legs.

I opened my mouth to speak but all that came out at first was a choking sound, so I drew air forcefully into my chest and tried again.

"What... what you want?" I asked as confidently as I could manage whilst my gaze searched the ground around me for something I could use as a weapon.

When I glanced back up at the chapel door, the thing was gone and I jumped back, a scream lodged in my chest, when I saw it was now standing a few feet away from me.

With my heart pounding horribly in my chest, I found myself staring in awe at the being standing before me in the guise of a man. And what a guise it was. Its face was perfect in every way. It had large, blue eyes, an aquiline nose, a strong jaw, and lips shaped like a woman's. Noticing traces of what looked like fresh earth on its clothes and hair, I took an involuntary step forward and I was so taken in by its beauty that I almost reached out and brushed some of that dirt away from its jaw.

Although my rational mind was urging me to run, I couldn't move. If anything there seemed to be some force between us that was tugging at my spirit, making me want to move closer to this being, and it took a great deal of will power to stop myself from taking another step forward.

It stood completely still with its head cocked to one side, its lips slightly parted as it regarded me in amazement, eyes like blue fire burning into me. Then it brought its hand up slowly toward my face.

I wanted to scream. I wanted to run, but fear kept me where I stood. Its fingertips, pale with torn ragged fingernails that had earth beneath them, were just inches from my face when it froze. Its eyes darted to a point behind me, into the trees as if it had heard something, and I used that opportunity to take a step back. That small movement brought its gaze back to me and in another of those quicksilver moves, it had closed the space between us again.

But it only gazed at me, looking slightly confused, and made no move to stop me as I took another step back. It was hard to resist the pull this being exerted over me but I forced myself to keep moving backward and away from the chapel, as I knew now that there was something else here in the clearing with us, something that swathed the hulking, decrepit chapel in evil. My senses were saturated by the being standing before me so it was hard to focus on the other entity. All I knew was that it had been here for a very long time and hate burned at its heart like a smouldering volcano.

There was something forlorn and incredibly vulnerable about the creature as it watched me move away from it. It made no further move forward but merely gazed at me in bewilderment, its stance one of dejection. The acute yearning in its eyes was as ancient as it was terrible. Unable to look into those eyes for even one second longer, I ran into the trees.

Chapter Five

I ran blindly, seeing nothing but its burning blue eyes, ragged clothes and torn fingernails just inches away from my face. I ran but I could still feel that mesmeric force, that heartbreaking lullaby, reaching out to envelop me, and I knew I would never be able to escape it.

My thoughts were wild and thin as I fled, the woodland I ran through eerie and surreal, every shadow or strange shape in the gloom sinister. It was no longer the woods I had grown up in or even the place I saw in my nightmares whenever I relived that day with Master Henry. It was now some otherworldly dimension where evil spirits and hellish incarnations resided alongside everything else I had long thought of as fancy but which were now as real as the thing I had left behind me in the clearing.

With my muscles burning and sweat pouring down my back, I raced through the trees until a dark shape came rushing out of the murky shadows and I collided with a hard, muscular chest.

Letting out a piercing wail, I squeezed my eyes shut as strong hands clamped down on my upper arms. I thrashed around wildly, not wanting to look into that hauntingly beautiful face and those wild, desperate eyes for even one second. But the thing held me tight and I screamed even louder, my chest on fire and dizziness beginning to sap the little bit of strength I had.

"Sister Luna! Sister Luna!"

It must have been the tone of his voice rather than the words itself which reached through the frenzy to quiet my screams.

"Sister Luna!"

I opened my eyes and was overwhelmed with pure joy when Jupiter's face filled my vision. He was looking at me as if his worst nightmare was being replayed right before his eyes.

"Jupiter?" I sagged against him.

For a few seconds I felt the same security I had on the day he'd run through the woods with me in his arms. It was the only part of that dark, traumatic day I could bear to remember.

The force I had felt in the clearing, and which had seemed to follow me through the trees, had dimmed and was now as faint as the background noise of the woodland around us, but I knew I wasn't safe.

"Sister Luna. What happened?"

"I... I saw something." I was crying now. "It ain't safe. We gots to go." I broke away, trying to pull him along with me even though I was disoriented and didn't know which direction would lead us out of the sinister company of the trees.

"No, Sister Luna." He had me by the arms again. "Tell me what frightened you."

Calmer now, I noticed that Jupiter wasn't alone. He was with his Master, Father Geoffrey, a short, portly white man with a cherubic face and small, twinkling brown eyes.

When he saw me gazing at him he came to stand beside Jupiter. "It's all right, dear. Why don't you tell us what you were running from?"

"I saw something," was all I could say at first, for dread as real as a hand clasped around my neck had quickly overwhelmed me again. Even though I couldn't see their faces clearly in the gloom, I could tell they were looking at me with the patient kind of wariness reserved for those

59

whose firmness of mind was in question. But I could still feel the creature's presence and I had to tell them.

"What, dear?" Father Geoffrey said, laying his hand on my shoulder. When I flinched at his touch he quickly removed it. "Tell us what you saw."

"It... it was a demon. I saw a demon. It be standing by that old chapel looking at me and I's thinking it gonna kill me but then it lets me go and... and..."

I saw a faint smile touch Father Geoffrey's lips as he glanced at Jupiter. Jupiter was still gazing at me but he had relaxed visibly, my words having no doubt sounded like nonsense to both of them.

"No!" I broke away from Jupiter's grip. "It's true. I ain't crazy. I saw it. It looked like a man but it a demon. I swear it be a demon! She told me, Mama Akosua told me not to go to the chapel but I didn't listen and now it's seen me. Please! You gots to believe me. It's still here. I can feel it. It's everywhere! Can't you feels it?"

"Luna, is it?" Father Geoffrey said, not bothering to hold back a small chuckle. "Listen to me, child. There's..."

"I do feel something," Jupiter said softly.

He was tense again now and brought his hand up to his chin as he searched the trees around us, a frown creasing his brow.

"I have felt something strange since we got here. Don't you feel it, Father?"

"Oh, Jupiter! Not you too," Father Geoffrey said, clearly amused.

"You are a holy man, Father. You should be able to sense it if you try. Use your sleeping mind and you will feel it."

He gave Jupiter the sort of indulgent smile a grown-up reserves for children who still believe in fairy tales although they are old enough to know better. But he closed his eyes theatrically as if he were playing a role for our benefit.

"Well, if it will stop you two and all this nonsensical

talk about..."

He stopped talking and the smile left his lips as his eyes flew open.

"You feel it now, Father?" Jupiter said.

Father Geoffrey looked troubled now. He too peered nervously into the intimidating shadows closing in on us.

"Father?" Jupiter asked.

"I... I don't know," he said slowly when his gaze met Jupiter's. "But I think we have lingered here long enough."

He took me by the arm, too busy looking around to notice me flinch. "Tell us everything that happened," he said and we began to walk as fast as we could while I told them everything that had taken place at the chapel.

Once we were out of the trees and under the sulky indigo sky, I walked on ahead, Jupiter and Father Geoffrey trailing behind and whispering earnestly.

I felt a little bit calmer now that we were out of the woods and nearing the lights and familiar smells of the slave quarters as the slaves prepared their evening meals. It felt like a semblance of normality was once more returning to my world. The terror I had felt at the chapel relaxed its hold somewhat, but I was sure it would be a long time before it ever really left me.

Mama Akosua had told me that the women in our family possessed the gift of second sight and I was starting to believe that the demon had somehow awoken it when it released its hold on my mind at the chapel. But without my fear focusing that second sight, I couldn't really sense the creature as strongly as I had before. I knew it was still near but its presence was faint, almost like looking at a figure in the distance and having to squint in order to bring it into focus.

"Sister Luna." Jupiter hurried to my side with Father Geoffrey at his heels as we neared the slave quarters. "We think we know what to do about this devil you saw."

"We?" Father Geoffrey interjected with a wry smile before he turned his gaze to me. "He wants me to go and consult with your mother about this thing you *think* you saw and which we *think* we felt." He looked at Jupiter. "How much of a congregation do you think I'll have if I start consorting with someone who is well known for dabbling in the dark arts?"

He spoke lightly but it was obvious the apprehension he had displayed in the woods hadn't left him.

"Father, please. She will know what..."

"Yes, yes," he said dismissing Jupiter's renewed arguments with a wave of his hand. "So you've said. Hopefully I'll have enough of a congregation left in order for us to eat this Sunday."

He was smiling again and it was obvious that there wasn't very much he could refuse Jupiter. I wouldn't exactly call what Father Geoffrey clearly felt toward his slave respect as you couldn't respect someone you didn't view as your equal. But there was definitely affection there and I was glad that what I'd heard about Father Geoffrey being a kind Master appeared to be true.

"So what we'll do before we go to her is warn everyone to stay inside and especially out of the woods," Father Geoffrey said. "You should be safe in your cabin tonight. We'll decide what to do tomorrow when we know more, so don't worry, dear. You're safe now."

He smiled kindly at me but I didn't feel as if I would be safe by any means tonight and it seemed as if Jupiter shared that feeling because he abruptly grasped my arm.

When I looked up at him his face was set in stone and he was glaring past me at something in the distance. I nervously followed his gaze, fearing he had seen the demon. But all I saw was a light burning in the window of my cabin.

I stiffened, feeling myself go cold despite the stifling heat.

No. It wasn't a threat from the demon that had turned his features to stone, but a human one.

Master John was waiting for me.

At that moment Father Geoffrey placed a restraining hand on Jupiter's, pulling it off my arm. It wasn't done unkindly as he was looking at Jupiter with a degree of pity, something I thought I would never see in the eyes of a white man. But it was there and I saw some of that pity extended to me when his gaze met mine.

"We'll be back tomorrow when we know more," he said patting Jupiter twice on the shoulder as he spoke.

"Thank you, sir." I turned to Jupiter and was dismayed to see that he wouldn't look at me. "Thank you, Jupiter."

He nodded and there was nothing left for me to do but walk to my cabin where Master John was waiting.

It had been a long day, one in which events had transpired to make Jupiter look at me again, instead of away as he had done ever since he found me lying in the dirt in my own blood. It was only now that I realised how much I had missed the feel of his gaze on me.

It was hard to walk up to my cabin door knowing what awaited me and also knowing that Father Geoffrey and Jupiter were still watching. But I steeled myself and didn't hesitate when I reached the door and opened it.

***

That night *was* filled with terror, but not the kind I'd been expecting. When I opened the door I stared at the ground, wanting to delay the moment when I would have to look up into Master John's smiling face, for he was always smiling. So the first thing I saw was Master John's riding whip on the floor. It had been broken in two.

In the time it took to look up, I felt the presence of the thing in the woods close around me and was tugged forward by an unseen hand at the same time that the door was slammed shut. When my gaze fell on Master John in the glow of the candlelight, he wasn't smiling and he wasn't alone.

He stood facing me with his arms hanging limply by

his sides. His head had been tilted to the right, leaving one side of his neck exposed. His eyes, which were frozen in terror, were locked on mine and a thin trail of tears ran down his face. His mouth hung open and I thought he was dead until I saw his lip quiver and he mouthed the words "help me."

The demon was standing behind Master John with one arm around his chest holding him up. Its eyes were closed and the bottom half of its face was buried in Master John's neck, an expression of pure bliss marking its features. It wasn't until I saw a trickle of blood run from the spot where the creature's mouth joined Master John's neck that I realised what it was doing.

It was drinking Master John's blood.

Drinking his blood and killing him in the process.

The comforting noises outside my cabin seemed to dissolve and I was back in that terrifying world I thought I had left behind in the woods. I couldn't move or speak and my mind seemed to have become completely locked in the terror of what I was witnessing in the furtive half-light of my candlelit cabin. I didn't think about trying to scream or run. I didn't try to think of a way to help Master John. I couldn't do anything but stand and stare at the atrocity that was taking place before my eyes.

I had seen all manner of cruelty and degradation on this earth. I had been a victim of rape, witnessed murder, and had even seen men treat their own children like cattle. I also believed in Heaven and hell, so I believed in the existence of demons. But what I saw before me now was beyond anything I could ever have imagined capable of the fallen.

What manner of creature on this earth or in hell could drink the blood of a man while he was still conscious and aware of what was being done to him? What manner of being could commit such an atrocity and appear to enjoy it?

At that moment the demon's eyes snapped open. It

regarded me for a moment and then, with an expression bordering on physical pain, it drew its lips away from Master John's neck, allowing me to see that its incisors were like those of a tiger.

It watched me for a few moments whilst the scarlet stain on Master John's shirt grew larger, then it moved its arm away from its victim's chest and I saw Master John's eyes roll back before he fell to the floor in a dead heap.

Now the thing stood watching me, its blue eyes assailing me with that same wild hunger and yearning I had seen before. That's when I found the strength to scream.

Everything that had happened over the last two nights seemed to overheat my brain and it began to withdraw, seeking refuge in darkness.

I had to get away. But I could already feel my legs giving way and darkness moving swiftly in on me.

The creature moved with that lightning-fast speed and was at my side to catch me before I hit the ground.

I knew I would surely die now.

The last thing I saw before I fell into darkness was its face hovering over mine with Master John's blood still on its lips, that bottomless blue gaze scorching my mind.

And then it was all gone.

Chapter Six

It seemed as though an eternity passed before the sound of raised voices began to penetrate the cool darkness. Those voices sent a white flare of anxiety into the dark and the more I tried to withdraw, the louder the voices became until I began to hear individual words.

"She dared to try and kill a white..."

"Her mama's a witch and she..."

"She's evil. We all know she done killed her own..."

What was this? Hell?

Then I was awake and looking up at the full moon gleaming like a pearl in the sooty night sky.

I felt something draw close around me and realised that I was lying on the ground outside my quarters, being propped up in someone's arms.

"Where...?" I whispered.

"Sister Luna. You are awake."

I grasped his hand, so relieved to hear the sound of his voice. It seemed that Jupiter was always there whenever I needed him most.

"What happened? Massa John?"

"He lives, Sister Luna," he spat. "We heard you scream and when we ran to your cabin we... we saw it. We saw the demon but it turned into air and was gone before we could even speak. I fear that if we had not been close by, you would be dead."

"Help me up," I said but his hold on me tightened.

"No. I do not want them to see you are awake. You're still in danger, Sister Luna. Not everyone believes that it was a demon that nearly killed Master John. They think it was you. And the ones who do believe what we say about the demon think you're the one who drew it here. And they don't believe any of us will be safe if you live."

For a moment I couldn't move. Then I slowly inched my head forward and surveyed the scene ahead.

A large crowd made up of slaves, the Master's family, and Mr Jenkins, a slaveholder from one of the neighbouring plantations, were standing about five metres from where I lay. I couldn't see the faces of all of the people gathered there but the ones I could see in the meagre glow of a few oil lamps were distorted either by fear or anger.

"Do you expect us to believe that some demon tried to hurt Master John? It was her! And I'm not going to let her live long enough to try again!" shouted Mr Jenkins, a burly, greasy man with a large moustache.

His words were met with a roar of approval.

Father Geoffrey had his hands held out as if to try and hold back the crowd and I could hear the low, imploring murmur of his voice but not the words. He was probably the only thing keeping them from putting a noose around my neck and lynching me from the large pecan tree that stood at the back of the slave quarters like a gnarled sentinel.

I searched the faces of the crowd. It didn't matter whether they were black or white, they were all glaring at me with varying degrees of antipathy and some even turned away in fear when my gaze met theirs as if they thought I could reach out and harm them in some way.

I closed my eyes, feeling completely alone, until Jupiter squeezed my hand. I hadn't exactly given the other Negroes on the plantation much reason to like me over the years, but it was still hard to face the fact that they believed me capable of something like this. At least Mary wasn't part of the baleful mob and hopefully she wouldn't be here to watch them kill me.

"Do not worry, Sister Luna. Father Geoffrey will calm them."

"Help me up."

"No. You must..."

"Help me up!"

When he didn't respond, I shrugged his arms away and sat up, turning to face him.

"If they gonna kill me, then let them."

I saw a sort of shrinking despair in his deep brown eyes before he lowered them.

"Sister Luna. You do..."

"No, Jupiter. You know what the demon be doing to Massa when I finds them? It be drinking his blood! I ain't gonna die that way. I ain't, so help me God!"

"Look! She's awake!"

It was Zila whose shrill cry interrupted us, her face a mask of unadulterated hated. Abruptly, she broke away from the crowd and came charging toward me. I quickly got to my feet but Jupiter was quicker and caught Zila by the arms just as she reached out to slap me.

"Zila, stop this! You know she did not hurt Massa John!"

But it seemed Zila's actions had broken the dam and the majority of the blacks that made up the crowd surged forward.

"She did this! She called that demon here!"

"We all gonna pay for what she did to Massa!"

"Kill her 'fore she calls it back!"

My head began spinning as I faced them, most of what was being said lost in the confusion of voices as they surrounded us. Jupiter pushed Zila back and moved to stand in front of me as I backed away, only to find myself trapped by the cabin wall. He appeared calm as he silently challenged all of them and perhaps recognising something in his gaze, something better not challenged, they held back.

The worst thing was that apart from Zila, who could barely contain her hatred, they were all genuinely scared. Scared of me.

"I told you all. She did not summon that demon. Listen to me..." Father Geoffrey had raised his voice now, but like a pillow pressed against a man's face, the authority in his tone was being smothered by the rising panic.

"Get out of my way!" Mr Jenkins pushed past Father Geoffrey. I remembered once that he had tried to get Master Henry, and then Master John, to sell me to him, and for a lot more money than a female slave of childbearing age was worth.

"You're not going to lay a finger on her."

A tremulous silence fell as everyone turned to the sound of the voice. The group of slaves who had surrounded us slowly backed away. It was Master John. In the midst of the uproar no one had noticed him and Master Peter walking toward the slave quarters. He was holding a bloody handkerchief to the wound in his neck, and had his other arm around Master Peter, who was supporting him. Even though his mouth was set in a determined line, he looked weak and pale. Master John and his brother were not alone. Mama Akosua was with them, and trailing behind her, with two horses in tow, was one of the field slaves.

Mama's expression was not one I'd ever seen before. I'm sure a lioness guarding her young wouldn't have been anywhere near as fearsome as she appeared at that moment. I was surprised to see her here but I shouldn't have been because she was always there in my time of need. Hadn't she found her way back to Mississippi when Master Henry sold her away to a plantation in Louisiana? And of course she had braved the storm on that night so she could deliver my baby and nurse me back to health in the weeks that had followed.

"This nigger wench is *my* property," Master John spat. "I, and only I, will decide what happens to her. Do you hear me?"

The appearance of Master John seemed to have given Father Geoffrey the confidence that was so obviously lacking before and there was a calm authority in his voice when he spoke again.

"Luna didn't do this. If you don't believe me then ask Master John. Ask him what happened!"

All eyes were on Master John again who seemed to be shrinking under the weight of those questioning gazes.

"It wasn't Luna," he said, his voice smaller than usual and his lip trembling with fear. "It... it was..."

"We don't know what it was," Master Peter said coming to his brother's rescue. "But it definitely wasn't human."

Mr Jenkins met this with a derisive grunt but although he clearly wasn't convinced, he wasn't about to call Master John a liar.

"We can't turn against each other now," Father Geoffrey said. "The thing we saw tonight is powerful and it's a common enemy to slave and slaveholder alike. We can't afford to be divided when faced with such a deadly enemy."

Mr Jenkins completely ignored Father Geoffrey and strode over to Master John.

"So if what you're telling me is right and this... demon...is after the girl, then why are we standing here arguing?" he asked incredulously. "We should take her back to the chapel and let that thing do whatever it wants to her!"

"And then you will have *two* hungry demons to fear," Mama Akosua said, her voice calm and steady.

Mr Jenkins turned to her, his eyes bulging in his round, meaty face. "What do you mean?

"This creature is no ordinary devil. It feeds on blood and it has the power to make other demons like it. If you

70

give her to it, you will have two blood thirsty demons on your hands."

A frightened hush fell over the crowd and then a male voice rose up into the night.

"We gots to kill her now 'fore it comes back!"

A murmur of agreement rippled through the crowd.

"I know how to kill it," Mama Akosua said quickly, stepping in front of Master John and speaking directly to Mr Jenkins. "But if any of you harm my daughter, I will do nothing."

"You'll do as you're told, nigger, or pay with your life!" the plantation owner hissed.

"Then I will pay with my life. My daughter is everything to me. Harm her and I leave this demon to slaughter you and your children as you sleep!"

"It won't come to that," Master Peter said gesturing for the field slave to bring the horses over to us. "Father, take them back to your home." He gestured to me and Mama Akosua. "The rest of us will..."

"No. She stays with us." Mr Jenkins had taken a hold of Mama Akosua's arm. "If there really is a demon and she knows how to kill it then I don't want her going anywhere."

I looked to Master Peter, pleading with my eyes, but all he did was make a furtive gesture for me to get on the horse. Jupiter was only too quick to heed the gesture and he pulled me along with him, only letting go of my arm long enough to mount the horse before quickly hoisting me up behind him.

"Be reasonable," Master Peter continued. "She doesn't need to stay. The demon will not trouble us with the girl gone."

"The witch stays here or her daughter dies," he said firmly.

Master Peter met his gaze for a few seconds and then turned to Father Geoffrey, who had mounted the second horse.

71

"I'll send someone with news for you tomorrow," he said.

"Massa John," Mama Akosua said. "I did not come to you so that you could let them take her away. Only I can protect her from this devil. You have to let me go with her."

But Mama's words were in vain, for although Master John no doubt wanted her to go with us, he was really in no condition to argue the case, for he looked even paler than when he had first arrived.

"You'll have to do what you can from here," he said before he turned to Master Geoffrey. "Make sure you bring my property back to me, *untouched*." His gaze flickered to Jupiter briefly on the last word before it returned to Father Geoffrey. "Go."

Jupiter urged the horse onward and Father Geoffrey followed. I kept my eyes on Mama Akosua, who looked completely bereft as she watched us draw further and further away from her.

She was and always would be completely devoted to me, and I realised with a sinking kind of shame that I had done absolutely nothing during the course of my miserable life to earn or even reward such a powerful level of devotion. Absolutely nothing.

When her forlorn figure finally disappeared, I began to cry.

I was sure I would never see her again.

Chapter Seven

I clung to Jupiter as our horse raced away from the comforting lights of the plantation into the night. The only thing that broke the emptiness of the stark landscape was the moon above and a ghostly black mass of woodland some distance to our left.

I had never felt so afraid, my gaze darting to every dark shape that swept past us and any sound other than the drum-like beat of the horses' hooves sending spikes of fear through me as we were carried deeper into the night. It was like a living thing, hostile and heartless in its absolute dominion and I longed for even the dim light of a solitary farmhouse to take away some of its power. But there was nothing; only the indifferent stars above and the awful realisation that I had lost everything, the only home I had ever known, and the few people that meant anything to me.

And it seemed the night held more horrors in store for us for we were only fifteen minutes into the journey when Jupiter abruptly brought the horse to a stop and turned it around. He was completely still, his body tensed like that of an animal that had caught the scent of a predator. Father Geoffrey, who was a few paces behind us, slowed to a stop and peered questioningly into Jupiter's face.

"What is it?" he asked, panting heavily.

"Look."

At first I couldn't see anything, but then I spotted a tiny amber glow in the distance struggling against the darkness that threatened to swallow it. It was obviously a lamplight, and on this night, it could only be bringing one thing upon us: Death. And now I could hear what had caused Jupiter to stop and whip the horse around. The faint sound of two, maybe three horses beating a ruthless path toward us.

A powerful, mind-numbing fear, as deadly as quicksand, clasped me as I watched that tiny orb of light steadily get closer. All my strength left me as that fear pulled me down into its cold callous depths.

"Massa John was not able to stop them," Jupiter said. "They are coming for us."

I watched the colour slowly drain from Father Geoffrey's face.

"We...We'll never make it," he said.

"We must try," Jupiter said fiercely. "Head for the trees. It will be harder for them to follow us once we are in the trees."

He spun the horse around and urged it forward as a sound like thunder tore the night apart making my heart leap so violently in my chest that I almost fell off the horse.

A gun. They had guns.

I clung even tighter to Jupiter as the horse tore across the barren countryside whilst the sound of gunfire chased us, each shot closer than the last. I could barely breathe, and the quicksand continued to pull me down leaving me lightheaded and trembling as the pursuing horses drew closer.

All I could do was pray. Pray that God would deliver us from the evil on our heels and let us reach the relative safety of the trees in time. But I already knew we wouldn't make it. In fact, what the events of this long, terrifying night had shown me was that God had forsaken me. I was being punished, not only for those babies I had killed in my womb, but for the child I had borne ten years ago and tossed aside like worthless trash.

Another gunshot rang out. This one was so loud it seemed to shake the very ground we sped across. I screamed but my cry was swallowed by the piercing shriek of the horse as it pitched forward and I realised it had been hit. My arms were wrenched from Jupiter and the world seemed to turn upside down in a whirl of gunfire and screams as the ground rushed up toward me.

I hit the dry earth with a bone-jolting thud that completely knocked the breath out of me and sent stars shooting behind my eyes. For a moment I couldn't move even though there was no pain, only numbness. The piercing scream of the wounded horse filled my ears. Closing in on that sound was the deadly tattoo of the approaching horsemen.

Bringing my head up, I looked around, my vision swimming sickeningly through a haze of tears, and saw the dim outline of Father Geoffrey limping toward me. He was covered in the same brown dust that clung to my face and clothes and there was blood streaming from a cut along his hairline.

"Quickly." He pulled me to my feet. "Where's Jupiter?"

"I am here."

He was standing a few feet away with his back to us and looking directly ahead. The three horsemen were upon us and we were all soon snared in the ominous light of the lamp as they slowed down to trot in a loose circle around us. The bloodcurdling shrieks of the wounded horse slowly began to fade, as if in response to the menacing presence of the three horsemen, until there was only silence. I wasn't surprised to see that the lead rider was Mr Jenkins. He stopped directly in front of us and held his lamplight up even higher before he turned his head in the direction of one of the other men.

"Eli," he said and nodded curtly.

The one called Eli, a thin, dark-haired boy of no more

than sixteen, raised his gun and aimed it at me. A low mewing sound escaped my lips. I tried to take a step back but I was now completely submerged in my fear-induced quicksand and I couldn't move. Everything seemed to slow down. I squeezed my eyes shut as Eli pulled the trigger and a deafening crack filled the air.

Instead of the blinding pain of a hot bullet piercing my flesh, I heard a strangled cry and something that sounded like a sack of coal hitting the ground. I immediately opened my eyes and saw Jupiter lying sprawled on his back at my feet.

"*No!*" I screamed as Father Geoffrey called out his name.

My legs turned to water and I fell to my knees mumbling Jupiter's name over and over again as I cradled his head in my lap. He tried to sit up but then inhaled sharply before he fell back down with a groan. Father Geoffrey was kneeling by my side looking just as horrified and helpless as I felt, especially when his gaze fell on the dark red stain that had appeared on the shoulder of Jupiter's shirt. It was spreading quickly down his arm.

Eli and the third assailant, a short, scruffy man, had dismounted, and as Eli stepped forward and aimed the gun at my head, the third man hoisted Father Geoffrey onto his feet and dragged him away.

I could only stare helplessly into Eli's sickle-thin face, taking in the malice in the mean, dark slits he had for eyes. I was sunk so deep in the quicksand of fear that I was beyond any kind of coherent thought or action that might have been able to make a difference. I could only marvel at how someone as young as Eli could be filled with so much hate. All the while, warm blood continued to gush from Jupiter's wound, soaking through my dress and running down my thighs.

It seemed Eli was determined to prolong the moment as long as possible because he slowly moved the gun down so that it was aimed at Jupiter's chest.

"Now, which one of these niggers do I kill first?" he asked in an amiable tone of voice.

A flare of anger sent my fear scurrying away and an odd focus quietened my mind in what I knew were to be my final moments. I pulled Jupiter closer and stared defiantly up at Eli. This boy may have had the power to take my life, but I wasn't about to let him have the satisfaction of seeing me quiver with fear at his feet.

With Jupiter in my arms, I was ready to meet my fate.

But it seemed my fate wouldn't be decided by Eli after all, because at that moment I was unexpectedly engulfed by the same sensation I had felt at the clearing when the demon first revealed itself to me. Everything sharpened just as it had then and I didn't need to see it to know that it was there in the same way that I didn't have to see the flames of a fire in order to feel the heat it generated.

If I thought I had felt fear a moment ago, then I was mistaken, because what I felt now was the paralysing shock of pure terror. I began to shake violently and my chest tightened painfully.

Eli, mistakenly assuming that I was reacting to the gun, smiled before bringing it back up to my head.

"It's here," was all I could whisper in warning. But it was too late.

Eli's attention was caught by a flicker of movement to his right. He let out a gasp and swung the gun away from me. The weapon was torn out of his hand and sent soaring into the air where it was swallowed by the darkness. I heard it fire once when it hit the ground some distance from us and then there was silence.

Fast, so fast that Eli barely had time to scream, the creature was upon him and violently hoisted him up off the ground by the neck with one hand. It looked up at Eli with inhuman rage, its fangs clearly visible whilst Eli gasped for air, his face turning red as he struggled like a fly caught in a spider's web. I heard the third man cry out as his gun flew out of his hand. Mr Jenkins was the last to be

77

disarmed. He dropped the lantern so he could clasp his gun with both hands and was nearly sent toppling off his horse when it was wrenched out of his grasp.

With barely a glance at the two men with whom he had arrived, he turned his horse around and galloped away.

In the fast diminishing light of the dying lamp, the demon reached for Eli's arm, the one that had been holding the gun, and grasped it above the elbow. Eli began to scream, a hoarse keening sound of raw pain, and then there was a sickening, wet snap as the demon tore Eli's arm away from his shoulder in one swift, brutal motion. Blood spurted in a crimson arc from the wound, splattering Jupiter and me. We could only look on in dazed horror as the demon casually flung the limb away and released its hold on Eli's neck.

Eli fell to the ground, his left leg, which was already soaked with blood, brushing against my arm. I shrunk from him in revulsion as his agonised screams melted away, leaving only the sound of his quick, pained breathing as he lay with one hand on the warm, steaming flesh where his arm should have been. The hot metallic smell of blood suffused the warm night air and made me gag, as Eli's eyes began to glaze over and he went into shock.

Screams of fear filled the air again and I looked behind me in dismay. The man who had been restraining Father Geoffrey had run off when the demon attacked Eli. He was screaming now as he was dragged back toward us by unseen hands. The demon materialised a few feet behind me and caught the panic-stricken man in its morbid embrace. His screams were cut short when the creature placed both hands at the sides of his head and picked him up. The acrid scent of urine mingled with the smell of blood in the air and I realised that in his fright the man had soiled himself. There was a horrifying crunching sound as the demon crushed his skull, causing his face to cave in. His left eye popped out of its socket to dangle on his cheek. Blood peppered with bits of bone and a spongy-looking tissue began to ooze down the side of his face. When the demon finally released him, the man's arms and legs twitched spasmodically for a few moments before he went completely still.

A fear-soaked silence hung in the air for a few moments and then the creature looked off into the night in the direction Mr Jenkins had taken. Its smile had no mirth in it, only cold ruthlessness. And then it vanished.

A few seconds later we heard another scream that was abruptly cut off. I stared into the dark and tried to imagine the horrific death that was being visited upon the man who had been so hell-bent on shedding my blood, and I knew, somehow, that the demon was drinking his blood, slowly.

I shivered. In a matter of moments, this thing had slaughtered three men in the most barbaric of ways, and that same fate might soon be ours.

I quickly stood up, and ignoring Jupiter's gasps of pain, dragged him to his feet. Father Geoffrey, who was still shaking, had started tugging at his hair and was staring fixedly in the direction Mr Jenkins had taken.

"Father," I cried. "We has to get to the trees."

It didn't seem as if he heard me. His complexion had taken on a greenish tinge, his lips were chalky white, and he was trembling as he continued to pull out clumps of his own hair.

"We... we can't outrun that thing. Did... did you see the way...?"

"Father! We have to go now!" Jupiter cried.

But it was already too late. As fast and as silent as I had always seen it, the demon appeared again about two metres from us. Its teeth were back to normal now but it had blood on its mouth and hands, the blood of three men. It stood before us with its hands held loosely by its sides, and although rage no longer marked its features, that tumultuous longing continued to blaze in its eyes as it stared at me.

The heat of its stare was hard to hold but although I wanted to look away, I couldn't. And in spite of the carnage I had just witnessed, I still felt my spirit come alive in the presence of this thing. Again, I had to stop myself from moving closer to it.

Only when Father Geoffrey began to mumble a prayer did I find myself able to tear my gaze away from the demon. The priest's hands were shaking violently as he held out the large cross that was hanging from a chain around his neck.

The demon turned its gaze to Father Geoffrey and a small frown wrinkled its brow as it stared at him with an almost human mixture of anger and pity. Then it took a step toward him, reached for the cross, and tore it away from Father Geoffrey's neck. It kept a steady gaze on him as it closed its pale fingers around the cross and snapped it in half, before releasing the fragments in much the same casual way it had discarded Eli's severed arm.

Father Geoffrey's voice had wavered when the cross was taken from him, but he steadied it and continued praying with his eyes closed.

I heard a roar then that was like a battle cry. Jupiter pushed me back with one hand and lunged at the demon. What occurred next happened so quickly that I didn't quite see everything that took place. The demon moved so quickly that he became a blur of pale white skin and coal black hair and when I fell to the ground, I saw Father Geoffrey lying unconscious at the demon's feet. Jupiter was now imprisoned in the demon's grasp and it was holding him up off the ground and snarling at him, its hands on either side of his head as Jupiter tried in vain to fight it.

"*No!*" I screamed and the demon stopped long enough for me to get to my feet, regarding me in confusion and distress. "*No!*"

I made to run toward the creature but before I could take even one step forward, hands clasped my upper arm and I was whirled around.

The next thing I knew I was standing in complete darkness with the demon's arm around my waist and my chest pressed against his. We were now closer to the trees, about twenty metres from where we had been and I could see Jupiter lying on the ground beside Father Geoffrey in the decayed ochre of the feeble lamplight. I could only assume that he was dead.

"*No! Jupiter! Noooo!*" I screamed, pain racking my mind and body at the sight of him lying dead in the dirt.

And then the scene before my eyes wavered and the demon and I were in the woods.

Chapter Eight

In the woods I fell silent, my senses completely overwhelmed now that I was in such close proximity to the demon. My heartbeat had sped up out of control, my breathing coming in quick shallow breaths and it felt as if my brain was on fire as the demon swept me along with it on a dizzying journey through the trees.

So far I had seen it disappear and then re-appear elsewhere instantaneously and thought it did so by walking or running, but moving far too fast for the naked eye to see. But that's not how it crossed distances in a matter of seconds. Instead it stood still with one arm around my waist and it was everything else around us that appeared to move. I can only surmise that the demon was able to exert some force, some power on the area around it and I watched wide-eyed as the trees, the earth beneath my feet, and the very air began to shimmer as if it were losing cohesion. It would look as if it was all being pulled in toward us and then it would abruptly push away and we would be in a completely different location, maybe miles, or tens of miles, from where we'd been before.

I had no way of measuring the distance we travelled, or jumped – if you want to see it that way, but a few minutes later we reached an area where the trees had begun to thin, letting the moonlight pool on the grass in lucent swathes. Towering over the trees was a gigantic rock and protruding from its base was a flat ledge about a metre high.

This is where the demon released me and I stumbled away from it until I backed into the rock face. It stood there studying me but I couldn't see its face as it stood with its back to the moon and so was just a shadow amongst shadows. Then it vanished.

I sank to the ground, my head swimming with all the horrors I had witnessed that night.

Was Eli still lying there surrounded by corpses, taking in those quick shallow breaths as the pool of blood he lay in grew? And Jupiter. Jupiter, who had stood by my side when the whole world was against me, was now dead.

A wave of misery swept over me and for a moment the whole world seemed to tilt threateningly. I felt my stomach constrict and I leaned forward and threw up. Then the tears came, hot, salty tears that did nothing to ease the pain or stop those images from filling my agonised mind.

I sat with my back against the rock and cried, feeling as if my mind was going to tip over into insanity as the images continued to crawl around my overwhelmed brain. They were dead. Five men had died horribly tonight because of me. I cried until all the tears had been wrung out of me and then I sat staring in silence until at last, my tortured mind began to form some sort of coherent thought.

I was still alive. God knows how or why, but I was still alive and I had to get away from here before the demon came back.

I climbed down from the ledge onto the soft grass and looked around. As I tried to decide which direction to take, I saw something in the distance: a dark shape moving to and fro.

I moved back against the ledge and peered into the dark. The creature was still here, pacing back and forth amongst the trees with its hands held to its head. Holding my breath, I started to back away. Abruptly, it stopped pacing and spun around to look directly at me.

I felt a surge of panic and quickly turned, intending to run, but before I could take a step forward, it was standing a few feet ahead of me, blocking the path. I froze, my heart thumping horribly in my chest, sweat trickling down my back.

After a few moments it made to move toward me and I scurried backward, tripped over a fallen branch, and fell to my knees.

"Please," I gasped and it immediately halted its advance. "Please don't kill me."

Some kind of turmoil crossed its features as it watched me trying unsuccessfully to fight back tears.

"I am not going to kill you," it said, articulating the words slowly and carefully.

I was surprised by how soft its voice was and noticed that it didn't speak like the other white men of the south. But I had never heard an accent like it before so wasn't able to place it.

"Then why has you brung me here?" I asked.

It seemed to shrink away from that question and lowered its gaze.

"Please," I said wiping away tears. "Please, take me back."

It was standing before me one moment, in the next it was gone. I gasped and brought my hands up to my chest when it reappeared kneeling on the ground a few feet away from me, fear marking its handsome face.

"They will kill you if I do that!"

I was silent, unnerved by the anger I saw, anger which seemed to drain away as it gazed at me.

"Then... then let me go on back there so's I can bury Jupiter and Father Geoffrey," I managed after a few moments of silence. "I can't... I can't leave his body there. Please, you gots to let me bury him."

It was gone again and when I looked up it was standing a few feet away, agitated and trying to avoid my gaze.

"No, no. They were not dead when I took you away."

"Don't lie!" I screamed, anger at the thought of Jupiter's corpse being left for some wild animal to scavenge overcoming my fear and I was only mildly aware of the fact that it had flinched in response.

"Even if you be telling the truth," I continued. "How long you think he gonna stay alive out there?"

"I... I..."

"He dead. Jupiter be dead and it's all cause of me!"

I cried without restraint now and the demon stood there with its hands curled into fists at its side, its expression one of helplessness.

Then it drew its lips together into a thin line and began to stare intently at me. I found that I couldn't look away. The dizziness that had overwhelmed me at the chapel returned along with that tantalising melody, and I realised what it was doing.

"No," I mumbled.

The dizziness took over and I closed my eyes, my head swimming with its sweet melody and then everything, my grief, anxiety and fear, began to disappear, until I sank into nothing.

***

The sound of birdsong drifted gently into my sleepy haven and I let out a heavy sigh.

Morning. Already?

It seemed as if I had crawled into bed only moments ago and it was already time to get up and make my way to the Master's house where I would spend the day at their beck and call. I was exhausted and there was also a hazy impression of terrifying blood-filled nightmares at the back of my mind.

"Luna."

It wasn't the sound of a male voice in my quarters at such an early hour that brought fear tiptoeing into my mind, but the way it said my name, wrapping its tongue around the word as if to savour it.

I opened my eyes.

I was lying on what looked like a loveseat by the window in the drawing room of a house I had never been in before. It was a large, stately looking room of the kind that can be found in most mansions of the south, but this one looked as if it hadn't been used in years. All the furniture was covered in a thick film of dust. There were cobwebs everywhere. It was dawn and the sun was beginning to break over the horizon letting a weak golden light into the room. I could see the demon standing at the door in the shadows the sunlight had yet to reach.

The memories of the night's events came tumbling down upon me one at a time, bringing with them a hopelessness that was deeper and darker than the depths of any ocean.

"It wasn't no dream," I moaned, tears filling my eyes.

"No," it said sadly.

There were a few moments of silence before it spoke again. "I... I have to leave you now, Luna."

I tried to sit up but a jolt of pain shot up along the left side of my body and I let out a gasp. Immediately the demon was away from the door and kneeling by the chair with its hands hovering over me.

"What is it? What ails you? Tell me!"

"Get from me," I cried and tried to bury myself deeper into the chair, tears springing to my eyes again.

It did as I asked, this time not by vanishing and reappearing. He simply stood up and took a small step back from the chair.

Now that it was standing in the meagre light streaming through the window, I found myself arrested by the beautiful guise this demon had chosen to wear. But those unfathomable blue eyes were still terrifying in their intensity and I was thankful when it looked away, as if it had been reprimanded.

The thing was even filthier than it had been the first

time I saw it. There was blood and dirt on its hands and clothes as well as small amounts of fresh earth. As I studied it, the creature appeared to notice these things for the first time. It looked down at its hands carefully as if it had never seen them before and then looked away, almost in shame.

"Please. Tell me what ails you," it asked in a whisper.

The pain was from the fall the night before. I hadn't felt it at the time but now that I had rested, those muscles had seized up and screamed in protest when I tried to sit up. It would be gone in a few days but I tightened my lips petulantly, refusing to ease the demon's worry. Let it think I was seriously hurt.

But something in my expression must have told it that I wasn't seriously hurt because it seemed to relax slightly even though I hadn't said a word.

"Where you going?" I demanded through my tears. "You can't be leaving me here on my own."

It was absurd that the thought of this creature leaving would fill me with dread, but it did. I had no idea where I was or how far away I was from the plantation or other people.

"You will be safe here, Luna, I promise you. No one ventures out this way so you will be safe."

I studied the gloriously handsome face of the demon. Did that mean that there were people relatively close by? And if so, would I be able to walk to them from here and maybe find my way back to the plantation?

"You will not be able to leave here, so do not try," it said, bringing its gaze up to meet mine again as a small frown creased its brow.

"I wasn't gonna," I said but it continued to frown down at me.

"Those two men. The preacher and the African. They will not die."

Despite my screaming muscles I sat up and swung my legs onto the floor. Leaning forward, I reached for the creature's arm but at the last minute withdrew. I just couldn't bring myself to touch it.

"They alive?" I suspected that this was a lie but I desperately needed to believe that Jupiter wasn't dead. "Please, tell me. How you know they alive?"

"I took them back to the plantation. They were unconscious but not hurt too much. They will live."

Its mouth turned up slightly at the corners. It wasn't exactly a smile but it took away some of the intensity in its gaze.

I closed my eyes, letting the relief sweep through me. Jupiter was alive.

Then I fixed him with a steady gaze.

"Why?"

"Because you wanted me to."

The tiny bit of hope and joy I had allowed myself disappeared, leaving only the overwhelming doom I felt at waking up and finding that the events of the night hadn't been a dream. "What you want with me?" I asked. "Take me back. *Please*."

He lowered his gaze again, took another step back and clasped his hands together in what looked like a punishing grip.

"I will return at dusk," he said looking briefly at the rising sun through the window. "I have already stayed far longer than I should have."

"No! You can't be leaving me here on my own. Take me back home, please."

He seemed completely heartbroken when he looked at me.

"Sleep now, Luna."

The last thing I saw before I was overwhelmed by the dizziness of that haunting melody were those searing blue eyes and whatever unfathomable emotion burned within them. As I drifted away I thought that what I saw there was loneliness. An intense, all-consuming loneliness and despair.

Chapter Nine

When I woke up again the sun was high in the sky and blazed through the window in a shaft of hazy gold. I was also completely alone.

I got to my feet and stretched carefully. Back at the plantation I had often sought solitude at the chapel but it was one thing to be able to choose brief moments of seclusion and another to have total isolation forced upon you as it was now. The silence in this place was so deep that it seemed to swallow everything. Not even the sound of the birds singing outside could come close to penetrating it.

Remembering what the demon had said about my not being able to leave, I ran out of the room and down a long, dusty corridor to the front door. Surprisingly it was unlocked and I flung the door open and rushed outside into the fierce sunlight.

The demon had left me in a large imposing mansion that sat between two oak trees. The red paint had faded long ago to a dusky pink; there were roof tiles missing, and the foliage surrounding the mansion had completely run amok. There was something pitiful about the mansion's current state of disrepair. It was like a once beautiful woman now in her autumn years, shying away from the gaze of the world behind the oak trees. Surrounding the mansion was a field of wild Queen

Anne's lace, so-called because the flowers resembled patches of white lace. At the back of the building was a cluster of trees, which thickened gradually into woodland further on.

Beyond the field of flowers at the front, the grassland seemed to stretch on for miles. I squinted into the distance at the green carpet, using my hand to shield my eyes from the sun. Was that line of brown a road?

I started running, ignoring the pain rippling along the left side of my body, taking long lunging steps through the field of flowers. Yes. I could see it properly now. It was a road, a dirt road that wasn't well used. But if it was there then it must lead somewhere, which meant there was a chance I would be well away from here and amongst other people before the demon returned at dusk.

I didn't know where I was or if I was even still in Mississippi. I also knew that even if I did find human beings, I was far from safe as it was likely I would be seen as a runaway and at the mercy of whomever I came across. And if by some miracle they believed my strange story of being spirited away by a demon, the plantation and Mama Akosua, who was probably the only person who could save me, were no doubt far away from here. This meant I would be endangering the lives of anyone kind enough to try and help me return.

But if there was a chance for me to get away from that evil being, then I would take it. So I ran, soaring and leaping over the field of flowers beneath my feet.

However, the closer I got to the road, the harder it was to keep running. My limbs felt heavy, as if they had been dipped in lead, and when I got close enough to see the road clearly reaching out into the distance and salvation, I was hit by nausea so intense I stumbled to a stop, a moan escaping my lips as I sank to the ground.

What was happening to me?

I moved away from the road and began to crawl back to the mansion. After a few paces, miraculously, the nausea began to drain away. I got to my feet uncertainly, expecting it to rise up again, but nothing happened. I took a few steps toward the house and found that it was completely gone. I felt perfectly well again apart from my hunger, thirst and aching muscles.

I faced the road as realisation dawned. Even looking at it made me feel ill. Turning to my left, I walked about five metres in a straight line. The queasiness left instantly. Then I did the same thing in the opposite direction. I still felt fine. I went back to the centre, took one step forward and then broke into a run.

This time when the nausea hit it was like running into a wall and I went crashing to the ground. I began to heave, the dry, hoarse sounds breaking through the stillness all around me. Relief came the moment I crawled away from the road toward the mansion and as I sat in the grass looking back at the road shimmering in the heat of the midday sun, I felt rage tempered with the nausea it had induced in me.

You will not be able to leave here, so do not try, it had said to me.

I let out another hoarse cry and pounded the earth with my fist.

I was a slave. That meant that I was used to having every aspect of my life under the control of another. But having this degree of domination forced upon me was intolerable. My mind was the only thing I had that wasn't governed by another human being. And this creature wanted to take that away from me too?

Angry, tired and feeling despair take over at the thought of my situation, I picked myself up and walked back to the house, for there was nothing else left for me to do.

In the kitchen I found food laid out on the table. Bread, fruit and vegetables, along with things like flour, herbs and spices. There was also meat, fish, milk and butter, which I found in a bucket hung down the well at the back of the house. I was so happy to see all that food that I pounced on the bread and crammed a fistful into my mouth before I had time to think. Back at the plantation, food for slaves consisted of rations of milk, cornmeal, some vegetables, molasses and a little bit of meat once a week. Even though we house slaves were often lucky enough to have whatever titbits the Master's family didn't finish at mealtimes, like every other slave on the plantation we never really had enough food to eat. I was so used to being deprived that I couldn't be sure all this food had been left for me. So although my stomach was grumbling loudly, I only took another handful of bread before I left the kitchen to explore the rest of the mansion.

Most of the rooms had not seen a living person in them in years; they were dark and dingy with cobwebs and thick layers of dust over all the surfaces. In the master bedroom, a particularly forbidding room with a deep red decor, I found water for bathing and items on the bed that had obviously been left for me. I saw the jewellery and dresses that I had found in the chapel along with other things like toiletries and shoes, not the sturdy leather boots a slave needed for long days of heavy toil, but dainty little shoes that my mistress would wear.

Without the fear I had felt in the chapel scorching my mind, I found myself seduced by the things that had been left for me. I ran my fingers down a particularly beautiful cerulean blue gown. All the clothes I had ever owned were ill-fitting hand-me-downs and the thought of wearing such a beautiful dress elicited a deep yearning in my deprived soul.

I carefully gathered up the necklace and held it aloft to watch the light play on the large ruby. It was simply breathtaking and when I placed it against my chest a shiver of excitement ran through me. That was what made me put the necklace carefully back on the bed and take a step back from all those beautiful things.

All of this felt like some kind of bribe and reminded me

of the way Master John had tried to entice me with a pair of Mistress Emily's old shoes and other little gifts in the beginning. He knew that none of the female slaves had a choice about bedding with him, but his vanity made him play these games so he could tell himself it was charm that paved his way into our beds instead of fear and intimidation. At first my refusal to accept his gifts had amused him and he had pursued me for months, the bribes and charm slowly being replaced with threats and slaps until he grew tired of my resistance and took what he wanted anyway.

The things I saw on the bed far outshone anything Master John had tried to give me, but I wouldn't sell my soul to this demon for a few fancy dresses and jewellery.

The only things I would allow myself to touch were the items I couldn't do without such as the toiletries. Those dresses I would never wear, though my eyes lingered on them as I left the room.

In the attic I found some very old clothes that were far too big, but they were preferable to accepting the bribes in the master bedroom. Then I took a bath, crying silently as I washed the flaking brown crust of Jupiter's blood off my skin. Overcome with grief, I could only hope and pray that the creature had not lied to me about taking Jupiter and Father Geoffrey back to safety. After bathing, I washed my dress and wore one of the ones I had found in the attic, not caring that it looked like a large green, musty-smelling sack.

After a very light lunch of an apple, and with nothing else to do, I began to clean the kitchen. By the time I'd finished, the bruised muscles from the fall were screaming in pain and I was starting to feel dizzy. So the most I could do for the rest of that afternoon was dust and sweep the drawing room. Besides, it was probably not a good idea to make myself too useful considering the situation I was in.

Now there was nothing left for me to do but wait. I was exhausted but my anxious mind wouldn't rest long enough to let me sleep, so I wandered the rooms of the weeping mansion and even ventured outside for a walk (being careful of course, to stay well away from the road).

At the plantation I was used to having my every waking moment filled with work. So finding myself with hours to spare, alone in a strange and silent house with only my thoughts to occupy me, was a terrible thing.

I was plagued with images of the night before and also the things I had deliberately kept from my mind. Thoughts and memories better left in the dark. And I had nothing to look forward to that evening but the return of a supernatural being that had unlimited control over not just my body, but my mind as well.

I was alone and doomed. At the plantation I had kept myself isolated from the other Negroes, apart from Mary. Now I realised just how much I needed the comforting presence of the other slaves, the sound of singing drifting from the fields whenever I walked past, and the pleasant murmur of gossip amongst the house slaves whenever there was a moment to spare. I thought about this now because the events of the last two nights assured me that I would soon die. Death was something I had never been afraid of. In fact, it had always seemed like a long-sought ally that would free me from the peculiar burdens of a female slave. No, I wasn't afraid of dying. I was only afraid of dying alone and of what I would have to endure before death came to my aid. So by the time the sun began to set I was frightened, angry, and utterly devoid of hope.

***

One hour past sunset and the demon hadn't returned. That's when fear became the dominant emotion in the thick melee going round and round in my head.

I was in the drawing room I had woken up in that morning, waiting for something that shouldn't be of this world. And I didn't know what terrified me more, the thought that he would soon return to do whatever he had brought me here to do, or that he wouldn't return at all.

Then I heard a noise outside.

I sprang to my feet and the fear reached fever pitch when I heard the front door open and then footsteps in the corridor.

That couldn't be the demon I heard moving down the corridor as he simply would have materialised in the drawing room. Panicked, I looked around the room, my heart pounding as those heavy footsteps reached the drawing room door.

Who could that be?

I thought about trying to hide but in the end all I could do was watch in abject terror as the doorknob began to turn and the door was pushed open.

A tall, handsome white man with shoulder-length brown hair entered the room. He was dressed in black trousers, a navy blue coat over a white shirt, a tan waistcoat and white cravat. He was also carrying a white box under one arm. He gazed at me, not in astonishment at finding a stranger in his house, but with an expression of hopeful anticipation, which slowly turned to bemusement and then outright concern.

"Luna?"

It was the same soft voice and if it wasn't for the unusual accent, in my fear I may not have recognised that the man before me was the demon I had been waiting for.

I sank down on the loveseat, and tried to get my breathing back to normal. He walked over to the table and put the box down, then stood watching me like a man waiting for the guillotine to fall. I felt myself explode.

"*What you do that for?*" I screamed as tears filled my eyes.

He flinched like a startled hare and it was a few moments before he answered.

"I... I do not..."

"Why you be *walking* in here like that – *and wearing*

95

them clothes?"

He looked completely mystified.

"I thought that if I came here today like this." He gestured to the clothes. "And moved like a man, you would not be so frightened of me. But I see now that you thought I was someone else."

"Yes!" I hissed.

"I am sorry," he said when I stood up abruptly. "But that is not the only reason you are angry."

"No, it ain't," I replied, furiously wiping away the tears.

"I see now."

I waited for him to ask what else had made me angry, but he didn't. He only continued to stare at me, looking more than a little uneasy the longer he stared.

"What you do to me?" I asked when it became apparent that he wasn't going to speak. I started pacing back and forth and gestured wildly. "At the road when I's trying to leave. What you *do* to be making me feel that way?"

"I told you not to leave, Luna. You know it would not..."

"I didn't ask that! I ask what you done to me!" I stopped and stood with my hands on my hips. "And why has you brung me here. What you want with me?"

He looked away at the last question and I could see that he was becoming agitated again.

"Luna..."

"Don't be calling me that!"

He flinched at the harshness of my tone then opened his mouth as if to speak and closed it again, his gaze falling to the ground as he considered what I had said. When he looked up again he was clearly confused.

"Luna, I do not understand..."

"I says don't be calling me that! You shouldn't know my name! *How* does you know my name?"

"You... You are angry and hysterical, Luna. I see that being on your own all day has not been good for you.

96

Sleep for awhile and then we will talk."

He locked his gaze on mine and I immediately began to feel the same light-headedness I always felt right before he robbed me of consciousness. But before it could overcome me and without giving myself time to think about what I was about to do, I lurched across the space between us and struck him across the face.

It was like hitting a tree and although my palm stung, I was sure that to him, the slap had felt like no more than a fly landing on his cheek.

But it seemed as if I had succeeded nonetheless because I felt him release his hold on my mind and my head began to clear.

"Don't you never do that again," I said bringing my stinging hand up under my arm.

He stared at me in amazement, a hint of fascination lurking in his gaze before he glanced down at the hand I was holding protectively under my arm.

"Your hand," he said and tentatively reached for it before he quickly withdrew.

We stood there for a few moments, me glaring at him and trying to ignore my throbbing palm whilst he struggled to regain some kind of equilibrium. Finally he spoke.

"You have a very strong mind, Luna. No one has ever been able to resist me for even the few moments it took for you to cross over to me. At the chapel, when you were kneeling by the stream, you did not know what was happening, yet you not only resisted, you were able to push against me as I tried to move the rock away from your face."

He said all this with an air of reverence that I found hard to believe.

"You think it is your body that I want. But it is your mind that interests me."

I took a step back, my wayward emotions somewhat calmed by my small victory.

"You's interested in my mind?" I scoffed. "Ain't no

white man I know ever been interested in a slave for her mind."

"I am not a man. Never forget that, Luna," he said softly, echoes of despair in his voice.

Those words should have scared me but it was hard to be afraid of this creature when he was being so docile and behaving as if he were a little bit frightened of *me*.

"You see," he continued, "I... I was in the woods and I heard you in the chapel praying and then when you came to the stream, I saw your face and I couldn't let any harm come to you because I have seen your face before."

"When?" I demanded.

"Many years... many decades ago. Before you were born. Before your mother was even born, I saw your face as if in a dream. And I have continued to see it ever since."

"You saw me before I was borned? How?"

"I do not know." He moved closer to me. "But do you understand now that when I saw what you meant to do by the stream, I had to stop you. I could not let you do anything to the face that has been haunting me for so, so long."

I felt uncomfortable with his nearness and the longing I saw in his eyes. It seemed to burn into my skull. But I remained where I was as he brought his hand to hover above my forehead, tracing a line in the air from my forehead, down my nose and across my cheek. It was exactly the path the rock would have taken if he hadn't stopped me.

"It would not have made a difference anyway," he continued. "You are exceptionally beautiful. Nothing can ever take that away." He made as if to cup my cheek and I stepped away.

"You says you heard me praying," I said as I went to the loveseat and sat. "All the way out there in them trees?"

"Yes. My hearing is a lot more powerful than a human's. I was standing outside by the trees but heard every word you said."

He could hear me from that distance? What else could this thing do? And what chance did I have of escaping him if he was as powerful as he said?

"I want you to know that I regret the way in which I sought you out. You see, I thought you would know me and know what I was. I did not consider the possibility that I would frighten you."

"Of course I's scared of you. You's trying to kill me!"

"Dear God, no, Luna. I promise you, I would die rather than harm you."

"You's waiting in my cabin last night and if Massa John ain't get there first, I be dead now!" I snarled.

"No. You have completely..."

"Liar!"

He took a step back and brought his hands up to his face in a gesture of helplessness that touched me in such a profound way that I was completely disarmed.

"I... I do not know how to do this," he whispered.

"Do what now?"

"This!" He gestured to his clothes. "I do not know how to converse with you. I do not know what to do with your fury or your sorrow. I have been alone for a long time. I do not know how to do this."

"You don't be knowing what to do cause I's mad at you?" I asked.

What he was saying was almost comical. No one cared about the anger of a slave. No one. And yet this all-powerful creature didn't know what to do with it.

"No. I have always killed those who were unfortunate enough to cross my path. I have never had to deal with their thoughts or emotions."

Those words sent cold tendrils of fear racing up my spine and although I tried not to let it show, it must have been evident because he immediately took a few steps toward me but then stopped.

"Please, do not fear me, Luna. You are safe with me, I promise you."

I kept silent.

"I did not lie to you. I was not waiting for you that night. I was waiting for your Master. I knew what he meant to do and I thought you would want me to kill him. But you were so scared that I could not finish what I set out to do."

He had intended to kill Master John for me! That surprised me. It also made me feel something I had never felt before in my twenty-odd years on this earth. Power.

"Then why didn't you just kill him? Why you be drinking his blood?"

He looked away and closed his eyes. I saw a deep agony pass over his features when he began to speak.

"This...what you might call magic, that gives me the strength you have seen and the other...gifts. It demands a price and that price is blood. Human blood. The only way I can continue to exist is by killing other men and women and drinking their blood."

"It seem like you don't wants to be doing what it is you do to keep alive."

That was something I understood all too well. I didn't like being subservient to monsters, spending my days and nights fearful and deprived of hope. I didn't like silently taking the abuse and degradation that they had heaped on me my whole life. But I did so just to stay alive.

"Who would want to exist in such a fashion?" he asked. "Can you comprehend the agony of being forced to live in the shadows, only able to come out under the light of the moon? Taking life after life? This body that you see is frozen in time. It is like a living statue and its only function is to kill. I have killed so many that I cannot remember the numbers. Can you comprehend being condemned to an existence like that? Living with the blood of so many, not just on your hands, but sustaining you? Can you imagine knowing that you are a walking aberration yet are compelled to keep existing? Alone for decade after decade, knowing that you will always be alone and that you will live forever?"

"You can't die?"

"Not easily, no."

"And you don't never go out in the sun?"

"Not for long, no. The sun weakens me. I can bear it for short periods of time but if I stay in daylight for long enough, it will kill me."

"How long be too long?"

I wondered, at first, why he would willingly tell me all this and if I could even believe what he was saying. But the longer I spoke to him, the more apparent it became that he was telling the truth. In fact he didn't seem to lie at all. I surmised that he had been alone for so long that he was almost like a child who hadn't yet learned the art of deception.

"I do not know. Maybe I would survive a few hours. Maybe even days. I do not know."

"You all alone? There ain't no others like you?"

Abruptly he turned and walked to the fireplace, keeping his back to me.

"There were. I do not know where they are now. They may have perished."

"So what you want with me?"

"I... I only want to be *near* you, Luna. Nothing more."

"Thank you... sir," I said and he turned to face me again, his eyebrows raised in surprise. "For taking Jupiter and Father Geoffrey back. And... and for helping me."

I saw hope blossom in his eyes and it was almost enough to melt the longing that seemed to have taken up permanent residency there.

"You gonna take me back now?" I asked.

The hope was gone so quickly that I almost doubted it had ever been there.

"I cannot take you back there, Luna."

He walked back over to the table. "And you do not want to go back. Do you?"

I didn't answer. Of course I didn't want to go back. But

how could I stay here with this blood-drinking demon?

"I have something for you."

He reached into the box on the table and brought out the bible I had kept hidden in the chapel.

I immediately left my seat. Taking the bible he held out, I placed it protectively against my chest. I noticed that while I had been thinking about his question he had placed a number of small white cards with things drawn on them on the table.

"I can teach you," he said waving his hand over the table when he saw me gazing at the cards. "I can teach you how to read your bible. You said that was your dearest wish, so let me teach you."

His eyes seemed to be pleading with me, but he needn't have been so worried. The chance to one day open my bible and read the words it contained for myself was one I would never have given up.

So I pulled out one of the chairs and sat down.

He moved quickly to the seat opposite and seated himself, maybe sensing that if he delayed, I would change my mind.

"Why's you wanting to teach a slave to read?" I thought to ask even though the answer didn't really matter to me.

There was an intensity in his voice when he answered. "You were never a slave to me."

He picked up one of the cards, which I came to learn had the letter "A" written on it.

What I should have asked was how he knew that my dearest wish was to be able to read my bible, for it was not something I had voiced out loud back at the chapel.

Chapter Ten

The next morning, I opened my eyes to suffocating disorientation and a strong smell of flowers, both of which quickly receded along with vestiges of a hazy dream. Then I remembered where I was and when I saw the sun steadily making its ascent over the horizon, I felt something I had never felt before on opening my eyes in the morning. Joy. To be sure that this day wasn't a painfully lucid dream, I reached under my pillow and pulled out the sheets of paper I had placed there before I went to bed. It was hard to keep tears from filling my eyes as I stared down at the alphabet, written in his neat, cursive handwriting. It seemed as if dreams really could come true, even for a slave.

Having been up until the early hours of this fine morning, I was still tired and needed to sleep for a while longer. But although I was alone and no one was expecting me to do any work, there was a lot that I wanted to get done before the demon returned at dusk.

So, after bathing and eating a veritable feast of bread and butter, grits and fresh fruit, I began to clean. In one of the bedrooms upstairs, the smallest one, I found new men's clothes neatly laid out on the bed. The jacket and trousers the demon had been wearing when I'd first seen him were in a heap on the floor with bits of soil still clinging to them and I made a quick mental note to ask him at dusk whether or not he wanted me to mend and wash them. Then I cleaned the whole room and spent the rest of the morning working methodically through the mansion. I slept for a couple of hours after my midday meal (sleeping during the day was a luxury that had never been afforded me up until that point) and then decided to tackle my main concern for the day, which was what to prepare for the creature's supper.

He had made no mention of what he wanted for his evening meal, but the amount and variety of food he had left for me suggested that it was not meant only for me. I didn't know what his tastes were and the sun would begin to set at around 7.30 p.m. That was much too late for dinner, which we always served at 3.00 p.m. back at the plantation. It was also too early for supper, which was usually a light affair made up of leftovers from dinner. But since this was the first meal I would be making for the demon and I wanted him to be pleased, I decided to prepare the type of food the Master's family normally had for their dinner. So I roasted the small pig he had left that morning, deciding to serve it with some greens and beans. I also made poached trout in a cream sauce. Dessert was an apple pie.

I had everything ready and the bowls of food on the table in larger bowls filled with hot water to keep everything warm by the time the sun began to set. Shortly thereafter, I heard the sound of a door closing upstairs, something that elicited mixed feelings of excitement and trepidation, followed by the sound of his slow heavy footsteps as he descended the stairs.

When he appeared at the door he was dressed just as immaculately as he had been the night before and his hair, which was wet, had been pulled into a ponytail.

"Good Evening, Luna."

"Evening," I said curtly, feeling slightly uncomfortable under the power of his lingering gaze. "Supper's ready. If you don't wants to eat now, I can keep it warm in the kitchen till you wants it."

He had been staring almost dreamily at me as I spoke and didn't answer right away.

"Well?" I asked, my tone a lot sharper than I had intended it to be.

He shifted his gaze to the table and alarm crossed his features when he saw the small feast I had prepared.

"If pork ain't to your liking, there be trout instead."

He hid his initial alarm and tried to smile. "No. It... It's all fine."

I breathed a sigh of relief when he walked gingerly over to the table and sat down. I hurried to prepare a plate for him and waited with a degree of anxiety as he picked up his fork timidly, speared some turnip greens, and put them into his mouth. He chewed awkwardly and swallowed, his expression more horrified than alarmed now as he looked down at the rest of the meal before him.

"You don't wants any of it, do you?"

I couldn't hide the dejection I felt at his reaction. He looked up, clearly pained and maybe a little bit embarrassed.

"No. I... I cannot eat normal food. Or at least I have not done so in almost fifty years, so it does not taste of anything to me. Blood is the only thing that can nourish me."

"Oh." I suddenly felt very stupid and a little bit sickened as well. "Well, I's mighty sorry but I ain't got no fresh blood left in the kitchen," I said in an attempt to try and make light of the situation.

Then I grew silent and a chill fell over me for there was a fresh stock of blood standing not far from where he was sitting.

Mine.

Oh, Lord. Oh Lord. *Please don't tell me he wants to drink* my *blood!*

He looked greatly amused when he answered.

"No, I don't suppose you would keep any blood in the pantry."

He laid the fork down on the table regretfully and I found myself feeling a little bit sorry for him. I couldn't imagine not being able to enjoy eating though I felt a sort of smug satisfaction at how much pleasure I would get when I had some of that pie once he was gone.

"Is this apple?" he asked gesturing to the pie and I realised that I had been staring at it.

"Yes."

"Why don't you sit down? *I* may not be able to enjoy this food, but you can eat if you wish, Luna."

"Um, no. I ate already and..."

"*Please*, Luna."

I couldn't resist rolling my eyes slightly when I reluctantly sat down.

I hated the way he did that; looked at me as if his very world hung on everything I said and did. It made me feel mean for even thinking about refusing him.

Cutting myself a slice of the apple pie, I bit into it and chewed quickly, giving him a few reproachful looks. But he didn't seem to notice and had a whisper of a smile around his eyes which barely touched his lips. Then he slowly cut a slice for himself and took a small bite out of it.

"So what is it supposed to taste of?" he asked.

Even though it made me feel slightly silly, I did my best to explain the sensations produced by the slightly tangy taste of the apple pieces against the sweetness of the crust and the way it all seemed to melt in my mouth. He searched my face intently whilst I described it to him and I found that I was really savouring the food and enjoying it all the more because I knew he couldn't.

"And it..."

"Vanilla," he said looking from the plate to me in astonishment.

"Vanilla? Yessir, I flavoured the sugar with vanilla."

"I can taste the vanilla and also some of the other things." He took another bite and chewed it slowly in

106

amazement. "Yes, I can taste it. Maybe not exactly what I should, but I can taste it."

He sat staring at the plate as if he had just witnessed some kind of miracle.

"Thank you, Luna"

There was so much gratitude in that thank you. Volumes of it, in fact, that I immediately grew uncomfortable.

"You gonna eat anything else?" He shook his head and I stood up. "I's gonna take it away then."

He nodded and I was grateful to get away to the kitchen for a few moments. Being around him was disconcerting to say the least. From the dizzyingly handsome face, sad eyes, and the little things he did that drew me to him like a moth to a flame. It was all very confusing.

He spent the next few hours teaching me how to read. He was very patient in his instructions and never made me feel stupid about the many things I didn't know. He was also very careful to respect the physical distance I kept between us. But by midnight, I was finding it hard to keep my eyes open, something he eventually remarked on.

"Perhaps we should stop now, Luna. I can see how tired you are," he said, although he looked at me as if it was the last thing he wanted to do.

"I is," I said through a yawn.

"You should have slept today instead of cleaning. I did not bring you here to be my servant," he said almost chidingly. "I have also been meaning to ask: Why are you wearing... that?" He gestured disdainfully to my ragged purple dress, which was marked by large brown stains. "Did you not like the dresses I left for you?"

I felt my heart stop at the mention of the dresses and my fears regarding those gifts came flooding back.

"N-no, and I ain't never gonna wear them."

He watched me carefully for a few moments as I tried to hide the dread I felt.

"I am sorry, Luna. I did not mean to scare you by

mentioning the dresses. I was merely..."

"I ain't scared," I said quickly.

"No, of course not." His tone was similar to the sort of tone you would use if you were trying to talk someone down off a ledge.

"I just don't see the use in wearing them fancy clothes when all I's gonna do is get them ruined doing chores." I realised that my voice had been rising throughout that sentence so that the last word sounded like a frightened squeak.

"Of course, of course. I will get some plainer dresses made for you."

I was so relieved at this and what it signified about his intentions toward me that for a moment I couldn't speak.

"Thank you," I said awkwardly.

He nodded, tugging absentmindedly at the cravat he wore as if he found it restrictive. When he saw me watching him he quickly stopped and placed his hands in his lap and that almost made me smile.

Maybe it was because of the soft, hesitant way he had of speaking, or the way he sat hunched over with his head down as if he wanted to disappear into his clothes, but I wasn't scared of him anymore. I actually felt sorry for him, as at times it was almost as if he felt unworthy in my presence. It was a very odd notion: a white man feeling inferior to a slave. But I was sure that it was true.

And then of course there was the form he had chosen, which was definitely the epitome of male beauty by any standard. It amused me to think of all those southern belles currently squabbling over Master John. I imagined that they would happily throw themselves into the fires of hell for even a glimpse of the vision before me.

"What you do in the day when you ain't here?" I asked, wondering if he maybe had a demon wife with whom to while away the long daylight hours.

"Um, no." He looked completely flustered for a moment then he seemed to regain his composure. "I normally bury myself in the ground to get away from the effects of the sun. It is the most comfortable I can be during the day."

"Oh," I said.

That got me thinking. I needed to find out what I could about his weaknesses and I had learned that the easiest way to get information from whites was to use the good old dumb slave routine. If you behaved as stupidly as they believed all Negroes to be, whites would tell you any and everything, right down to their toilet habits.

"I expect it be all nice and cosy in the ground like that. But don't you gets scared none? I mean, Lord forbid, what if somebody finds you one day? They could hurt you some, couldn't they?"

His watched me steadily for a moment and I got the distinct impression that he was not in the least bit fooled by the dumb slave act. In fact I got the feeling that it had offended him in a way that I couldn't possibly begin to understand.

"If there is something you want to know, Luna, you should ask. I promise I will answer truthfully."

"I wants to know what can kill you."

The briefest of smiles touched his lips before he answered.

"Well, I am considerably weaker during the day and if I am exposed to the sun for long enough, it will kill me. But I find that the older I get, the longer I can tolerate its effects. The only other thing that can kill me is probably decapitation, but that would be a difficult thing for someone to achieve as only certain metals can pierce my flesh. Fire can hurt me, and maybe it can even kill me, I do not know for certain."

Instead of appeasing me, I found that his response had irritated me slightly and an odd protectiveness stole over me. What on earth did he think he was doing telling me the best way to kill him? That sort of honesty would only lead to one thing: An early death.

He seemed slightly amused. "I tell you these things because I want you to know what to do if you ever come across one of my kind. I also tell you because... well... There is still so much that I do not understand about why I saw you long before you were born, but for some reason I have been led to you and it seems as if nothing is closed to me where you are concerned.

"For example beings like myself can only enter a person's abode if they are invited in. But I was able to enter your cabin even though you were not there to do so. I do not have an explanation for any of it, but somehow, I know I am safe with you, Luna."

"I reckon you's right."

Of course I would kill him if I had the chance. And if I did, this idiotically trusting creature would think he was safe with me even as I twisted the knife in his chest.

He looked as if he was trying to suppress a smile as we sat in silence and although I wasn't sure why he appeared to be amused, I smiled sweetly at him.

He really did seem so harmless now and I felt confident that I had nothing to fear from him, least of all sexually. It wouldn't surprise me if I learned that he wasn't even able to perform that function. He was after all "not a man", as he had instructed me never to forget.

An ironic smile passed over his lips.

"What's so funny?"

The smile disappeared and he quickly shook his head.

"So do you want to continue or retire to sleep, Luna?"

"I's gonna go on up to bed now," I said. "I can't see straight no more." I yawned again and stood up.

"Until tomorrow evening then. Good night, Luna," he said sadly.

"Good night," I said and left the room.

It was a relief to be upstairs and away from him even though I got a small measure of comfort knowing that he was still downstairs in the drawing room. Being around this strange being was proving to be a very unsettling experience for me, especially since I found myself staring at him far too often and for far too long.

Chapter Eleven

So if you were wondering how an illiterate slave could write an account of her life, you now have the answer. The demon that had terrified me so, the same one I had seen slaughter three men in a matter of minutes, the very thing I thought was going to kill me, began teaching me how to read. And that is how the following nights passed by.

Most of the time we sat in the drawing room but on other nights we sat outside on blankets under the gentle radiance of the night sky with three or four lamps creating a soft amber cloud around us.

My mind, which had been idle for so long, ate up everything I was taught and I learned quickly. He would often leave a few hours before the sun rose, but I would continue to pore over everything he had showed me and spent hours writing out letters, and then words, until what I wrote came close to his elegant script. I spent as much of the day as I could spare learning the little tasks or homework he set. But if I wasn't sleeping, the slow task of cleaning the many rooms of the mansion occupied my waking hours.

My life had changed completely in a matter of days and for the first time my needs were not only met, they were made a priority. Hunger, which had been a sensation as familiar as the feel of the sun on my skin, was completely obliterated. And food of all varieties was so plentiful now that much of it was wasted. I fretted whenever I threw food away as I knew that nearly all the slaves on the plantation I had been rescued from would be going to sleep with the sharp ache of hunger in their stomachs. I was also clothed properly in brand new garments and had so many dresses, simple though they were, that I often felt guilty when choosing what to wear.

After a short while I found that I didn't like being awake during the day and was often restless and agitated during those hours. The fierce glare of the sunlight irritated me now and the sound of birdsong was far too shrill, unlike the almost hypnotic drone of the crickets after nightfall. Everything looked far too harsh without the moon or lamplight to cast soft shadows over them and I told myself that the reason I pined for nightfall was because at night I got to feed my mind, a mind that had been starved for far too long. At that stage, I couldn't be honest with myself about why I would rush to the drawing room window at sunset or why I would sit outside watching with breathless anticipation as the sky began to darken, the shadows lengthening and deepening as night crept softly into view. Yes, on those days I waited and watched until he appeared. I would usually hear the sound of his footsteps on the stairs and then he would be at the drawing room door. Other times he would simply materialise wherever I was. But most of the time I would see him walking toward the house under a vermillion sky, whilst the sun, which looked like a golden fireball, dissolved into the horizon. And the part I looked forward to the most was that gentle, hopeful smile of his whenever he saw me waiting for him.

I wish I could say I looked forward to nightfall and his presence merely because he taught me how to read, but it would be a lie if I did.

At first I was slightly uncomfortable about the fact that he stared at me constantly. But I got used to him searching my face as if there was something hidden there for him to

113

find. Sometimes he looked slightly puzzled as he watched me. Other times a whisper of a smile, so slight, would creep over his features. Sometimes he looked sad and at times I thought I saw anger as he studied me.

Once I glanced up to see him looking at me as if I had said something to anger him and felt dread touch my heart for the first time since agreeing to stay at the mansion. Part of that instant prickle of anxiety was because my mind had been plagued that day with thoughts of life at the plantation, and in particular, the abuse and degradation I had suffered at Master John's hands. And I worried that I had done something that would make the demon take me back to that nightmare.

"Why you looking at me like that? Has I done something wrong?"

He snapped out of his anger immediately.

"No, Luna. I am sorry." He frowned. "I was merely thinking about something I wish I had been able to prevent from happening."

When he looked up at me again, the frown had disappeared. "You could never do *anything* to make me angry," he said and I was able to relax under the steady light of his gaze once more.

I have to say that I began to not only enjoy the adoration I saw in his eyes whenever he looked at me, I began to crave it, and when he left in the early hours of the morning, it was as if I had been plunged into a deep dark hole.

It may seem strange to you that I was able to adapt to being in the presence of an otherworldly being so quickly and even come to crave his presence, but you have to understand that I was used to being noticed because of my beauty and of being an object of lust. But I had never been the object of the kind of adoration I received in the company of the creature, nor have I experienced it from another living being since.

Being under the gentle reverence of his gaze was like a

114

balm to my battered, tortured soul. And what was more, I felt a sort of kinship with him as I recognised a slave's broken spirit when I saw one. Whilst I was bound by my white Master, this creature was bound by the need for blood that compelled him to kill and so I no longer saw him as something other to me. It didn't occur to me then, but I realise now that it was much deeper than that for we had a connection to each other that denied any kind of rational explanation.

I didn't start to have misgivings about my decision to stay with the demon until the end of that first week. Still flattered by his devotion in ensuring that all my needs were met and in an effort to see how far he would go, I had mentioned the apple tree behind the chapel on the plantation and how those apples were probably the sweetest in the whole of Mississippi. You can't imagine the warm glow that melted through me when I came downstairs the next morning and found a basket of those apples waiting for me.

There was nothing that he wouldn't do for me, I thought to myself as I wrapped my fingers around one of the apples, remembering with longing the time I had placed one in Mama Akosua's hand and held it between us. It was hard to believe that I had ever thought he meant me harm, as I was so sure now that he would rather die than hurt me.

And maybe because my thoughts were, to a degree, on Mama Akosua as I brought the apple to my face and inhaled it, I heard her voice clearly in my head.

Be careful, my child. I fear your vanity blinds you.

"Mama?"

I dropped the apple. Tears immediately sprung to my eyes and the longing grew into a fierce ache at the sound of her voice.

He will not kill you, no. But there are worse things than death. Remember that.

Closing my eyes, I pressed a hand to my chest and tried

115

to concentrate.

Mama, can you hear me? I'm all right. He won't hurt me. I'm all right, Mama. I'm...

I opened my eyes with a start, thinking about what I had been about to say. *I'm happy*. Was that really how I felt?

I listened and tried to concentrate, but if she had been there, she was gone now, and I had no way of knowing if she had heard me.

Her words however, lingered that day like the smell of rain in the air before a storm.

That night, he looked harmless as always as he sat on a chair a few feet away whilst I copied out lines of script. When I looked up at him he immediately lowered his gaze and began following the path of a spider as it scurried along one of the books that lay across the table.

I groaned inwardly at the sight of the spider. This house seemed to be a veritable playground for them. They were everywhere and I had lost count of how many I had killed over the last few days. As the spider inched nearer to the paper I wrote on, I moved my hand closer to one of the books, ready to slam it on top of the spider when it got close enough. But before I could do anything, the demon cupped the creature in his hands and took it over to the window, where he released it on the sill.

I continued to write, but my mind was elsewhere. Glancing at that impossibly beautiful face, half-turned toward the open window, I asked myself if all I saw in his actions and countenance could possibly be a lie, an elaborate deception. There was also the issue of the form he had taken. I had to admit that I was captivated by the beauty he wore and maybe that made it hard to see the truth about his intentions toward me.

If I was to stay here, I had to free myself from the deception that was the handsome man and see this being in his true form.

"Demon," I said somewhat imperiously, and tried to

116

ignore the swell of anxiety I felt as I swivelled around in my chair to face him. "I wants to see what you really looks like."

I braced myself for the horns, scales, or whatever it was that I would soon see, and promised myself I wouldn't scream or show repulsion in any way.

When he turned from the window he was smiling slightly, as if I had amused him.

"I do have a name," he said. But then sorrow passed over his face. "Or at least I used to."

He faced the window again, seemingly wrestling with some private pain.

"Then go on and tell me this name," I said.

At first I thought he wasn't going to answer me.

"Avery," he said finally. "My name was... is Avery Wentworth."

Avery Wentworth.

I don't know why I never thought to ask him his name before. I said it a few times in my head while he stood brooding by the window and if I'm honest, I was actually disappointed. Avery wasn't exactly the kind of name you would expect a demon to have.

"And what you see is my true form," he said whilst I was still toying with the sound of his name.

I gaped at him.

"That... that can't be," I said.

There was no way that what I was looking at could be real. It was too perfect.

"It *is* real," he said and moved to the fireplace where he stood with one arm on the mantelpiece.

"You lying. You... you hiding what you really looks like 'cause you don't wants me to be scared of you," I said.

"If that were the case, do you think I would have chosen the form you fear and abhor the most? That of a white man?"

Of course I had no answer for him. But how could what

117

I was seeing be his true form?

"This is what I looked like when I was a man. When the change..." He closed his eyes as if to shut away some horrendous memory, and when he opened them again he looked so sad that I felt a pang of sympathy for him. "When the magic was worked on me, it froze me at the age I was at the time and this is the way I have stayed for the past few decades."

"You was a man?" This was not what I was expecting to hear at all. "When? How long you be this way? And what happened to make you what you is?"

Silence pervaded the room for the longest time and when he finally spoke, he was looking off into the distance as if he could actually see his past human self. A range of human emotions quickly passed over his features. Anger, disbelief, and most of all, intense longing.

"I was born in England in 1730. A few years after I completed my formal education I was ordained a priest and served as a vicar in my local parish. I came to the Americas with my new wife in 1757 when I was offered the opportunity to start a parish in Mississippi. But we soon came to see that the chapel I was asked to take over was a pretence for something evil. There were three of them. They ravaged my body and stole my soul, turning me into what you see now."

"You was a priest? What happened to your wife? And the three you be talking about, where is they now?"

He moved away from the fireplace, moving much faster than a man was supposed to move, his form a blur of green and beige clothing. I guessed that in his agitation he had lost a measure of the control he used to mimic human behaviour. He regained it fairly quickly and when he sat down his movements were normal again.

"I do not remember," he said quickly.

"Sure you do. You just don't wants me to know."

He gestured to the piece of paper on the table in front of me. "Show me what you have done?"

"You know how come the chapel got burned down?"

It seemed that question was more than he could bear. His mouth became a hard line and the agony in his eyes flared into burning blue pools.

"Do not ask me anymore, Luna. I want to see what you have done."

I had only spent a week in his company but I wasn't used to having him deny me anything. And it wasn't something I intended to let become a habit.

"Tell me, now," I said with steel in my voice.

"No."

"If you ain't gonna tell me then... then you better go on and take me back home right now!"

He looked up in alarm. He appeared to be so shaken by my words that I almost felt bad. It was cruel to threaten him like that, but a part of me was also overjoyed at the power I wielded over such a powerful being, leaving him as defenceless as a lamb in my presence.

He studied me in that way he had of doing and in those few seconds he managed to control some of his alarm.

"You... you should not toy with me so, Luna. I know you do not want to go back to the plantation, so do not ask me to take you there."

"You's right. I don't wants to go back and be worked from sunup till sundown like some mule. But it don't mean I wants to stay here with you neither. Especially if you gonna keep things from me."

He remained silent, lost in his thoughts. I decided to press him further.

"This where you's living with your wife?"

"No. This is not my house."

"This ain't your house? Whose is it then?"

"It belonged to an old woman. She lived in this crumbling house with two Negroes until I came across her one night."

As he spoke I began to feel apprehensive, first at the knowledge that this mansion, which I had come to love, was not his, and also at what I knew was coming.

"Don't tell me you done killed her?"

"Yes, I did," he answered simply, and I wished, not for the first time, that he would lie sometimes to spare me from the gruesome details of what he was and did in order to stay alive.

"She died quickly, Luna. I did not let her suffer."

"That don't mean nothing, *Avery*!"

"Luna, I do not make excuses for what I do to sustain myself. But of all the lives I have taken, that one haunts me the least. You see, her family fell into disgrace a long time ago. Her father was a lawyer who at first delighted in being able to acquire the free labour of slaves to build his fortune. But he soon saw that keeping his fellow man in bondage was a sin and began to educate his slaves so that he could eventually grant them, not only their freedom, but also a way in which to earn a living. As you can imagine, this did not fare well with the rest of the community. The family were ostracised and she lost any chance of gaining a husband. They fell into ruin and in the end she was left with only two Negroes who stayed and cared for her out of loyalty to her father. His decision ruined her life. She was old and her days were filled with thoughts of hatred, not only for him, but for the Negroes who cared for her out of pity. She knew death was prowling the night I came to this mansion, but she invited me in. She wanted to die, Luna. And I made sure her last moments were filled with pleasant thoughts. She did not suffer."

"Why in God's name you done told me all that?" I asked, picking up a pile of books and slamming them down on the table.

I was heartbroken because I had come to love the mansion mainly because it seemed to embody him in so many ways. Now it was only a house. An old, musty house belonging to some dead white woman.

"Luna, you know I do not want to be what I am. But I cannot help what it is I must do to survive."

"I don't care! How you expect me to stay in this here house when you done killed somebody in it."

He looked ashamed for a moment but when he spoke there was an air of impatience in his tone.

"Luna, all of this has nothing to do with what... with the previous owner of this mansion. You're simply throwing a tantrum because I won't tell you what you want to know. If..." He faltered for a moment as if he was on the verge of changing his mind about what he was about to say, but then pressed on. "If you really do wish to leave then... then go."

A heated silence hung in the room and he refused to meet my glare. I slowly got to my feet.

"Where are you going?" he asked, clearly confused.

"You says I should go, and that's what I's doing."

"You are leaving. Now?"

In order to prove that I was serious, I moved away from him to the door, where I paused, expecting him to stop me. But he merely sat there looking bewildered. Irritated by how calm he appeared to be at the fact that I was leaving, I flounced out of the house and into the balmy summer night.

I looked toward the road but the memory of that incapacitating nausea was too strong for me to even attempt to move in that direction, so I walked around to the back of the house where I intended to stay for a few minutes until he came to his senses.

He was already standing at the back door when I got there. He made no move to stop me, just stood staring at me in consternation. Unwilling to appear as if I was unsure of what I planned to do, I walked (slowly) in the direction of the trees. When I looked back, he was still standing by the back door, his expression hidden in the dark. Feeling my heart quicken at the thought that he meant to let me leave, I pushed my anxiety away, knowing he was merely calling my bluff. Once he realised I was serious, he would come after me and tell me whatever I wanted to know.

Chapter Twelve

And that is how I found myself tramping through the undergrowth under a sheet of darkness that made it impossible to see anything, only looming shadows. I had been walking for an hour by that time and the thin smattering of trees had already thickened into dense woodland. I was dead tired, my feet were aching. I had no idea where I was going and the unfamiliar noises were becoming menacing. When I felt something brush past my face, I screamed in terror, only to realise that it was nothing more sinister than the leaves of a low-hanging branch. Even so, I had to stop for a few moments to steady my breathing before moving on.

A week ago I'd been terrified of being on my own in woodland during the day, let alone at night. But that stupid demon had given me such a strong sense of security in the few days I had spent in his presence that I had been stupid enough to march into this living cavern of unseen threat without a moment's thought.

I desperately wanted to turn back, but how silly would I look if I returned to the mansion with my tail between my legs, or even worse, had to call out for him to come and rescue me? I shouldn't have left the mansion, but I hadn't expected him to just let me walk off alone.

I almost smiled to myself at the timidity I kept seeing in him. Some predator he was turning out to be. It was hard to believe I had ever been scared of him, this kind and gentle demon of mine. It was actually a miracle he had even survived as long as he had and I could picture him as a timid wolf with those large blue woeful-looking eyes of his hungrily trained on the chicken coop, too concerned about upsetting the chickens to actually make a meal of one. I found myself giggling at the image and then stopped abruptly.

What a naive thing for me to even think. Of course he was dangerous. I had seen that for myself only a week ago.

I am not a man. Never forget that, he had said and yet I *was* forgetting. All I saw when I looked at him nowadays was a gentle person. I didn't even see a white man anymore, only another lost and floundering soul.

I heard a loud rustle of leaves above my head and screamed again, ducking as a large bird, most probably an owl, darted toward the canopy of leaves and into the night sky.

This time it took a lot longer for my breathing and heart rate to return to normal and I was scared now, so scared that I was going to have to swallow my pride and call out to him.

But what if he didn't hear me, or even worse, chose not to come and find me?

"Are you ready to go back now, Luna?"

I spun toward the sound of that voice, my heart fit to burst with relief when I saw him leaning against a tree with his arms folded across his chest.

"Go away, Avery," I said and strode off.

I heard him sigh in exasperation and for a moment fear ran through me at the thought that he would disappear and leave me alone again. Then I heard the welcome sound of his footsteps, slow and steady like a heartbeat some distance behind me and I breathed a sigh of relief.

"This is silly, Luna."

I rolled my eyes, stopped and turned to watch him approach.

"Avery, I never asked you to follow me. So you go on home now," I said, fairly confident he would do no such thing.

"And leave you to be attacked by some wild animal? "

"The onliest thing I gots to be scared of is you."

"Really? So you have nothing to fear from that snake?"

I looked down and saw a large, fat snake disengaging from a rock not that far from my left foot. It took immense willpower to keep the scream in my chest from escaping as I jumped back, quickly searching the foliage at my feet to make sure I wasn't stepping on anything else.

"There are a million things I would have preferred to spend the last hour doing. Instead I've spent it following you to make sure there was nothing dangerous lurking in your path. Enough is enough, Luna. Stop this and let me take you back to the mansion."

I turned on my heel and carried on walking.

"I done told you to leave me be, Avery."

He had been here the whole time. My heart warmed at that thought and I wondered why I had ever been worried. And strangely enough, now that I knew he was about five metres behind me, the night seemed to open up. The moon came into view when the trees thinned and I paused to gaze at the stars, which were like smatterings of ice on dark, oily water. For a moment everything seemed to stop and it felt as if Avery and I were the only two people on the face of the earth, an image I found somewhat pleasing. Is this what it had been like for Adam and Eve in their Garden of Eden?

Feeling safe in the knowledge that he wasn't far behind me, I moved on.

About ten minutes later I heard Avery chuckle softly.

I spun around.

"What you doing?" I asked sharply.

"Walking," he replied without taking his eyes away from his feet.

He laughed again and then met my questioning glare.

"I remember now," he said still smiling. "I remember that I used to like walking. I often went for long walks with my dogs. I had two of them."

He came to a stop a few feet away from me. "I had forgotten what a simple pleasure it is to walk."

He beamed at me then, the first time I had seen him smile properly, and for a moment it felt as if my heart had come to a complete stop.

It was such an innocent, beautiful smile and I was the only one in probably fifty years to have had the privilege of seeing it.

"Take me back," I said, abruptly folding my arms.

The smile faded as he obediently came to stand beside me. He held out his arms and I moved gingerly into them, feeling the breathlessness I always felt whenever I was close to him. As before, I saw the very air around us appear to rush forward and then everything was pushed back and we were standing in the sumptuous glow of the lamplit drawing room.

I stepped away from him immediately. He sat down at the table and looked up at me expectantly.

"Should we continue?"

"No," I said and retreated to the chair by the window where I sat glowering at him whilst fear trilled through me.

Mama had been right to warn me. There was a lot more at stake here than my life. My very soul was at risk.

When I sat down he had looked slightly apprehensive, but a soft smile touched his lips.

"What?" I demanded after a few minutes of silence.

"Oh, it is nothing. I was only thinking about what a pleasure it is to be allowed to be near you."

I felt my anger begin to boil. Was he making fun of me and my seemingly futile attempts to annoy him? Of course there was no point in asking for I knew he would be the picture of innocence as he denied doing anything of the sort. I hadn't even said anything yet and he was already gazing at me with those puppy-dog eyes as if I had said something to wound him.

"I mean everything I say to you, Luna. Being near you is a joy."

So earnest and sincere. It was sickening.

"You really have no idea how *fascinating* you are," he continued. "You are a witch and yet you are barely aware of the power you have. Your strength astounds me and you can be so headstrong at times that it is easy for me to forget how frail you are. For example, you have been extremely obstinate tonight, but when I see how fatigued you are by such a short walk, I remember that you are as delicate as a flower. And your mind. Your mind is like a diamond. It has many facets to it, some of which even you are not aware of. And the rate at which you are learning to read and write astounds me. You are blessed with all of those qualities as well as the beauty of a queen. You are simply unique. There will never be another like you."

I stood up at that point, sure that he *must* be making fun of me.

"I's going to bed!"

He appeared as deflated as he always did whenever we parted in the mornings but was still able to maintain that sickeningly sublime smile.

"Goodnight, Luna."

I didn't answer, only paused long enough to glare at him before I left the room.

Upstairs, I found that exhausted as I was, I could not sleep. I kept thinking about the dazzling smile he had given me in the woods. When I did manage to fall asleep, I dreamt of Avery. Avery teaching me how to read. Avery standing by the fireplace with one arm resting on the mantelpiece. Avery walking towards me in the woods. Avery, Avery.

Avery.

Chapter Thirteen

I spent the following day in the most frightful mood. I was beginning to see now that I hadn't thought through the possible consequences of being here with Avery. And when he arrived at sunset, I didn't want to see his face or that irritating smile that spoke of such hope.

When I ignored his "good evening", he gave me a puzzled, wary look and sat down at the table.

"Would you like me to take a look at the work I set for you?" he asked.

"No! I's sick and tired of all this!"

"Do not be disheartened, Luna. You are making extraordinary progress but it can still take..."

"I don't mean this!" I said and swept the books and paper off the table, leaving him looking at me in consternation.

"Luna! Do you mean to spend *another* night quarrelling with me?"

"Yes, if it make you see I can't stay here with you."

He got to his feet.

"Do not say it," he said sounding a little bit angry himself. "Do not say you want to go back to the plantation unless you mean it, for I may just do as you ask."

A chill settled over me at the thought of once more being at the mercy of Master John but I wasn't about to show him how much those words had affected me.

"Oh, you making threats now? And all this time you's pretending you all kind and gentle. Huh! A wolf in sheep's clothing if I ever did see one! Go on and make your threats, or why don'ts you take the lash to me just like any other Massa?"

He looked completely mortified.

"Do not call me that. I am not your Master."

"Ain't you? You took me from everything I ever knowed and you won't turn me loose. That what slaveholders be doing all over Mississippi."

"You... you should not tire my patience in this way, Luna. It is cruel. Besides, I am not a man. If I want to force you to do something, I need not beat you into doing it. I have only to think it and I can make you do and feel anything I wish."

"What you say?" I hissed, closing the space between us.

He immediately took a step back. His words had ignited a fire that had lain dormant during those nightmarish years at the plantation. And although it was calmed somewhat by that small back-step he had taken, I wasn't finished with him.

"I done told you to never do none of that devil stuff on me again. You's lucky I ain't strong enough or I'd done knock you down for even saying that to me!"

He flinched as if I had actually hit him.

"Luna, stop this," he said softly. "You do not mean half the things you are saying and we are wasting the evening. So please stop this."

"You threaten me with that devil magic of yourn again and God help me I's..."

"I said, stop this."

And I did, for I was suddenly overwhelmed by a dizziness much stronger than I had felt on the other occasions in which he had used his magic on me. It lasted for only a few seconds and then a warm, mellow dreamlike feeling began to fill me. It was again like listening to that

128

sumptuous lullaby but it had changed slightly. Instead of the unending waves of unsurpassed sorrow, undertones of a timid joy had crept into the melody. And again I was completely enthralled by it. As always there was a very small part of me still present but it was a tiny bubble of anger that had no hope of finding its way to the surface.

He was firmly in control of me now but even though I stood motionless, unable to move or speak, he looked as fearful as if he were fending off an angry lion and I yearned to be free of his spell so I could show him that fangs and claws were nothing compared to my rage.

Trying to disguise his apparent nerves, he straightened his shoulders and moved to stand only inches away, knowing full well I would never willingly let him be this close. I expected the bubble of anger to grow but it was hard to concentrate on anything other than his handsomeness when he was this near. His face was perfect from every angle. How could anybody or anything on earth, or in Heaven and hell, be this perfect?

And under the irresistible pull of his spell it was hard to be sure if those thoughts were a result of what he was doing, or merely things I normally fought to suppress.

"Can you see what I can do, Luna?" He looked sad as he brought his hand up towards my face. Even then, he hesitated before letting his fingers lightly graze my cheekbone for a few seconds.

"So please, Luna. Do not..."

He stopped for I had moved closer to him and my chest was now pressed against his. It seemed as if he wasn't sure whether this was an act of his will or my own because he looked slightly taken aback and more than a little confused, especially when I laid a hand on his cheek. I had seen how strong he was yet when he covered my hand with his own, his touch was as gentle as the lightest feather.

He closed his eyes as he inhaled. He looked so sad, but all I could think about were his lips and whether they were as soft as they looked. Inching up on tiptoe, I slowly brought my lips closer to his but before they could meet, he brought his hand up to cup my cheek, and when he opened his eyes I saw vast, unending circles of sorrow and felt myself melt. I wanted nothing more at that moment than to ease his pain with a kiss, but the hand cupping my cheek was meant to restrain, not pull me in, even though I could see that he wanted my lips on his as much as I did.

As frustration battled against the mellow dreamlike feeling he had induced, I strained against his hand and would have kissed him if he hadn't prevented it.

"Sleep, Luna."

It was said tenderly, but I felt crushing disappointment as everything went black.

***

When I woke up again, I was lying on the loveseat by the window and it was still dark outside. For a moment I felt nothing and then rage coursed through me. I sat up with my hands clenched into fists at my side and screamed in anger and frustration before leaping off the chair to go in search of him.

I didn't need to go far for he was standing in the corridor outside the drawing room door when I wrenched it open. He looked stricken and then terrified when he saw how angry I was.

"I am sorry. I am sorry, Luna. I..."

I lunged at him and began to pound my fists against his chest and the arms he held out to try and ward me off.

"You wicked, no good dog!" I cried in between the blows, which were no doubt hurting me a lot more than they were hurting him, if he even felt them at all.

"Luna, please stop. You will hurt yourself."

I hit him one last time and then stopped because it was pointless trying to hurt him physically. Words were the only thing that could harm him.

"I am sorry, Luna. I do not... I did not mean... You do not know how angry I am with myself for having done that to you. Please, Luna. Can you ever forgive me?"

He moved toward me with his hands held out and I jumped back.

"Get from me!" This was something I could never forgive him for.

"Please, Luna. Do not say you will never forgive me for I cannot bear that. If you knew the turmoil in my heart you would forgive me in an instant."

I felt myself grow cold and stared at him as a horrifying realisation slowly dawned on me.

He had heard that. He had heard what I was thinking.

For a moment I couldn't say anything. I could only stare at him and ask myself if I hadn't completely lost my mind.

"I never *said* I ain't never gonna forgives you," I said finally. "But I be *thinking* it."

He opened his mouth, then quickly clamped it shut and then looked at the ground.

Can you see into my mind, Avery?

At first I thought I must have been mistaken because he was silent for what seemed like the longest time.

"Yes."

"You's looking into my mind? *All this time*?"

"Yes." He finally looked up at me. "At first I only listened to your surface thoughts, but the more I heard, the more I wanted to know and I found myself delving deeper into your mind."

"How could you?" I shouted and took a few steps forward. He instantly backed away.

"Luna, this... gift. It is something that comes as naturally to me as taking a breath comes to you. It is not something I can stop doing."

"But you never says. You never told me you could see in my mind!"

"No, because I knew you would try and block me if I

131

did or at least censure your thoughts and... and... I only wanted to get to know you, know your thoughts and your memories."

"My memories," I gasped.

I felt almost close to tears now. He knew everything about me. There wasn't any part of me that was hidden to him. He had access to all my memories, all those things that I did not want to think about, let alone utter to another human being.

"You's evil and I *hates* you," I said.

I didn't like the fact that he was looking at me as if his world had suddenly come to an end, but I didn't let that stop me.

"I's a slave. I ain't got nothing for my own. I can't even call my body my own 'cause it belong to Massa and any children I has be his. My mind, my thoughts, my feelings, they the onliest things I has for my own and you takes that from me too?"

"Luna... Luna...I..." Anguish no longer came close to describing his expression as what he had done began to dawn on him.

"Taking them thoughts is the worst thing anybody ever did me. It be even worse than... than..."

I searched my memories for something awful to compare it to so I could make him understand. I thought of the time I had been at a slave auction with Master John. The trip had been during his period of bribery and flattery and the purpose of taking me with him was to hang a silent threat on my resolve to resist his advances.

It was the most soul-destroying thing seeing those men, women and children up for auction whilst slaveholders hung around them like flies, pinching their muscles to test their strength or forcing their mouths open to look at their teeth. At times it was like watching a sick version of "Simon says" in which they were ordered to bend over in a manner of ways or made to walk to and fro. All so that those potential buyers could be satisfied that they hadn't missed a hidden wound or defect that would mean they paid over the odds for their flesh-and-blood commodity. It was heartbreaking. Especially when I saw the behaviour of a slave who thought he was standing before a kind slaveholder. The begging – for that was the only way to describe it – was humiliating as he strove to persuade the slaveholder to purchase him.

All the while Master John was at my side, his icy blue eyes pitiless as he beheld the slaves for auction, his gaze continually finding its way back to me as he smugly searched my face for signs that his little lesson was having the desired effect.

But even that memory wasn't enough to make Avery understand how I felt in that moment so I searched for another, my thoughts lingering briefly on that day in the woods as I lay in the dirt with blood seeping through my legs whilst Master Henry walked back to his horse. I was still searching when a strangled noise escaped Avery.

"Is that how you see me?"

I looked up at him. Of course it wasn't how I saw him. I had already forgotten that he could see everything I was thinking as I tried to gather my thoughts in order to articulate the depth of my feelings. The image of that day at the woods had been a random one I had been in the process of discarding when he had interrupted me. But, seeing a chance to wound him as much as he had wounded me, I stayed silent.

I was torn as I watched him, but I still did my best to keep my mind blocked to his prying eyes. He took a step back, dazed and completely bereft. Another of those choking sounds (was it a sob?) escaped him, and then he put his head in his hands and vanished.

I immediately ran out of the room to the front door.

"Avery," I screamed, as I pulled the door open and ran outside. "I ain't finished with you! So don't you be running away from me!" He was nowhere in sight but I raced out into the night anyway. "Avery, get back here!

Avery!"

There was no answer, so I came to a stop, breathing heavily in the night air. I couldn't sense his presence at all now. All I felt was a strange pull in the pit of my stomach, which made me feel weak.

"Avery! *Avery*!"

In the end, screaming at the night sky didn't bring him back. There was nothing I could do but return to the mansion.

I waited for him in the drawing room and at one point even sat down at the table to try and work on my reading, but my thoughts wouldn't settle long enough for me to be able to do anything constructive. So I threw my pen down in frustration and began to pace the room as the hours ticked by.

I was so *angry*. How dare he do that to me and then have the audacity to get upset and run away? I strode out of the drawing room to the front door and threw it open again.

"Avery! Get back here. I ain't finished with you... you no-good snake!"

The only response to my cry was the croak of a frog and the distant hoot of an owl, perhaps the same owl that had frightened me the previous night.

Back in the drawing room I stood at the window, wringing my hands. I may have been angry, but there was something niggling at me, making it difficult to order my thoughts. That something was the look of total despair on Avery's face before he'd vanished.

I moved away from the window and sat down at the table again.

Stupid man. If that image in my head had hurt him, then so be it.

But the niggling persisted because I believed him when he said it was something he couldn't stop. Besides, I should have realised that he could read my mind before tonight. I could think of so many instances now when he had given himself away by responding to my thoughts instead of my words and yet I had missed them all, too wrapped up in the silken threads of my own vanity to see what had needed to be seen.

My anger began to drain away, leaving me weary and tearful. He had looked so tormented.

I rose and went to stand at the window. My mood dipped even lower when I saw that the sun was starting to rise.

Rubbing at my temples, I went down to the kitchen to find myself something to eat, and stopped short when I saw the kitchen table laden with fresh food.

Alarmed, I stood staring at it for a few moments. He had been back to the house and hadn't even come to see me?

I experienced a sense of impending doom at what this might signify. Maybe he intended never to return.

I pushed that thought away and strode over to a basket of fruit.

Of course he would be back this evening, I thought as I bit into an apple. He had to come back, for we only had each other. There was nowhere else, and most importantly, no one else for him to run to.

I threw the half-eaten fruit away and made my way out of the kitchen and upstairs.

He would be back this evening, I repeated to myself when I was in bed.

But I found that sleep was a long time in coming and when it did, I had a terrifying nightmare that I was back at the plantation, standing at the edge of the cotton fields at dusk, long after all the slaves had gone back to the slave quarters. I was three in the dream and I stood there alone and lost, calling for Avery and wishing with all my heart that he would come walking out of the cotton fields. But a part of me knew he was nowhere near the plantation as he had been sold and I would never see him again.

I woke up covered in sweat in the stifling heat of a lazy

afternoon. The house was silent, eerily so. Knowing that there was no point in trying to go back to sleep, I got up and wandered around the house, and eventually found myself outside in the field flowers. I let the sweet scent of the flowers envelop me but couldn't clear my mind of Avery and how close I had come to kissing him. This scared me because it was bound to be the first thing he saw when he returned at dusk.

The only way I could take my mind off what had happened was to picture Master John in Avery's place every time my mind returned to it. It wasn't the ideal solution as I knew Avery would wonder why I kept doing that, but it was the best I could do until I found a way to close my thoughts off from his prying eyes.

The afternoon seemed to stretch interminably, but eventually it drew to a close. I sat in the drawing room wiping my sweaty palms against my dress. I wanted Avery here because I wanted to talk to him and explain the little misunderstanding I had let take root with my silence. I was desperate to see him but worried about what would happen once he got here. If he read my thoughts and decided to kiss me, would I be strong enough to keep my desire for him in check?

I wasn't so sure, so I waited, wanting nothing more than to lay my eyes on beautiful Avery, but frightened of what would happen once he got here.

Chapter Fourteen

But Avery didn't return that night. I waited in the drawing room anxiously counting away the hours and when it struck midnight I ran to the front door and stood in the doorway looking out into the unfeeling night.

"Avery! Avery!"

My voice sounded so shrill and the desperation I could hear in it was like a knife cutting into the shadows. And yet there was still nothing, only that pull and the terrible certainty that he wouldn't come back.

I stepped away from the safety of the mansion and into the dark, stopping when I was halfway across the field of Queen Anne's lace. Searching the night anxiously for some sign of his presence, I called him again and wanted to venture further out to look for him. But tonight the darkness all around me seemed impenetrable, especially as the moon was hidden behind a cloud. Everything was forbidding and seemed to whisper of danger now that Avery wasn't here. So I rushed back into the mansion and put the bolt against the door, the first time I had done that since my arrival here.

Back in the drawing room, my fears took on lightning clarity.

Where was he? Had something happened to him?

I was about to go outside and call him again when I noticed a pile of papers in the corner.

I picked them up and leafed through them. More of the poems and short stories Avery had copied out for me in large writing so I could practice reading. They had not been there yesterday.

Had he been and gone without my being aware of it? That was certainly possible. He could have appeared, placed the papers there and disappeared in an instant whilst I sat at the window looking out for him. I would have been none the wiser. This could only mean one thing. He didn't want to see me, and maybe he intended never to return.

That made me so angry that I tore the papers in half and threw them on the floor, sweeping everything else off the table to join them.

But I couldn't hold onto that anger because a mind-numbing fear was drowning everything out.

He wasn't coming back.

Getting to my feet, I decided that there was no point torturing myself with such thoughts. The best thing for me to do was to get some sleep.

Not wanting to closet myself in the gloomy red velvet room upstairs, I lay out on the chair by the window.

But I didn't sleep at all that night and when the sun began to rise, I stared out of the window in quiet despair. First the indigo sky lightened to a dark blue, which melted away to streaks of turquoise and burnt yellows, making the clouds that hung below it look like puffs of floating gold. I hated the sun as it came and robbed me of the possibility of having Avery with me again until sunset, though it was unlikely he would appear even then.

I lay there with that pull in my stomach, tired but unable to sleep, until at midday, I finally got up and dragged myself to the kitchen.

Like every other morning, the kitchen table was laden with fresh food, including a plate of what I was certain was a peach pie. Back at the plantation whenever I was down, Mary would bake a peach pie for the Master's family to have at dinner in the hopes that there would be some left over for me, even if it was only the tiniest slice. And I was sure that she was the one who had baked the one I was looking at.

It really was the last straw and I felt the sliver of self-control I had been fighting to hold onto disintegrate.

"Where is you?" I cried as tears filled my eyes. "Where you be, Avery?"

The pull in my stomach was bordering on pain now and my throat felt swollen and sore. In fact, I felt terrible all over, almost feverish, and my mind was ablaze with nothing but thoughts of Avery and how much I wanted to see him.

I eventually strode back out into the hallway.

"Where is you?" I cried out again to the silent, miserable house as I wiped away my tears. I ran up the stairs and down the long corridor into the small room in which he kept his clothes. I went straight to the jacket and trousers he had been wearing when I first saw him and held the jacket to my face. I thought I would be able to detect a scent of some sort, but there was nothing, only the faint smell of earth that still clung to the fabric and this made me even more miserable. It was as if he didn't really exist.

"Where is you? I ain't gonna stay here. If you ain't coming back then, I's leaving."

I said that even though I knew he was no doubt too far away to hear me.

But I meant what I said and ran out of the room. I held the jacket against me as I ran out of the mansion, only barely aware of how dishevelled I looked and that I was in the grip of a mounting frenzy that bordered on mania. I expected to feel that incapacitating nausea the moment I got near enough to the road, and, as unpleasant as that feeling had been, it would at least be a sign that Avery was still nearby.

So I ran as I had done on my first morning here, trying

to run toward him instead of away. But this time I didn't feel my limbs grow heavy the closer I got to the road and I was able to run past the point where I had been weakened by nausea the last time. My feet hit the brown, baked road before I stopped, this time not because Avery had used his powers to halt me, but because I realised he wasn't going to.

I sank to the ground and wept bitterly, my emotional turmoil coming out in long, rasping sobs.

"Where is you?" I managed to choke out again as I held the jacket against my chest and rocked on my knees. "Please, don't leave me here. Please, come back to me."

I wept and wept until it felt as if every last bit of moisture had been wrung from my body, leaving behind only the dry husk of a woman in mourning. Then I stood and began the walk back even though I was walking back to nothing.

When I reached the mansion, I didn't go inside. I couldn't bear the thought of being in that large, silent house without him so I sat outside in the field of white flowers, still holding his jacket to my chest.

It seemed as if the childhood memories of Mama that I had repressed for so many years were coming back to me. I could remember everything. I would be sitting under one of the trees by the slave quarters playing marbles with the other children when I would feel something warm and loving envelop me like a warm breeze and smell Mama's scent. She always smelt of cinnamon. I would jump up and run down the hill to the edge of the woods and seconds later I would see her, often looking angry or simply exhausted. But the moment she saw me waiting for her, it was as if the arduous day she had endured ceased to exist and she would laugh and ask how I had known she was coming. My answer was always the same. Your spirit came before you and kissed me on the cheek.

I remembered other things as well, like the time she had come home with one small heart-shaped chocolate wrapped in shiny red paper, which had fit perfectly into the palm of my tiny hand. Mistress Joan, Master Henry's first wife, had given her two of those expensive chocolates and she had saved one for me. I sat by her and ate the chocolate whilst she cooked our dinner on a small fire in front of the cabin, and even though she appeared to be absorbed with the task at hand, I knew she was thinking about those chocolates. Puzzled by a strange image that had popped into my mind, I had asked her if she would be bathing me in chocolate that night. She had laughed and laughed before explaining to me that she had been thinking that the chocolate had been so sweet she could have eaten more and would have loved to swim in a bath full of it.

She used to take me with her to find herbs and I remember she would teach me the names of the different herbs and flowers. "This one is called bloodroot," she explained in the woods, and when we came across a small cluster of Queen Anne's lace, she had smiled sadly as she picked a few and stared at them for a few moments. I was bored and didn't want to know the names of these plants but it was time with Mama so I tried to look interested. "This is called Queen Anne's lace. I was searching for this when I met your father."

Sorrow clung to her as she handed them to me and moved on. I didn't question her as I had no real interest in a father. Mama was everything I needed.

I also remembered the aching anguish that had befallen me when she was sold. I had been so distraught that a week later I crept out of the cabin in the dead of night and stood at the entrance to the woods. I desperately wanted to try and make my way to the cotton fields in the hope that I would find her there, but was too frightened to go into the woods by myself at night. A frightened Mary had found me and was trembling when she pulled me into her arms. She had held onto me fiercely, her voice breaking as she spoke, and she had eventually coaxed me away from the woods and back to the slave quarters.

Oh, Mama. When you were stolen away, a part of me went with you. The part that was loved and knew how to love in return.

That devastation I felt then had been terrible because I could only see things through a child's eyes, and even though it had been explained to me that Master Henry had sold her, I couldn't really accept the fact that Mama was gone for good.

I asked myself if what I felt in Avery's absence was merely those repressed emotions being replayed but I knew the answer was no.

Then what was this? Why was I feeling this way over someone, or I should say, *something* I had only been with for about a week? I desired Avery, but was my desire for him so strong that it could leave me in such an acute state of angst and despair now that he was gone?

What I felt for Avery was more than mere physical desire for a man. A lot more. And yet I couldn't bring myself to say it. That word I didn't want to say, even to myself, was not something that happened overnight. It was something that could take years for people to feel for one another, especially if the feeling was as intense as this. But I couldn't deny that that's what it was because my mind, body and soul told me so.

I placed my hand on my stomach on the spot from which the pull seemed to originate and all I could think about was the story in Genesis that Miss Emily had read to us one evening. The story of God taking one of Adam's ribs and using it to create Eve, a woman for him to love. I knew I was half mad with longing and lack of sleep but that pull seemed to make perfect sense when I thought of that story because I was sure that it was exactly what Eve would have felt if she had been separated from Adam. She had been made from him. A part of him had formed the core of who she was. She was bonded to him irrevocably and there was nothing on this earth that could ever have broken that bond. Only God, and if He had ever chosen to do so, she would have ceased to exist.

I had to find him. Being here, being anywhere without him, was intolerable. I had to find him or die.

He had told me I had a powerful mind and Mama Akosua had said that I would have been a powerful seer if I had nurtured those gifts. I had always been able to feel his presence whenever he was near so maybe if I concentrated I could reach him, just as Mama had been able to reach me when she'd needed to.

I closed my eyes and tried to focus. I tried to remember the force that always emanated from him, tried to hone in on it so I could maybe speak to him as Mama had spoken to me. I concentrated on him with all my being and for a while there was nothing, only my pain and desolation.

And then I perceived what I can only describe as a spark, like a match flaring in the dark. It went out almost as quickly as it had come but I opened my eyes and looked out toward the trees at the back of the house.

He was somewhere in that direction. I didn't know how far or if it was close enough for me to reach, but I had to try.

I got up and began to walk.

It took roughly three hours in the relentless heat to get to my destination. I hadn't thought to bring any food or water with me and had only taken Avery's jacket, which I clutched to my chest the entire time. Luckily, I came across a small stream on my way and was able to gulp down a few mouthfuls of water. The whole time that I was trudging through the woods, I asked myself if I had lost my mind. I was half delirious from the heat and hunger, so maybe I was only imagining that I could sense where he was. But the thought of going back to the mansion and waiting until dusk only to spend the night alone again quickened my steps.

It seemed as if the spark I had seen and felt was getting stronger and the pull that had tormented me so began to loosen and then disappeared altogether. Finally I began to feel the force he generated, faint at first, and then stronger, until my senses were engulfed with the sound of that sweet lullaby drawing me ever closer to him.

At last, I emerged from the trees to a still, clear blue lake glistening in the light of the afternoon sun.

I smiled, probably for the first time in nearly two days and relief, so strong and so sweet, filled me. He was here under the water somewhere.

I walked to the edge of the lake, took off my shoes and waded into the cool water up to my knees, not caring that I got my dress wet. He was here. I had found him at last. Letting out a shaky breath, I waded out of the water and sat down on the grass.

The feverishness I had felt was gone now and the burning in my brain was nowhere near as intense as it had been.

I lay down on my side still clutching his jacket to my chest. He was here; I had found him. He was bound to see me waiting for him when he came out of the water at dusk and I could only hope he wouldn't be cruel enough to leave me here on my own.

I thought about everything I had felt over the last two days and finally decided to say aloud that dreaded word: "Love."

I had fallen in love with Avery, fallen fast and hard. I couldn't even pinpoint how or when it had happened as it seemed as if it had always been there, waiting for a moment to show itself. I had spent my whole life trying not to form strong attachments to anyone and yet here I was, hopelessly and desperately in love with someone who, by his own admission, was a walking aberration.

Yes, I was in love.

I thought about using the time I had before the sun went down to try and find a way to shield my thoughts from him. But I was too tired to even try. When he came out of the water at dusk, he would find me here, look into my mind and know what I felt for him. That thought gave me a certain amount of peace because what I felt was too strong a burden to carry on my own.

It was a burden I would happily share with him because once he saw everything I had suffered over the last few days, he would never leave me. And I knew now that I would follow him to the ends of the earth for as long as he allowed me to.

With that last thought, and knowing that he was only a short distance away, I fell into an exhausted sleep, probably the deepest sleep I had ever had in my life.

Chapter Fifteen

I was standing outside the chapel under storm clouds so thick and black that almost all the daylight had been frightened away. But this wasn't the burnt ruin in which I had so often sought refuge. It was the chapel of the past, a glorious white mass looming out of the shadows cast by heavy black and purple clouds.

Even from this distance, I could feel an aura of evil surrounding the chapel that was as pervasive and noxious as the black smoke that must have billowed from it when it was set alight. This is what others sensed here, the thing that kept them away. I knew this even though I was in a dream. I also knew that, although I had picked up this evil on a subconscious level during my many visits here, something else had drawn me, something that had made me feel safe and comforted whenever I was there. Avery.

Somehow, I had sensed his past connection to this place long before he came into my life, and I was beginning to see that we were tied to each other in a way that neither of us could hope to understand.

Although the evil swathing the chapel sent fear shooting through my mind, I knew I had to go inside. So I walked steadily to the door and stepped into the cool, bright interior.

The inside was just as beautiful as the outside. The polished wooden pews, whitewashed walls, and the warm glow cast by the stained glass windows were a far cry from the carnage of burned wood, blackened walls, and gaping holes where the windows should have been. But none of those things mattered, for I could see a man standing at the altar with his back to me.

I ran down the aisle toward him, every fibre in my body coming alive and when Avery turned around in response to the sound of my footsteps, I almost wept with joy.

"Avery? Avery! Thank the Lord!"

A slow smile passed over his lips, one that was somewhat furtive and totally unlike the open, simple smiles I was used to seeing from him. But I didn't care. I ran into his arms even though everything around me screamed of danger and a dark, soulless yearning.

"Avery, I's scared I wasn't never gonna see you again."

"Hm. Yes, I have missed you too, can you not tell?"

He had his arms around my waist, crushing me to him, and I was shocked to feel his rigid manhood pressing against my stomach.

Desire flared within me and I grew weak in his arms, especially when he began to trail a line of soft kisses down my neck. And yet there was something horribly wrong. I knew this but now that I had found Avery again, nothing was going to tear me away from him.

Pulling my head back by my hair, he gazed down at me, his eyes hard like blue steel.

"Kiss me," he demanded.

I was slightly confused by the change in him, the mean edge in his voice that was so unlike the Avery I had fallen in love with. But my desire for him burned out of control and I pulled his head down and kissed him, entwining my fingers in his hair as I searched his mouth with my tongue. He met my passion with his own, crushing his lips to mine as he lowered me to the floor. I was on fire and reason deserted me along with any sense of propriety I might have had about what we were doing and where. Weak with lust, I could only cling to him as he loosened the top half of my dress and began to explore my bare skin, his cool touch agitating the heat of my desire rather than slaking it. When his mouth left mine and moved down to my breast, I writhed and moaned beneath him like a woman possessed as his hand reached under my skirt and up to my thigh.

When his teeth clamped down a little too vigorously on my nipple, I gasped and would have tried to pull away if his fingers hadn't at that moment reached the warm darkness between my thighs that was aching for his touch. I arched my back as he stroked it, completely enthralled by the fire that raged within as he brought his head up to mine once more.

At first all I saw was blond hair obscuring his face but when I brushed the hair away to look into his eyes, they weren't the shade of blue I was expecting to see.

I went rigid with fear as I stared into the face I hated, and when Master John smiled, I saw that his teeth were as long and sharp as Avery's when he was ready to kill.

To my horror the fire within me continued to rage and I threw my head back in wild abandon as Master John entered me, a cry of triumphant pleasure escaping me as his teeth tore into my neck.

Completely lost, I continued to writhe beneath him as he drank my blood, abandoning myself to desire as death slowly consumed me.

I woke up stifling a scream. I was lying in the lamplit red velvet bedroom and it was dark outside.

Even though I was wide awake, the dream continued to lie on me like packed earth. I found myself unable to move for a few moments as I pondered its significance and whether it was some sort of warning. But the cloying uneasiness it had induced was nothing compared to the raw panic I was faced with when I realised I was once more alone at the mansion.

Avery must have brought me back and left again. To make things worse his jacket, which I had carried with me and held onto like my life depended on it, wasn't in my hands. Tears began to gather as I contemplated another night in the mansion without Avery.

"Luna."

I sat up, my heart leaping with joy at the sound of the voice, that voice, coming from the direction of the half open door.

"Avery?"

His poked his head around the door, and looked more than a little bit nervous.

"Please, Luna. Do not start shouting until I have had a chance to speak to you."

"I ain't gonna shout. Just get in here."

He emerged fully from behind the door, brow slightly furrowed. Then he took a hesitant step forward and another until he got to the foot of the bed, where he stood gazing down at me. I remained silent, trying not to embarrass myself with the tears that desperately wanted to show themselves.

"Are you well, Luna? You look a little bit peaky this evening," he said after a few awkward moments.

"I's fine. It's the heat, that's all," I said quickly and then looked down and chewed my bottom lip as I knew he could no doubt see how much of a lie that was.

After studying me for a few more moments, he sat down gingerly on the end of the bed.

"You really are not going to start shouting at me?"

I shook my head.

He smiled timidly.

"Right then. So tell me, what are you thinking?" He said this with an almost childlike air of excitement.

The tears that had been threatening to overwhelm me disappeared almost as quickly as I had seen him vanish in the past.

"Is you... *mocking* me?" I said, using the same word he would have used. "You done left me on my own for nearly two nights and now come walking in here so's you can *mock* me?"

The smile left his face immediately and he looked at me, eyes wide.

"Oh no, I promise, Luna. I do not mock you. I do not know what you are thinking." He waited for the words to sink in and the smile reappeared. "That is why I stayed away. So I could learn to close your thoughts off from my mind."

I gaped at him and swiftly felt complete and utter hopelessness.

"You don't know what I's thinking?" I asked. *You don't know that I love you?*

He shook his head in delight. "No, Luna."

He stood up abruptly then and started gesturing excitedly as he spoke.

"You see, when I realised the magnitude of what I had done, I knew I could not come back unless I found a way to correct my error. So I went into town and practiced blocking off the thoughts of those I came across. And I did it, Luna."

"So you can never see in my mind again?"

"I can if I choose to. I cannot explain exactly how it is done but it is like gazing out of a window. I can turn away from the view if I want to but it will always be there. Of course I have to concentrate on looking away, so please, try not to tire my patience as much as you used to."

He smiled gently down at me and although my heart was breaking, it was hard not to respond to that smile.

"Well, I can't promise nothing. But I's gonna try."

He became serious again.

"I hope you know how sorry I am, Luna. I promise I will never invade your mind like that again."

I could only wave away his apology as I was too upset to speak.

"I must say I was exceedingly surprised to find you by the lake when I woke up today. How did you know where to find me?"

I shrugged and looked away. "I just knowed where to

go."

"Remarkable. You never cease to amaze me. And I think I'm beginning to understand why I saw your face so many years ago. You see, I think you were meant to save me, Luna."

"Save *you*. How?"

He sat back down on the bed and gave me the softest, sweetest smile.

"Well, when I left here a few nights ago, I could not stop thinking about what you said to me about killing and I was filled with anguish because, like the mindreading, I have always believed it was something I could not control. Then I began thinking about the night in your cabin when I was about to kill your old Master, and I remembered that I was able to stop feeding on him when I saw your horror and revulsion. I have never been able to do that before, stop in the middle of a kill. But I realised that if I could stop then, because of you, then I might be able to do it again.

"So that night, as I fed, I envisioned your reaction and I was able to stop before I completely drained my victim."

He appeared sad for a few moments. "It was a big accomplishment, but I fear I may still have killed him as he was very weak when I left. But the following night I was able to succeed in drinking enough to sustain me but not enough that my victim would be harmed. Can you imagine how I felt when I let him go his way without any memory of what I had done and with the simple command to hide the bite marks until they were healed?

"The fact that I still drink blood to survive will no doubt always be repulsive to you, but do you understand what it means to be able to do so and not kill? I have been tormented by the souls of the lives I have taken over the past fifty years and you do not know the joy, the peace that comes with the knowledge that I will never have to kill again."

I smiled. The relief and joy he felt was obvious. He

looked lighter somehow, and for the first time he appeared to be at ease with himself. He wasn't fidgeting or pulling at his shirt collar as he did so often.

"I may not understand exactly how I saw your face the night I died or why I continued to see it over the years, but there is one thing I am certain of, Luna. You were meant to save me. Only you could save me from an eternity of torment. Only you, beautiful Luna."

"Avery, I... I wants you to know that what you seen in my head, that ain't how I sees you. You shoulda stayed long enough to see the rest or so's I could explain it to you when I quit being mad."

"You... you do not need to explain anything to me, Luna. I only hope that you will be able to truly forgive me in your heart for my transgressions."

"I already has, Avery."

We sat in silence for a few moments in which he gazed at me thoughtfully. But he seemed a lot more confused than usual.

"Do you know, Luna, I am only just noticing how expressive your face is. Your eyes alone can say a thousand words with a mere glance. Reading your expression is like putting together the pieces of a complicated puzzle, and I think I have the answer to the one I see now."

He continued staring at me but for all his words it seemed as if he didn't have the answer to the puzzle. Then he brightened and that wondering smile appeared again.

"You... you are looking at me as if you wished I would stop talking and leave you by yourself in peace."

I sighed inwardly knowing that this was going to get very tedious, very quickly. But he was here. Avery was here and smiling at me.

"No, Avery," I said with a faint smile. "In fact, I's thinking..."

I paused, reluctant to say anything that would ruin the simple pleasure of having him returned to me. But he had to know that he could never leave me like that again. So my next words were said as tenderly as I could manage.

"I's thinking that it be mighty mean of you to leave like that and for so long."

"I... I am sorry, Luna. But I could see no other way to mend my trespass apart from staying away until I could learn to never do so again."

"I understands that," I said. "But next time you has to go away, you gots to tell me you's coming back cause... cause..."

"Luna, I would have never done that even if I wanted to. I love you. Not being near you is like dying. You are like air to me, like the water and food that humans need to keep them alive. I would die if I could not be near you."

I could only stare at him for it was as if, despite his promises, he was still reading my mind and reciting back to me my own thoughts about his absence.

His anguish seemed to deepen.

"I apologise. I should not have spoken so, for I see that I have made you uncomfortable. I have to remember that the love I hold for you is that of an immortal. It is too... too immense... and all-consuming for any woman to be able to bear let alone return in kind, so please forgive me for speaking it out loud to you."

Oh, Avery, I thought, my heart aching for him. *I love you too. If only you would read my thoughts, for I can never tell you I love you even though I want to with all my heart.*

"It frightens even me sometimes, the intensity of my feelings for you," he said as he stood and moved to the window. "It is so strong that I want to reach out and crush those who tormented you even though they can no longer do you harm. And it does not matter how many things I do to your old Master, it is never enough to assuage the hate that smoulders within me."

"What you mean by that, Avery?" I asked, slightly alarmed by the intense fury I saw in his eyes at the mention of Master John.

He moved from the window and came to stand before me.

"Oh, it's nothing really," he said waving his hand in the air as if to dismiss the seriousness of his actions but I could see in his eyes that he knew exactly how serious it was. "I have merely sent him a few hallucinations, brought some of his worst nightmares to life, so to speak."

"Like what?"

"Nothing so frightening that it would actually unhinge his mind or kill him. I merely made him think he had been buried alive a few times." A soft smile curled the corners of his mouth and he looked away. "Do not worry, Luna. I did not permanently injure him. Only his pride was hurt at the fact that he woke up the whole plantation with his high, childlike screams."

"Avery, I wants you to stop doing them things to him."

"Oh, come now, Luna. Asking me not to torment John Holbert is like asking the sun not to shine. It is impossible not to have ill feeling toward that man. Do you know that everyone despises him? Even his own mother and brother? What you are asking is simply impossible."

"You listen to me now, Avery, and listen good," I said reaching out and grasping his wrist.

He seemed to forget everything for a moment and stared at the hand clutching his wrist with a kind of awe.

"Avery!" I shook his wrist and he met my gaze again, a sublime expression of pure joy in his eyes. "You wants to be a man again, don't you?"

He nodded, his gaze returning to the hand grasping his wrist.

"You know that scares me?"

I saw confusion and uncertainty in his gaze when he brought it up to mine again.

"Why?"

"Cause I've watched white mens be cruel my whole

154

life and I's scared that that's what you's gonna be. So, please, stop 'cause I don't wants you to ever be like them."

He seemed to understand and he smiled sweetly at me when he sat down. "Luna. Beautiful Luna. "

"You gonna quit?"

"If it is your wish, then I am obliged to try, for who can refuse the request of such an angelic, selfless being as yourself? Your old Master is a worthless excuse for a man but you are right. What I do is nothing compared to what your mother has planned for him but..."

"Mama? What she gonna do?"

"I do not know for sure, but maybe she means to lay sickness on him as she did his father."

"You fooling me?"

"No, she cursed him. It was meant to kill him but unfortunately he survived the stroke."

"That can't be."

"You have never believed in her skills but am I not proof that powerful magic exists? Your mother is very powerful. If her attention was not taken up with trying to kill me, she would have taken care of Master John by now."

The emotional turmoil of the last night and a half came swooping down on me at the thought that Mama meant to kill Avery.

"I can see that you still do not believe she is powerful enough to do harm, but she is," he said and I was relieved that he had again misread my expression.

"But she don't be knowing how to kill you. Or do she?"

"I believe she does. She knows that certain metals can pierce my flesh and that the sun weakens me, because that is when I feel her the most. She can also summon things. Spirits that may be able to hold me for long enough for someone to inflict a mortal wound."

He said all this with an air of fascination at the thought of his death, whilst the blood turned to ice in my veins.

"She felt your distress a few nights ago when you

realised that I was looking into your mind. And it has made her determined to find you. She can see that you are in this house but she does not know where it is or how to get to it yet. Do not be alarmed, Luna. I may not be able to hear your thoughts but I can hear your heart racing. I will not hurt your mother." He smiled again at that moment. "I could never hurt anyone who cares for you that deeply. And besides, I have seen her through your eyes and through the eyes of that boy Ebenezer and... I love her too now."

I sighed. Only Avery could love the one woman on this earth who not only knew how to kill him, but wouldn't hesitate to rip his heart out if she got anywhere near him.

"I should let you get some sleep. You look exhausted, Luna," he said, concern creasing his brow.

"No, I's fine," I said, terrified of letting him out of my sight even for a moment.

"I noticed you did not eat the peach pie Mary made." He searched my face as he spoke.

"I done told you it's the heat. I couldn't eat nothing."

He nodded even though he appeared puzzled.

"Is them clothes new?" I said to change the subject.

His face lit up. "Yes. I went into town and had new clothes made. The last time I did so I made them do what I wanted without showing myself. But I was able to move amongst them yesterday and no one suspected that I was anything other than what I was pretending to be. A few noted the paleness of my complexion but none thought I was anything other than a wealthy man."

"What about the womens? What you see in they heads?"

He paused and looked at me questioningly, perhaps wondering at my tone, so I bit back my jealousy and added light-heartedly, "Women always see more then mens."

"Yes, of course. No, they did not appear to notice anything unusual. But I must say it was amusing being around them as their thoughts are often very different from

156

the things they say and the way they act."

He chucked lightly and frustratingly did not elaborate on the thoughts of these women or his interaction with them. But I could imagine all too well how they must have fawned over him. It was a sickening, painful thought.

But the thing that dominated my mind as I sat talking to Avery was the news of Mama and how desperate she was to find us. I promised myself that I would sit down with Avery at some point over the next few nights so we could decide how best to let Mama know that I was safe where I was.

But I'm ashamed to say that I never did. The news of Mama's distress troubled me, but being around Avery was at times like being at the heart of the sun. It blinded me to everything but him. I also put off discussing the issue because I knew in my heart it would mean doing battle with Mama. A battle I had no hope of ever winning because nothing would ever convince her to let me be with Avery. Besides, I knew now that my time with him would soon come to an end.

I was in turmoil that night as I listened to him and watched him, delighting in his achievements but also despairing at the small changes I kept seeing. I despaired because ironically, the more of his humanity that he was able to regain, the humanity he credited me with helping him to rediscover, the less of a possibility there was for us to have any kind of future together.

He was changing. I saw it in the way he stood, the way he walked, and the way he talked. He was slowly becoming a man again. A white man. And I could never tell him I loved him because there was no place in this society for a white man and a Negroe woman unless she was his bed wench. A Negro woman was less than nothing to the world at large, a world in which women were judged by four virtues: piety, domesticity, submissiveness, and purity. And although I had spent most of my life striving to meet those virtues, there was one I could have no hope

157

of attaining. And that was purity, the one virtue that had been stolen from me one bright spring day in the woods and which would always have been denied me by my position as a female slave.

Once Avery regained his humanity and took on the values of the society in which we lived, he would soon see me as nothing but his property. And if I let him treat me as such, it would completely poison the love and respect I had for him. So I kept quiet, knowing I had to make do with the time that I had with him, to live each day as it came, until he was gone.

"Can I show you something outside?" he asked.

"Sure, but you gots to let me have a minute to bathe and change outta these dusty clothes," I said.

"All right. I will wait for you by the stables."

"Make sure you don't go nowhere now, Avery," I blurted out.

"There is nowhere else that I would want to be."

He studied me intently for a long moment. "How I wish I knew what you were thinking right now, Luna."

"You saying you want take a look?" I asked.

If only he would, I thought, *and end my agony*.

"No," he said with a sheepish smile. "I have learned my lesson." He grew serious again. "I will be waiting outside."

He walked to the door then paused as if he were about to say something more, but then changed his mind and left.

I bathed quickly and chose a sky-blue dress to wear, one of the nicer ones he had given me. Then I ran down to the stables at the back of the house and was relieved to find Avery waiting for me as he said he would be.

***

The "something" that Avery wanted to show me was a light brown mare, which I took an instant dislike to, probably because Avery seemed to have fallen in love with it.

"What in God's name is that?" I asked.

He faced me, amused by the question and, no doubt, my displeasure. "A horse."

"I know it be a horse, Avery," I said archly. "What I's asking is what the hell it be doing here?"

"I found her a few miles from here." He went back to stroking and patting its neck. "Most animals can sense that there is something different about me and so steer clear. But she approached me and I have no idea how she knew where to find me, but she was waiting here when I brought you back this evening. There's something special about her. Can you not feel it?"

"Why it be looking at me like that?"

I wasn't being difficult this time. It was looking at me with its eyelids half lowered, a look I found particularly sinister.

"Looking at you how, Luna? She likes you, I can sense it. Come closer so she can say hello properly."

I stayed where I was. There was no way I was going anywhere near that thing when it was looking at me like that.

"You are not scared, are you?" he asked, amused.

"No! I just don't like the way it be looking at me."

"I do not believe it." He laughed, and stroked the horse's head. "The same Luna who fearlessly tried to fight a vampire twice her size is scared of a horse! Unbelievable!"

"I says I ain't scared of it," I said and stepped up to the horse to prove my point, only to jump back when it swung its head into my chest.

"Ah, look how playful she is with you, Luna. She loves you."

I wasn't so sure but I stroked its mane anyway to avoid any more accusations that I was scared of a horse.

"Will you look after her for me during the day?"

"Sure, Avery," I said, and tried to direct a dirty look at

the stupid horse without Avery seeing.

It pulled its lips back from its teeth and whinnied, almost as if it was laughing at me, something Avery found hilarious and took as another sign that the horse liked me.

"A vampire?" I asked stepping away from the horse so I could avoid any more "playful" tosses of its head. "Is that what you is?"

The hand that was stroking the horse slowed and the smile left his face.

"That is what the ones who turned me called themselves. Vampires. But it is just another word for demon in my eyes," he said morosely.

I wanted to ask him again about his past and what had happened at the chapel, but he looked unhappy now and it would be foolish to risk another argument so soon after he had returned.

I asked anyway.

"Avery, tell me what happened."

He sighed and stopped stroking the horse. He turned to me, eyes heavy with years and years of sadness.

"Luna, I cannot talk about what happened at the chapel. It is too painful for me. Those things killed my wife right before my eyes and then turned me into this!" He was silent for a while before he spoke again. "It is hard to talk about her because I am consumed with guilt whenever I think about it. I was not a good husband to her. I only had one love at that time and that was God. There was no room for anyone else and she knew that. Maybe in time I will be able to talk about all that happened. But I will not talk about it now, so please, do not ask me."

I tried to give him a look of acceptance, but knew I was scowling.

"I wish you could see how adorable you look at this very moment, Luna."

"You be thinking everything I does is 'adorable' 'cause you gots nothing to compare it to. I wonder what I's gonna do when you start seeing that there ain't nothing special or 'adorable' about nothing I says or does."

"Or maybe you cannot see just how enchanting you are. How beautiful, how strong, and kind. No one can ever compare to you."

I couldn't look at him. The pain was acute at the thought that although he probably meant what he said, he would soon be gone, so I changed the subject.

"So what you gonna call that thing?"

"Julia," he said, growing sad again. "In memory of my wife."

"You naming that horrible thing after your dead wife?"

He faced me, more than a little exasperated.

"I's asking that's all," I added quickly. "Calls it what you want."

"I will, my dear, adorable little Luna."

He was, as always, so sincere but I felt sure that the day would soon come when he would not only start comparing me to other women, but would find me wanting in contrast. I could only promise myself that when the time came for him to leave, I wouldn't return to a life of bondage.

"Avery. I seen some guns here the other morning. Can you teaches me how to use one?"

He mulled over this for a second and then he vanished. I gasped. No matter how many times he did that, I couldn't get used to it. He reappeared a moment later with a gun and a box of bullets in his hands.

"You gonna teach me?" I asked.

"Well, of c..." He stopped and stared at me apprehensively.

"What, Avery? You think I's gonna shoot you once you show me?"

"Well, yes."

"Oh come now, Avery! I ain't gonna shoot you!"

"It is not my safety that I worry about, Luna. A bullet cannot pierce my flesh. I only worry that you will try to shoot me in a rage one day and the bullet will ricochet off

161

my hard skin and hit you instead. How do you think I would feel if that happened?"

He had been leading the horse back into the stables as he spoke and I was glad to be rid of that horrible thing and the sinister way it had of looking at me.

"I says I ain't gonna shoot you, Avery, now give me the gun," I said when he returned.

"Let me show you something first." He loaded the gun. "Stand back, Luna."

I rolled my eyes and took a few steps back.

"Further back please, Luna."

"Avery!" I folded my arms.

"Please, Luna, just a little further back," he said, clearly amused.

I took a few more steps back and then waited, hands on hips, tapping my foot.

He nodded, seemingly satisfied, and then brought his hands up and aimed the gun at his palm.

"Avery?" I said uneasily, taking a step forward.

"It is all right, Luna. Just watch."

I jumped when the gun went off and then ran to him. The hand at which he had aimed the gun was closed in a fist and he opened it slowly to show the misshapen bullet sitting in his palm. He let it fall to the ground and held his palm out to show me.

"See, I am completely unharmed."

"Yes, that's mighty fine. You gonna show me how to use the gun now?"

"I will, but you have to promise not to try and shoot me. My skin is completely impenetrable..."

"Yes, yes. So you said."

"... So you will only hurt yourself if you try and shoot me, so promise me now that you never will."

"Avery! I says I ain't gonna shoot you."

"Promise me, Luna," he said sternly.

"I promise."

"Good, because as you have seen, there is a very real

162

possibility that you will hurt yourself if you try."

I rolled my eyes again and was so annoyed by his long drawn out warning that the first thing I did when he (finally) gave me the gun was aim it at him, even though I had no intention of pulling the trigger.

In an instant he vanished, reappeared at my side, and wrenched the gun out of my hand. Then he flung it away and I could only watch as it arced high and disappeared into the night a great distance from where we stood. When he turned to face me, I was a little bit scared when I saw how furious he was.

"Luna! What did I just tell you? What have I just spent the last few minutes explaining and even demonstrating to you? I am telling you now, Luna, I will not tolerate this foolhardy, reckless behaviour. I won't stand for it!"

I could only stare at him as I put a hand over my mouth to stifle the laughter. He was angry. Avery was actually angry with me. His eyes were blazing, his cheeks flushed, and his mouth was fixed in a hard, thin line.

I couldn't help it. I started laughing, even though it was bound to make him even more furious. But the anger immediately left him as he watched me, a smile of his own tugging at his lips. Only when my laughter had subsided did he speak.

"I believe that is the first time I have heard the sound of your laughter. And what a beautiful sound it is," he said, gazing at me adoringly.

"You's hopeless, Avery," I remarked, marvelling at his inability to stay angry with me for long. "If I really be looking to shoots you, I's at least wait for you to teach me how to use the gun first."

He laughed. "I suppose that does make sense. I had better get the other one. But before I do, you must promise that..."

"Avery!" I cried but saw that he was merely teasing me.

Avery spent that night showing me how to use the gun

and a few hours before the sun came up, he decided to teach me how to ride Julia. At first I didn't want to go anywhere near that horrible creature, but from the moment he helped me up onto the horse, I felt completely at home. He spent a couple of hours showing me what to do, leading the horse in a walk and then allowing me to progress into a trot on my own whilst he stood back and watched. Already enjoying my first horse riding lesson and wanting to go faster, I tried to squeeze the horse gently with my lower legs in order to encourage her to go a little bit faster, but ended up kicking with my heels instead, which made her shoot forward. Not knowing how to slow down and not particularly wanting to, I kicked with my heels again and before I knew it we were galloping through the night. I held on tight, terrified but exhilarated and a giggle escaped me, followed by a scream of pure joy. The speed, the feel of the wind sweeping past me, the thrill of being in control of such a powerful animal was pure euphoria, and I knew this was what it felt like to be free, really free.

"Luna, stop! That is too fast."

He had appeared to my right but we sped past him as I urged the horse to go faster. But all too soon he reappeared a few yards ahead and I knew he was controlling the animal because she started to slow down and came to a stop a foot away from an extremely angry Avery.

This time his tirade was longer and far more heated than the last and ended with him stalking off saying that if I was this determined to kill myself, he saw no reason to stand in my way. I was laughing so hard by that time that I fell off the horse into a heap on the floor, still struggling to control my laughter. He was kneeling at my side in an instant, his anger replaced by concern and intense remorse, which only made me laugh harder.

Poor Avery. I abused and wore out his patience on those nights as he taught me how to ride and shoot. He threatened to stop those lessons on more than one occasion but he could never quite bring himself to carry out his threats. So as well as teaching me how to read, he taught me how to ride and shoot better than most men. He often said he regretted teaching me such dangerous pastimes, as I seemed determined to injure myself. But in the end, when our lives were threatened, those lessons would be our only hope for survival.

Chapter Sixteen

And so the days slowly turned into weeks, the happiest of my life. I spent a lot of those long, warm nights with Avery, often sitting on a blanket amongst the sweet perfume of the Queen Anne's lace. I ate up everything he taught until, at last, I was able to read small sections of the bible out loud to him whilst he sat watching me like a proud parent. If I struggled with a word, he waited patiently for me to tease it out on my own and the smile that lit up his face when I finally managed it always made my breath catch and it would be a few moments before I was able to continue.

Avery also continued to teach me how to shoot and ride and, after some persuasion, he let me ride off into the night on my own. Once he was out of sight, I would recklessly urge Julia on as fast as she could go, thrilled by the speed and the feeling of freedom. It was always a magical moment and felt as if I were shedding my skin and becoming one with everything around me. Out in the empty countryside, with only the moon looking down on me, I could pretend I was invincible and laugh into the rushing wind as I sped on to nowhere under a boundless starlit sky. But I was never completely alone for Avery was always nearby. I would often catch reassuring glimpses of him out of the corner of my eye and no matter how far from the mansion I rode or eventually found myself, he would always be waiting for me, relief in the weary little smile he gave when I dismounted and let him take me and then Julia back to the mansion.

On some of those nights we took long walks under the loving magnificence of the moon. Sometimes we would talk for hours but at other times we merely walked in silent reverence for the beauty all around us. I was able to find out little bits of information about his past life during those walks and discovered that he had been the one who had started the fire at the chapel and then fled, without knowing whether or not the other demons had survived. He also told me that he first saw me "as if in a dream", as he put it, immediately after he was turned into a demon and kept on seeing my image over the years. But most of all he spoke of the many, many years alone in a wilderness of despair at what he, a God-fearing man, had been turned into: a creature that was perhaps on a par with the devil himself. My heart cried out for him when he told me those things and I desperately wished I could have been there to comfort him during his travails. I was also eternally grateful that he had eventually found me.

I was a different woman during those weeks, the lowly slave whose every moment had been dogged by fear now a phantom of the past I barely acknowledged. I felt vibrant, fearless and most of all, loved. Loved. And there was nothing in this world that was closed to me now, so long as Avery was by my side.

I should have thought more about those I had left behind, particularly Mama. But I was selfish in my newfound love. You see, love and happiness had previously been as unreachable to me as the sky. So now that I had been given those things, I was selfish with them and left no room for thoughts of anything else. And in the grip of that all-consuming fixation, like Icarus, I flew too close to the sun and sealed my long fall back to earth.

The first signs I had of the threat to our happiness were the dreams. In those dreams I was always at the chapel and although I could never remember the content when I awoke, I always had the sense of some malevolent terror, an insatiable evil lurking in the darkness waiting for a chance to devour. I sometimes felt that presence during the day and found it hard to sleep especially since Avery's absence was already like a festering wound.

On one of those days, nearly a month after Avery took me away, I was alone in the kitchen having been frightened out of an uneasy sleep by another of those dreams, the third one in a row. Already brooding over Avery's daytime absence, I couldn't shake the feeling that there was something watching me, something that hated me and wanted to see me bathed in blood.

At that moment there was a loud thump at the kitchen door that had me scrambling to my feet. Trying to control my terror, I hurried to the kitchen window and peered out in time to see Julia rear up on her hind legs and bring her front hooves crashing down on the kitchen door again.

I sighed in exasperation. God only knows why I had promised to look after that stupid nag for Avery. I made sure she was fed, had fresh, clean water to drink and even spent a lot of time grooming her so that when Avery arrived at dusk her coat was gleaming. But it still didn't stop the dumb beast from tormenting me and doing things like getting a hold of my skirt between her teeth and dragging me backwards until I cried out for a laughing Avery to help me.

"Stop that now!" I cried as I leant out of the window. I wondered how the hell she had even managed to get out of the stables.

I quickly ducked back when she came toward me. Then she stood at the window neighing and shook her head at me as if in agitation.

This was just my luck, I thought as I backed away from the kitchen window in fright. The horse had gone mad and Avery was too far away to come to my rescue. Julia looked at me in that menacing way she had and then

168

trotted away. Relieved, I crept warily to the window to see where she had gone, gasped when I saw what she was doing, and ran out of the kitchen into the wilting afternoon heat.

"You dumb beast! Stop that now! I says stop it!"

She ignored me completely and continued trying to pull the clothes I had hung out to dry off the clothesline with her teeth. She yanked so hard the line snapped and fell to the ground along with the clothes I had washed that morning. I ran up to her and grabbed the other end of the trousers she still had in her mouth and pulled, surprised when she let it go.

"You know how long it took to wash them clothes? Stupid, stupid horse!" I cried and swiped at her with the trousers. She backed away and trotted toward the trees at the back of the house, then stopped and turned to look back at me.

Realising what this behaviour was about, I dropped the trousers and walked over to her.

"So you misses him too, huh?" I said, resting my head on her neck.

She neighed again and walked forward a few steps and then looked at me again.

"All right, Julia. Let's go find him."

***

She took me to the lake in which I had found Avery that day. He wasn't in the water this time but I could sense him nearby, so I let Julia wander off whilst I looked out over the water which stretched out like blue glass in the drowsy afternoon heat.

There was no one around, save Avery, but he wasn't likely to make an appearance whilst the sun was up, so I stripped off to my underclothes and waded into the clear crisp water. Having never learned how to swim, I couldn't go out as far as I would have liked to but the cool water, the stillness all around me, and Avery's presence nearby gradually began to calm me down, so that by the time I came out of the water, I had left behind the sense of foreboding caused by the nightmares.

I put my dress back on over my wet undergarments, leaving it undone at the back as I stood in the shade of the trees and looked out across the lake.

All at once I had the sensation I used to have as a child whenever I knew Mama was on her way home, but this time it was much stronger. In my mind's eye I saw Avery standing a few feet behind me, reaching out a hand toward the bare skin exposed by the undone dress. I turned my head slowly and there he was, his hand hovering only inches from my back, his gaze troubled as he studied the bare flesh. He brought his eyes up to meet mine and slowly withdrew his hand.

"Avery? What you doing out in the day?" I asked and noticed that he was a lot paler than usual and that there were dark circles under his eyes. "You all right? You look sick."

"It is only the sunlight." He glanced ruefully up at the sky through the canopy of leaves.

"Then what you doing out here?"

"I felt you nearby and I suppose I did not want to wait until dusk to see you. The sun will go down in a little over two hours. I have stayed out a lot longer during the day without too many ill effects."

I still had my back to him and I noticed that he kept glancing at it as he spoke. Feeling self-conscious, I looked away and began to fasten my dress.

"All that happened a long time ago, Avery," I said when my back was covered.

"It... it's just that I have only seen the whipping through your eyes so it was a shock to see your back marked in that way."

I sat down on the grass and he joined me.

I had never seen the scars on my back but I imagined

that the puckered, twisted flesh must have been a repulsive sight. He was lost in thought as he looked out over the water and although it scared me to see him looking so unwell, this was the first time I had seen his face clearly in the brilliance of daylight and his beauty took my breath away. When he faced me, I lowered my gaze quickly, slightly embarrassed at being caught admiring him so openly.

"Luna, when I used to look into your thoughts, I noticed that the ones of your child and the whipping did not come to the surface often. Why is that?"

"Somebody who don't like talking about they past shouldn't be too quick to get in everybody else's business, Avery!"

The silence stretched on until I finally had the courage to meet his gaze. He was looking at me in that gentle, patient way he had, which spoke of his total and unconditional devotion and I was ashamed, not only of the way I had snapped at him, but of what I was about to say.

"It... it's cause I hated her. I hated her, so I told Mama to take her away so's I never has to lay eyes on her. She be dead now for all I know and that makes me happy, Avery. It makes me happy."

"Yes, I saw your conflicting emotions when I came across the memory, but like so much that I heard and saw in your mind, I did not understand the reason for it. Tell me. Why do you think you hate her?"

"Cause she be *his*!"

"No, Luna. She is yours," he said simply.

"No, she ain't. She be his. His child, his *slave*. His blood and mines runs through her, tying me to him and what he did and kept on doing for years. Us! Forever, in *her*. How can I loves something that be made from his unnatural lust for the child I was when he got at me in the woods that day?"

He only looked at me thoughtfully as if he were still trying to understand, and that careful scrutiny in place of the condemnation I was expecting made me look away.

"Mary be thinking I ask Mama to take the child away cause I ain't want Massa Henry to get his hands on her. Child of his or no, we knowed he woulda done the same thing to her the minute she be old enough to walk. But Mama knew. Mama knew I hated the child and she done never forgive me for that. I see it in her eyes and... and I expect it be the reason she done never told me what she did with her."

"I have looked into your mother's mind. She does not hate you for it. She is merely angry at what she sees as weakness in you for not wanting your own child."

It hurt to hear that and not for the first time I wished Avery was like most human beings who would have lied and said what they thought would make me feel better.

"Letting your guilt and shame run its course is her way of punishing you," he continued. "So she will not tell you unless you ask."

I shook my head slowly and wondered how Mama could know so much about my character even though she rarely saw me. My guilt and shame *had* been tormenting me. I could see that now and it was a fitting punishment, much worse than the feel of the lash across my back.

"I have seen your mother's memory of that night," he continued. "And I know what happened to your baby. But do *you* want to know?"

I was quiet for the longest time and he gave me the space to make up my mind as I struggled with the hate and repulsion I felt for the thing I had heard take its first breath in my tiny little cabin. I could not look at Avery when I answered.

"Yes," I mumbled. "Yes, I does."

"She gave her to a family of runaways she had been giving food and medicine to. They were the reason she did as you asked and took the child away. She knew that they would agree to take her with them up north and raise her as their own."

172

"So she be alive? And... and *free*?"

"I do not know those answers, Luna. But your mother seems to think she is alive. She would know if anything happened to her, as she knows whenever you need her."

To my surprise, I began to cry, silently at first, and then the dam broke and I was almost choking on my tears as they ran wild and free. It felt as if a great many chains had been lifted from my soul and I wept in relief for her, for my daughter, and the fact that she had been given a chance at a bondage-free life. I also wept for myself and the sweet freedom this knowledge had granted me.

When Avery realised the tears were cathartic, he relaxed and let me be.

"What her name be?" I asked when I could speak again.

"I do not know. There was no time for your mother to think about naming the baby. And no way for her to find anything out about her either. She told the family that they should never try and come back or contact her in any way because if Master Henry ever found out who the child was, he could claim her back as a runaway."

I nodded slowly. Yes, as sick as he now was, he would still move Heaven and earth to retrieve his property if he ever found out where she was.

"But I will find her for you one day, Luna. I promise you that."

"And what good that do her?" I asked, on the verge of more tears. "She be better off not knowing nothing about me. I's happy she ain't dead, but I still hates her. And I expects I always will."

"You think you hate her because you never saw her, Luna. If you had seen her, you would not feel as you do now. Yes, there were elements of Master Henry in her features but it was mostly you I saw through your mother's memory of her. She was beautiful. You will see. When you are able to lay eyes on her for yourself one day, you will see that you could never hate such a beautiful little thing."

We sat side by side in silence for the rest of the afternoon, looking out across the lake as the day yawned and the sun began to set.

It was only then that Avery stood up and, with one last glance at the sky, held out his hand to me, forgetting as he did from time to time the careful distance he placed between us physically. He remembered, however, and was in the process of withdrawing his hand when I reached up and grasped it. He looked stunned for a moment and stared in awe at my hand in his before he helped me to my feet.

He held onto my hand as we walked away from the lake, and kept finding reasons to take it again over the course of the next few nights, an expression of such sweet joy and hope in his eyes whenever I gladly entwined my fingers in his.

But the sense of foreboding that had been plaguing me for the last few days came back stronger than before when we returned to the mansion that evening. When we stepped inside, Avery stopped at the doorway and looked out into the gathering night with an air of apprehension. He insisted that we stay indoors that evening, something we rarely did on such warm, balmy nights, but for once, I didn't argue. He was distracted, and kept going to the window to peer outside, his expression more troubled every time he did so. I wasn't surprised when he left a few hours earlier than normal that night, and he looked anxious at the thought of leaving me on my own.

Yes, he could feel it too. But even though I could sense that danger would soon be reaching out for us, when I went to bed that morning all I could think about was the feel of my warm hand in Avery's cool one, and when I fell asleep I had nothing but sweet dreams of us walking hand in hand in our very own Garden of Eden.

We loved each other so much, there had to be a chance for us and the happy ending I kept dreaming about.

There *was* hope for us.

Wasn't there?

Chapter Seventeen

The following night Avery returned to the house two hours later than usual, two hours I spent in an orgy of wordless panic. When he finally materialised at the drawing room door, his expression was as fearful and frantic as I'm sure mine was, until he saw me sitting in the chair waiting for him. He relaxed then and looked so relieved that it made me wonder if he'd expected something to have happened to me in his absence.

He apologised for being late and explained that he'd had something important to do, which had taken far longer than expected. I didn't ask where he had been even though I wanted to and he didn't volunteer that information.

He was distant for most of the night and left early again. He told me that he might be late returning that evening. This time when I went to bed, I found it very hard to sleep and when sleep did finally pull me into its arms, the nightmare was there waiting.

When he returned the following evening he was in a bad mood. Amused by a previously unseen aspect of Avery's personality, I allowed myself to forget my fears about the increasing number of hours he was spending away from me. Having insisted that we stay inside again, he sat slouched opposite me with his eyes lowered and his mouth pursed. And instead of listening to me read, he decided that I needed to memorise maps of the area and learn what seemed like a random assortment of words and their meanings, getting impatient if he thought I wasn't taking the lesson seriously. When, after one reprimand too far, I shouted at him, he gave me a long wilting stare before he abruptly left his seat and moved to the window.

I stared at him as he stood with his back to me and, feeling my gaze on him, he turned and glowered at me.

Still amused by his little mood, I gave him a grin that never failed to draw one from him in turn, no matter how sorely I had tried his patience. And sure enough, his scowl melted away and a soft adoring smile crept onto his lips. Then it seemed as if he was reminded of something painful and the smile vanished. He drew back from whatever it was as if he had been burned and quickly faced the window again, his misery lingering like an earthbound spirit.

A wrenching sadness came over me as I watched him. I thought the anguish that had previously been so much a part of him had been banished. But now it seemed it had returned and I felt crushed. I was no longer enough to keep his pain and misery away.

That night he stayed with me until the sun began to peer over the horizon and even then, he was reluctant to leave. That should have allayed some of my fears but I went to bed wreathed in misery, certain that my heavenly nights with Avery were almost at an end.

***

The next day I was sweeping the kitchen floor when I heard a sound from the front door. Startled, I dropped the broom and grabbed a large knife just as Avery materialised causing me to scream out in fright.

He sighed. "If I walk in here as a man would, you scream. If I appear out of thin air, you still scream. Please, Luna, make up your mind so I can at least be consistent in scaring you out of your wits."

177

"Avery! What you doing out in the daylight? Get on out of here!"

"I need to talk to you."

"You can talk all you wants when the sun goes down. Now get!"

He made no move to leave.

"Avery, I ain't fooling! You look half dead. What am I gonna do if you drop dead on me in this here kitchen?"

He rolled his eyes. "Your... concern for me is touching," he said, his tone dripping with sarcasm. "But you forget that I am already dead. Besides, it is most unpleasant spending the day buried underground, especially now that I have your mother's presence with me daily whispering as tenderly as a lover, all the different ways in which she means to kill me."

"Mama?" Even at the mention of her name, I was instantly struck by the now familiar feeling of longing mingled with heart-clenching anxiety. "And you's only telling me this now?" I threw the broom I had just scooped up back onto the floor. "We gots to go and see her so..."

"It is too late for that," he said quietly, deep in thought. "Far too late. She would think that I was controlling you and making you say those things. Anyway, I did not come to talk about your mother. I came to talk to you about Jupiter."

"What about him?" I asked sharply.

He fixed me with a direct gaze, one I found hard to look away from. "Do you love him, Luna?" he asked with a pained expression. "I have promised I will never look into your mind again and I mean to keep that promise, so please be honest with me because I need to know if you love him."

"Why you asking me that?"

"Because it seemed as if you were beginning to fall in love with him. That is why I almost killed him that night. I hated him because you felt things for him that I knew you would never feel for me. I will always be grateful to you

178

for preventing me from doing so, for if I had slaughtered such a courageous man merely for loving you, it would have been a sin that would have haunted me all the days of my never-ending life. So tell me. Do you love him?"

I did and always would feel something for Jupiter. A powerful bond had been formed between us the day he gathered me in his arms and raced through the woods as my blood ran down his coal black skin. That bond had been cemented when I held him in my arms and prepared to meet death as his blood pooled in the dirt beneath us. But as powerful as my feelings for Jupiter were, it was merely a shadow of what I felt for Avery, and it would always be that way.

"I don't know," I said.

"Luna, I need to..."

"Love? Huh. That ain't nothing no slave can affords to own. We can't afford ourselves so how we afford to love each other?"

He gazed at me for a long moment, his expression one of searing impatience and I was forced to answer as truthfully as I could manage under the circumstances.

"Maybe. Maybe I coulda loved him if... if... things is different."

He was sad again, seemingly deep in thought for what seemed like the longest time before he spoke again.

"Luna, can you prepare a meal for both of us tonight?"

I gaped at him. "But you don't eat!"

He rolled his eyes and pursed his lips. "A simple yes or no would suffice."

"All right," I said. "If you wants me to spend my afternoon cooking for a man who don't eat, then I guess I has to."

He gave me another of his withering looks. "Fine. Do not waste the afternoon cooking on my account. But perhaps you could have some bread and water ready for me instead. Even the lowliest prisoners are given bread and water once a day, or is even that meagre a meal too much to ask for?"

"Bread and water sounds mighty fine to me," I said with a smile. "Now get on out of here!"

He glared at me with the sulky petulance of a spoilt child, an expression I found quite endearing, and then vanished.

I could hardly contain my excitement. He wanted me to cook for him. I quickly ran through a list of things I could prepare, deciding that variety would be the theme for Avery's second dinner in over fifty years. If only he had told me this yesterday. Counting down the hours to dusk, I decided I had enough time to go into town to get a few more things. Rushing out of the mansion, I started singing to myself as I saddled up Julia and rode into town.

But the further away I rode from the mansion, the more fearful I became and the singing soon petered away to a glum silence punctuated only by the sound of my fluttering heartbeat. As a precaution, I had taken one of the guns with me and hidden it in a satchel strapped to the saddle. But even if I did encounter trouble, I knew I could never use that gun as the consequences of a Negro shooting a white person would be so severe that not even Avery would be able to protect me. So it was a very nervous, timid Luna who entered the busy main goods store that day. And when the proprietor, a red-faced gentleman with a receding hairline, regarded me in that intimate knowing way I was used to seeing at the plantation, I was flooded by the same helplessness that had been at the core of my existence for many years. For a moment I couldn't speak.

"What do you want, girl?"

I lowered my gaze and cleared my throat. "Mr Jacobs. I's Luna. Massa Avery Wentworth's slave."

He straightened up immediately and I noticed that the gaze of all the women in the store immediately fell on me at the mention of Avery's name.

"Sir, I's needing one or two things and Massa says..."

"Yes, yes. Of course. What do you need?"

I told him what I needed and waited patiently to one side whilst he leisurely gathered the things I had reeled off and tossed them into a paper bag. In the meantime a short stocky man who had been watching me since I'd entered the store sauntered up to the counter.

"We were wondering what our young Englishman does up in that old house by himself. I see now he has something to keep his bed warm at night."

I felt the blood rush to my face but did not react or look up even though anger began stirring like a hungry snake.

"Now, now, George," the store owner said with a smirk as he returned with the last of my order. "You heard young Mr Wentworth in that girly accent of his the other day. He said if his slave comes into the store he wants us to – what was it he said? – Yeah, that's it. He said: 'I want you to extend her the same courtesy you would to me'. These English have some mighty strange ideas. Imagine treating a nigger wench the same way I'd treat a white man. But if he's as rich as he seems then I'll be more than happy to humour him and his strange ways. So long as he plans on bringing some of that money into my store."

"He hasn't been here long anyway, but he'll soon get used to the southern way of doing things," the other man added.

The store owner handed me my package and although I meant to whisper a thank-you before scurrying out of the store, a stillness came over me and, remembering the reverence I saw in Avery's eyes whenever I was in his presence, I spoke up without thinking.

"Yes, Massa Wentworth has some mighty big plans for that old house, and boy does he has money to spend. So long's he ain't got no reason to spend it elsewhere."

I pretended not to notice the stunned silence that fell across the store at my veiled threat and left quickly, keeping my gaze from meeting anyone else's.

It was only when I got to Julia that I realised I had been holding my breath since leaving the store and I wasn't able to fully relax until the town was far behind me.

***

Avery arrived as I was bringing the food into the drawing room. At first I didn't notice him standing by the fireplace, his gaze on the feast I had spent the afternoon preparing. I had made three different types of soups along with meat, fish, greens, cornbread, and two different fruit pies. And judging by his expression of amazed delight, he really had been expecting just bread and water.

"Luna, I... you didn't have to do all this," he said.

I shrugged casually and although I was hot and tired from rushing around all afternoon, I was elated by his appreciation.

But then it all changed and dejection settled over his countenance like a dark cloud.

"Avery, what the matter?"

He didn't speak for a few moments, merely stood staring at the table, taking deep breaths as if struggling to stop something from tearing him apart.

"Avery?"

I stopped what I was doing and moved toward him. After a few moments he finally met my anxious gaze.

"I... I... have to take you back," he blurted out.

I stared at him in horror, feeling as if I had been thrown to the bottom of a deep chasm.

"Wh...what?" I whispered.

The day I had been dreading for weeks was finally here. Avery was leaving me to pursue a life of his own and all I could see ahead of me now were days, months and years of nothing but the road to a long, torturous death.

"Do not look so, Luna. I am not taking you back to the plantation to be a slave again. I would never do that."

He moved forward as if to place his hands on my shoulders but I backed away, angry at what I saw as his rejection and betrayal. His reaction to my response was that of a man nearing the finish line of a particularly gruelling race who has been told that he has to go back and start the race all over again. But he composed himself and made no move to touch me.

"Please, sit down, Luna. Let me explain what has happened."

I was thankful for the hard chair beneath me when I sat down because I felt like a weak and fragile flower that had been uprooted from the nourishment and strength of the earth. Watching my reactions carefully, Avery slowly sat opposite me, the food completely forgotten.

"These past few nights, and sometimes during the day, I have worked at securing your freedom by placing suggestions, so to speak, in the mind of your old Master and those around him. I have led them to believe that the only way to secure the safety of everyone on the plantation is to sever your ties to it by freeing you. He has done that now and you are no longer a slave. Unfortunately, it is still not enough for your mother."

"Mama?"

Why oh why didn't I try to do something about her fears before?

"I have been so selfish, Luna. When I took you away I knew your mother would move Heaven and earth to get you returned to her and yet I kept you here anyway. And that selfishness has put her life, her very soul at risk."

"What you mean?"

"She knows where we are now and she is coming for you."

"How that make her be in danger? You... you ain't gonna do nothing to my mama is you?"

"No, Luna. I would never do that." He reached for my hand but I drew it away and after a few moments in which he seemed to flounder like a wounded bird, he placed his hands in his lap and sat back.

"Do you remember me telling you that your mother knows powerful magic and that there is always a price for using that magic?"

I nodded.

"Well the women in her family have always known how to counteract this, and protect themselves from some of the more malevolent spirits that are drawn to powerful witches. But she was stolen from her people before she could learn how to do this, and every time she draws on the power of these spirits they drain her of her life force in return for what they do for her."

Of course, I had seen the signs in the physical pain that had plagued her and the fact that she had seemed to be aging so fast.

"In her desperation to find you she has been tapping into much darker, powerful energy, and last week she did the unthinkable. She sought out the spirit that has haunted the chapel for centuries and it has a hold on her now. This thing, from what I have learned of it, is an ancient evil, pure evil, and it is feeding on her fears. It has shown her where we are now and they will set out to find us tomorrow morning. It will take them four days to reach us and by that time, there will be nothing left of your mother but evil. So I have to take you back."

I sat in silent turmoil as I mulled over what he had told me. Mama was the strongest person I knew and she was in danger, a thought that clawed at me with cold, spiteful fingers. I was also ashamed of my selfishness.

"This is the hardest thing that I have ever had to do," he continued. "When I found you, I can say that I had forgotten who I was during those years of despair. I was barely a man. But I remember who I am now and the more you come to accept me as a man, the harder it is to keep you here. The danger your mother is in is my fault. I should have never taken you away. I love you, Luna. I have from that moment, all those years ago, when I first saw that vision of you in the chapel. But I should have let you go with Jupiter and Father Geoffrey that night and found a way to let you stay with them as I have now done.

But I let myself believe you wanted to stay here with me and that you could grow to love me too, even if it was only the love of a friend. But I realise that I am no better than those slave holders if I continue to do as I have done. You are free now, Luna. Free to go back to Jupiter and pursue the life you want."

I didn't believe that he was being completely honest about his motivations for sending me away. If he wanted to, he could find a way to save Mama and us. But he was choosing to send me away instead, which meant he could see no possible future for us. And perhaps he now saw me for all that I was. A mere slave.

I was convinced of all those things but my soul still yearned to confess my feelings for him. I would be his if he wanted me, mind, body and soul. And I might have told him if Mama's life did not hang in the balance.

I could not let her die, especially to keep chasing after someone who was already lost to me by virtue of the colour of my skin.

"Luna, *say* something." He was looking at me earnestly, some of the desperation and anguish that had characterised him upon our first meeting already back in his eyes.

"What happen to Mama ain't your fault, it be mines," I said. "When... when you gonna take me back?"

He gazed down at the hand I had pulled away from him with so much yearning that I couldn't look at him.

"We will leave an hour before dawn, the same time they intend to set out. That means we will intersect them in the woods.

"Tomorrow morning?" I gasped, almost unable to choke back the tears that were fighting to surface. "You shoulda said this gonna to be my last night here!"

"I meant to. God knows I meant to take you back a few nights ago but I have been struggling with the thought of letting you go. This afternoon when you confessed that you do, or could love Jupiter, it made it much harder to

185

continue to keep you caged here. I love you. I love you more than I thought possible to love another and you have given me so much. But all I have done is take from you. I can no longer keep you here and let the years eat away at your chances of happiness whilst I continue to hope and dream."

He was silent for a few moments and just stared at me, appearing perplexed.

"I fear I am talking far too much, Luna, for you seem... bored?"

I narrowed my eyes at him. I felt completely bereft. All of this would soon be taken away from me: the love, respect, and quiet joy I had basked in this past month. Most of all, I would miss him constantly misreading my expressions.

"I *is* bored," I said and stood. I did not look to see his reaction to my heartless words. "And all this food be getting cold. I's gonna go upstairs for a minute, you go on and start without me."

I walked to the drawing room door and then faced him. "And, Avery." He looked up at me hopefully. "Don't you never tell me you loves me. 'Cause you don't!"

I gave him another "bored" look, which would have looked suspiciously like a glare to anyone else, before I stormed out of the room.

Once in the hallway, I clamped my hand over my mouth to try and stifle my moans. There was no stopping the tears now and I ran away from the drawing room as fast as I could. But even when I entered the room I had come to view as mine, I couldn't let go as I would have liked to in case Avery picked up the sound of my sobs.

So, crying silently, I took off my dress and pulled out the fancy ones Avery had left for me on my first day here. I chose the red one and also put on the ruby necklace that had captivated me so on that warm dusty morning. When I glanced at my reflection, I saw the beautiful woman so many others saw whenever they looked at me. I saw

186

sadness and dejection in her eyes and in the way her shoulders seemed to droop forward slightly. She carried an unnatural burden, the burden of a female slave not easily lifted.

When I re-entered the drawing room, Avery was sitting at the table staring forlornly at his hands. His face lit up when he saw me in the red gown and he got to his feet immediately, smiling sadly as I moved to the table. Then he surprised me by bowing.

"Luna. Why, you look as you should. You look like a queen," he said when he straightened.

I fought the tears that tried to return at his words and curtsied awkwardly, which seemed to delight him. He pulled out a chair for me and I sat down whilst he took a seat opposite.

The meal was a largely silent one. It seemed he had lost all interest in the food (as had I) but he still took a bite out of everything. Sometimes he said he could taste some of the ingredients. At other times I had to describe the taste and texture as I had done on that first night with him. But for the most part he would gaze at me with that bereft look in his eyes whilst I did my best not to look at him or let my turmoil show.

After our solemn meal, we stayed in the drawing room for a while and I read aloud to him. But even that was too hard for me, so at around 11.30 p.m., I stood up.

"I's gonna go on up to bed. Tomorrow's gonna be a long day."

He made as if to speak but then merely nodded, his face a study in sorrow.

"You... you ain't gonna go nowhere tonight, is you?" I asked anxiously.

"No, I will stay here until it is time to wake you."

I nodded, grateful for that small mercy.

"Luna."

I spun round hoping that he was going to tell me he had changed his mind and that we would find some other way to save Mama. I at least hoped he would ask me to stay with him during these last few hours we had together. But he said none of those things.

"You have nothing to fear when you return to the plantation. Everything has been taken care of. Even if your old Master were to try and go back on his word, he cannot for he signed a legal contract giving you your freedom. I would never let him anyway, and neither would your mother."

I merely stared at him for a few moments then left the room.

Once upstairs, I sat in the soft light cast by a single candle and wept softly. The longer I sat there thinking, the more distraught I became, until raw panic began to set in. It felt as if I was falling, falling, falling, with no end to this hideous plummet.

I couldn't let him leave me.

I got up and moved to the bedroom door.

When I entered the drawing room he was standing at the window with his back to me. His hands were resting on the window sill, his head bowed and his shoulders hunched. I'm sure he heard me enter but he didn't move as I came to stand directly behind him.

For a moment I felt uncertainty overwhelm me and considered turning around and leaving him in the shadowy silence of the drawing room. The step, the *leap* I was attempting to make was maybe one too far. If I did this, if I committed myself to him, I would be choosing to turn my back on God. And I didn't know if I could trust him, for I had seen so many Negroes put their trust, and at times their lives, into the hands of whites, only to be betrayed. Perhaps that is what the dreams had been trying to show me.

But as much as I wanted to turn around and go back upstairs, I couldn't envisage any kind of life without Avery. I would die if he left me.

Hesitating for only a fraction of a second, I closed the

space between us, lay my head against his back and wrapped my arms around him. He stiffened for a moment, then relaxed into me, his hands coming up to clasp mine tightly as I held him.

Please don't leave me. Please don't leave me, I said over and over again, hoping he had maybe forgotten his promise and was listening to my thoughts.

When he pulled away and faced me, I thought for a moment that he had heard that desperate plea. But the years of despair that had lived in him before he found me were laid bare for me to see and I felt myself die a little inside. Slowly, as if expecting me to resist him, he pulled me gently into his arms and held me close, resting his chin on the top of my head. Nestled in his arms with my head against his chest, I felt safe and secure.

"I promise, I will not let anything happen to you, Luna," he said. "I will die to protect you, so do not be afraid of what awaits you at the plantation."

I pulled away and looked up at him, struggling to find the courage to say what my soul demanded. The seconds passed and he stared at me, growing increasingly concerned as I stood struggling to even draw a breath.

"Luna?" he said softly, placing his hands on my shoulders. "What is it?"

Feeling as if the opportunity to change the course of my destiny was slipping away but desperate to at least show him how I felt, I reached up on tiptoe and kissed him. At first he was so surprised that he merely stood there. Then I felt his arms around me and he kissed me back with a fierceness that surprised me. That's when I realised the extent to which he had held back during his time with me, how well he had hidden his desire. It was all there in that kiss, decades of longing and a passion that had me trembling in anticipation under the gentle pressure of his cool soft lips. But all too soon he pulled away.

Staring at me intently, he softly traced his thumb across my lips whilst cupping the back of my neck with his other hand.

"What are you thinking?" he whispered. "Tell me what you are thinking, Luna."

There was a slight air of desperation in his voice and an intensity in his eyes that spoke of so much pain that I couldn't bear to see it.

"I's thinking of you, Avery. Only you," I said.

It seemed he wasn't satisfied with that answer and he made as if to speak, but I stopped him by placing my fingertips against his mouth.

"Take me upstairs," I whispered.

When he didn't respond I pulled his head down into another kiss, a long slow smouldering kiss that left me gasping when he pulled away. I clung to him as the room rushed in on us before pushing back and then it was swept away and we were left standing in the candlelit red velvet bedroom. He kissed me again as I pressed myself against him, tugging away his cravat and undoing the buttons of his shirt. He loosened the fastenings on my dress, slowly pulling it down over my hips and onto the floor. For a few moments he stood there gazing at my nakedness with some raw emotion I couldn't identify. Then he reached out and traced his fingers across my face as if I were some rare and precious jewel. Kissing me again, he pulled me down on the bed, his lips eventually leaving mine to travel down my neck, each kiss sending frissons of molten ecstasy as he caressed me.

Never before had I been touched like this. Never before had my body, which had always been a tool for others' enjoyment and gain, been used to give *me* so much pleasure. And it frightened me because I was completely caught in this dark web of desire as he explored every inch of me with his mouth, his touch like icy flames that threatened to devour me whole.

He stood up and removed his clothes. The sight of him naked before me left me completely breathless. The soft light of the candle danced across his muscular chest, which tapered to a narrow waist and strong powerful legs. I moved to him and he gathered me in his arms, kissing me with a fervour that left no doubt about the urgency of his desire as he picked me up and lowered me onto the bed.

But as his weight pinned me and he positioned himself to enter me, I recalled that ugly feeling when trapped beneath Master Henry and then Master John, like a moth slowly being smothered under a fingertip. I tensed, squeezing my eyes shut and my arms fell away from him to my sides. I balled my hands into fists as I lay there bracing myself for the inevitable assault.

He noticed the change immediately and grew still. I could feel him staring at me but I couldn't bring myself to open my eyes, and for one horrifying moment I was in that dream again, frightened that when I did look at him, I would find myself staring at Master John. When I eventually opened my eyes, Avery was looking at me with such a sad, sweet expression that I almost burst into tears.

This is Avery, I said to myself as he reached for the fist at my side and brought it to his mouth, bestowing a soft kiss against my knuckles. *This is Avery*, I told myself again as he gently uncurled my fingers, entwining them in his. I grasped them, and realised that he had been expecting something like this.

I felt the tension leave me as he kissed me gently on the nose. I sought his lips again, needing to find solace in those sweet kisses, letting him know that the moment of terror had passed and that I wanted him more than anything on this earth. When he slowly eased himself into me, I cried out, welcoming the pain, which bloomed for a few moments before being swiftly replaced with pleasure. Time seemed to stop as we gave ourselves to this primal dance only lovers know, and it felt as if we were caught at the heart of dark sensual waves. And just when I thought that the force of those waves would overwhelm me, a soft explosion below left me weak and quivering in its wake.

He came a few moments later, and when he made to

191

withdraw, I held onto him, unwilling to break the bond of flesh that joined us in that moment. I lay beneath him, my arms clasped tightly around him, soaking in the aftermath of our lovemaking and the soft sweet kisses he lavished on my face and neck.

To my delight, I felt him hardening within me a few minutes later but instead of continuing in the same position, he picked me up and flipped over onto his back so that I was sitting astride him, enabling me to control the rhythm and pace of our lovemaking whilst his hands travelled over me, frequently returning to knead my tender breasts. I had never even conceived that this much bliss was possible. Everything ceased to exist but Avery and the world of pleasure in which we were suspended. The resulting explosion was even more intense than the last and left me reeling in delicious spasms of ecstasy.

I lay in his arms, basking in what had been the culmination of a love and friendship that was sure to last an eternity and the last thing I heard as I slowly succumbed to sleep was Avery whispering "I love you" as he tenderly smoothed back my hair.

It was the perfect end to a perfect night.

***

When I woke up it was still dark outside and the candle had burned down to nothing, letting darkness steal in. Feeling slightly cold, I shifted to my left, expecting to fold myself into Avery's arms, but there was only an empty space beside me.

"I am here, Luna."

I peered into the gloom in the direction of his voice and saw him sitting in the chair by the window, nearly hidden by the shadows in the room. I began to smile, but then felt a stirring of alarm when I saw that he was dressed and had one hand beneath his chin as if he had been deep in thought. He stood up slowly and moved to the bed where he stood gazing at me for a few seconds. I was unable to read his expression in the dark.

"It is still early but I wanted to speak to you before we leave," he said as he sat down on the bed.

Before we leave? He was still planning on taking me back to the plantation?

I sat up, pulling the sheets around me as something within me shrivelled up and died. I didn't move when he cupped my face in both hands and kissed me on the forehead. Now that he was closer, I could make out his expression. He appeared shaken and upset. Feeling as if my world was disintegrating all around me, I couldn't understand why *he* appeared to be so distraught.

"Luna. I need to know why you let me make love to you," he whispered.

As much as I tried to still my emotions and not let my anger and dejection break through, I found that I couldn't stop the tears from welling up. He had been inside my head for a whole week and had seen that my body had never been mine to give. How could he not know what he meant to me after I'd willingly chosen to give myself to him? How could he not know?

"I don't know," I said angrily and took his hands from my face.

"Luna, I need you to tell me," he said, anxiety mounting in his voice. I scrambled away from him, dragging the sheets along with me.

He was already standing before me when I got to my feet and he grabbed my arms to keep me from walking past him.

"Luna, please. I need you to tell me what you were thinking about before you kissed me. I need you to tell me."

"I says I don't know!"

I tore myself out of his grasp and he let me go, watching helplessly as I made my way to the door, tripping over the sheet I had hastily wrapped around myself. When

I got to the door I spun round and fixed him with a long lingering stare, hoping he wouldn't be able to see the tears that had spilled over onto my cheeks.

"I don't know why, Avery. But it be like I wasn't in control of myself."

It was a few seconds before he grasped what I was trying to say.

"Luna!" he gasped, clearly appalled.

Not waiting to hear anymore, I stalked out of the room.

I waited for a few minutes and when I could be sure he was no longer in the bedroom, I let myself back in. After staring at the bed for a few moments, I dried my tears and got ready to leave both my only home, and the only man I had ever loved.

Chapter Eighteen

When we left the mansion under a mantle of darkness that morning, Avery and I were silent and miserable. He had gone back to keeping a careful distance between us, something which stung after what we had shared only a few hours before. I was determined to be strong, however, so I contained my feelings and avoided meeting his bewildered, dejected gaze. Realising how much I was going to miss Julia, I asked Avery if I could ride her for part of the journey into the woods. Never one to deny me anything, he readily agreed. As I saddled her up, something he insisted on doing until a dirty look forced him back, I hid the gun under her saddle for no other reason than I was used to doing it and it made me feel secure.

When it was time to dismount and leave Julia to find her way back to the mansion, I considered asking Avery if I could take her with me. He would, of course, have said yes, but I couldn't do that to him. Besides, Julia wouldn't have wanted to come with me. She knew where her place was and that was with Avery. So I said goodbye to her in the tomblike darkness of the woods and we went on with our journey.

Once more in his arms as he swept me along through the dark woodland, I remembered how terrified I had been the night he had torn me away from everything I had ever known. I had been so sure I would meet death at his hands before the end of that long confusing night. Now I couldn't imagine living without him.

All too soon we reached our destination, which was the large rock face he had taken me to that night. It towered above us like a surly giant under a peach and violet sky as the first few rays of light struggled to seek us out. Reluctantly, I moved out of the comfort of Avery's arms but when I felt his fingers tentatively reach for mine I grasped them gratefully and we walked hand in hand into the thinly populated trees.

"So, what you gonna do with yourself now that I's going?" I asked, glancing anxiously up at the sun, which was now high enough to bathe his face in a soft golden glow.

"I am uncertain. I was thinking of perhaps going back to my native England. I left siblings behind when I came to America and would like to find out what happened to them and their children, my nieces and nephews. I may also decide to travel and see what else the world has to offer me." He was silent for a few moments. "The world is open to me again but I am reluctant to leave America now."

He looked at me meaningfully before he continued.

"I have left a few things for you in the chapel where you used to hide your bible. I've left money, a copy of your freed papers, and a map that will lead you to a house quite some distance from here. I have left similar little boxes of money scattered in various locations, including the mansion, in case you should need to venture out this way again."

We had stopped walking by this time and as he stared at me, images of various places began to flit across my mind. One was of a farmhouse, the other was a tree with dead, twisted branches, and although I had never seen it before, I knew it wasn't that far from where we were now. I also saw a small spot behind Mama's quarters at the

Marshall plantation along with many other locations, most of which were unfamiliar to me.

"Do you see them?" he asked and I nodded. "You will remember how to get to those locations in more detail if you ever need to. I will always be near but I have taken these precautions in case you need to get away and I am not around to be of any assistance. But you do not have to worry, Luna. I will stay out of sight and never darken your future with my presence again."

"So I ain't never gonna see you again or know where you is?" I asked, dreading such a clean-cut amputation.

"Well, maybe your extra senses will detect my presence. But I will never intrude as I have done thus far."

"No, Avery. If you's gonna leave me then... then stay away for good."

I tried to take my hand out of his but he held on.

"Do not ask that of me, Luna. What I am doing is going to be hard enough. You *cannot* ask that of me," he said, his eyes alight with anger.

I said nothing, wouldn't even look at him.

"Luna, please. I do not want these last precious moments with you to be like this. Please. I will never intrude in your life again but allow me to be able to know that you are safe and happy. Please, Luna."

Hating that way he had of making me feel as if his whole world hung on the smallest thing I said or did, I nodded. "I's sorry. You know I don't mean what I just said."

The smile that touched his lips spoke of so much gratitude that it completely disarmed me and I was left bare and trembling whilst the sun rose even higher in the sky.

"I have some gifts for you, Luna."

Reaching into his pocket, he took out a gold chain with a cross on it and placed it in my hand.

"This was given to me by someone long ago. She gave it to me in the hopes that it would keep me safe. And I believe it has. I want you to have this now, Luna. The other gift is the farmhouse you saw in your mind a moment ago. I had it built for you, so no matter what happens, you will always have a home. The last thing concerns Jupiter, or I should say, Dembi. That is his real name. I saw it in his mind, but now that he is a slave he no longer feels worthy of it. You should know this if the two of you are... well..."

He trailed off and looked into the distance, his face a tapestry of untold misery. I stared at the gold chain for a few moments, my thoughts on the farmhouse I had seen, and for a moment I couldn't speak. Then I reached up and placed the gold chain around his neck, tucking it under his cravat.

"No, Avery. I's gonna be fine so long's I knows you out there somewhere even if I don't never sees you. Thank you, for everything you done for me." I let my hand rest on his chest. "You gots to go now, Avery. I don't want this moment ruined when you drops dead at my feet."

I tried to smile but it hurt too much.

He nodded, covering my hand on his chest with both of his, looking down at it as if all his hopes and dreams were contained in there. It seemed hard for him to do, but he slowly let it go.

"It will take them about three quarters of an hour to reach here," he said.

When he looked at me again it was as if the life was draining out of his eyes while the ancient longing that had lived in them slowly stole in to take its place.

"Goodbye, Luna."

I looked down and tried to mumble a goodbye but somehow the words wouldn't leave my lips. Then he quickly kissed me on the forehead and by the time I looked up and reached out to grasp his arms, to grasp anything of his to keep him with me, he was gone.

I would never see him again.

I stood there, feeling completely listless and bereft.

198

Although I couldn't feel that pulling sensation yet, I knew it would soon come. A breeze had picked up by this time, rustling the leaves above me and making the tall grass cower under its might, but I hardly felt it.

He was gone and I would never see him again. My life would now be lived in the harsh glare of the sun and without him it would kill me as surely as if I were the light-fearing demon.

I stood like that for a while, wallowing in my misery and weeping at the thought of what I had lost. And he didn't know. He didn't know how much I would suffer without him.

That was when I came to my senses.

What was I doing?

I was no longer a slave. I was free now and had been free ever since the night Avery had spirited me away with him into the woods. I was free and yet I was still thinking and acting like a slave. How could I not believe that Avery loved me? He had seen into my mind, had heard my stupid, vain thoughts and all the ugly little things most people would have held against me, and yet he had not judged. So how could I believe he would want anyone else?

What he felt for me was obvious, but having lived a life filled with insecurity, the voice of doubt still tried to tell me I was wrong. *He should have known I loved him*, it insisted. *I showed him only a few hours ago*. But no, he didn't know, I realised. He didn't know what it meant because as he had said so often, it had always been my mind that interested him. My mind, my thoughts, my words. But like the lowly slave I still thought myself, I had believed my body mattered more than those things. The chains keeping me in bondage may have been shattered, but the ones that had bound me mentally would take far longer to cast off, if it was indeed possible to completely break them. That is when I began to realise the enormity of my foolishness.

He thought he was doing the right thing by letting me go and by allowing him to do so, I had failed him terribly. He needed me as much as I needed him, no, even more so, and yet I had allowed him to walk away to live in solitude and desolation.

I looked around frantically and began to run back towards the rock face, the tears flowing freely down my cheeks as I thought about all I had given up because of my own stupidity.

"Avery, Avery," I sobbed as I came to a standstill in the wilderness.

The sun ducked behind a cloud and an ominous gloom settled around me. For the first time in a month, I felt fearful of my surroundings. Covering my face with my hands, I wept in the graveyard silence that had crept in unnoticed, knowing that I would suffer for the rest of my life. What made it even worse was that he would suffer too, and for that I knew I would never forgive myself.

Chapter Nineteen

"Luna!"

Was I imagining that voice? It was distant but sounded unmistakably like Avery. I looked up to see him running toward me, running much faster than a man but running nonetheless.

"Avery?"

My heart filled and then overflowed with elation at the sight of him. I had a chance to make everything right again.

I ran toward him, so caught up in the joy of the moment that I didn't stop to think about the unusual fact that he was *running*, although so fast he was almost a blur, instead of crossing the space between us in the blink of an eye.

He reached me a few seconds later and looked completely taken aback when I ran into his arms, still crying. He pulled me away from him so that he could look into my face, his own expression one of fearful concern.

"What happened, Luna?" he asked looking in the direction from which I had come. "Are they here? What happened?"

"It ain't them, Avery. I just... I just..."

I still couldn't say it. I still couldn't say those three little words that had the power to change everything, but I had to try.

"When... when you asked why I made love to you last

201

night, it... I's wanting you to know I don't want to leaves you."

He cupped my face in his hands.

"Oh, Luna. I promised that you had nothing to be afraid of when you go back..."

"Naw, Avery!" I cried, appalled at the conclusion he had drawn. "That ain't my meaning. When you asked about Jupiter, I lied. I do feels for him but... but it ain't nothing compared to what I feels for you, and I wants you to never leave me, ever."

It seemed as if he couldn't speak. He simply stared at me in quiet joy and wonder as I carried on talking.

"I wants you to know that I's gonna follow wherever you go and for as long as you'll has me. If you won't let me be with you, then promise you gonna let me see you from time to time over the years."

"Luna, Luna," he whispered, drawing me to him. He kissed me on the forehead and I sank into him, holding on as tight as I could. "You do not understand how much what you have said means to me."

"Then promise you gonna come back for me in one week. A week be all I need to convince Mama. You has to 'cause I can't live without you."

"Oh, Luna." He looked radiant with happiness but sadness marked his eyes. "My dear, Luna. It... It is too late. They are coming."

He glanced away into the trees again whilst I gazed up at him in confusion. And then I realised what he'd meant.

The sunlight. I had called him out into the sunlight when he was at his weakest and they were coming.

"Oh Lord! Avery, you has to get away before they sees you."

"It is too late. They are already here. Can you not feel them?"

I looked around me and noticed for the first time that the temperature had dropped. The wind sweeping through the trees was almost violent and seemed to whisper of malevolence. I realised that the gloom that had settled on our surroundings had nothing to do with the sun being hidden by a cloud. It was also far too silent and there appeared to be no sign of any living thing apart from us.

"Your mother has sent them for me. They've caught my scent now so I won't be able to escape."

I could hear something in the air around us now, a faint but clearly audible murmur, which sounded like something creeping beneath a decaying tomb.

What had I done?

"No," I moaned. "Why you stay when you knowed they be coming for you? Why, Avery?"

"I could not go until I knew that you were safe, Luna. Please, don't cry."

The murmuring was much louder now and I heard low unearthly sniggering that filled me with a black fear. I couldn't see its source, but I could sense that the air was thick with them and their malicious energy as they drew strength from our fear.

"No! I ain't gonna let this happen. I's gonna die before I lets anybody takes you away from me."

"You will do no such thing," he said sternly, but when he spoke again his tone was gentle.

"You have to understand, Luna. I have been in the grip of this bloodlust for over fifty years and I have done so many terrible, terrible things because of it. But if not for this demonic power I would not have lived long enough to find you or be in a position to take you out of bondage as I have now done. These past few weeks with you have been the happiest of my life. But this is my time to die. No, listen to me, Luna. It is my time to die and because of you I can die a man and not the beast I was when I found you. And the best thing is that I'll die knowing I was somehow worthy of your love."

The tumult surrounding us had grown stronger now. It was as if we were standing in the eye of a hurricane and I could hear more of that vicious-sounding laughter in the air.

"You have to get to a safe distance now, before they attack," he said looking anxiously around us.

"No, I ain't gonna let them kill you!"

"Those men will be here any second now. If they see us like this they will kill you and I will be too weak to stop them, so go!"

He tried to push me away but I wrapped my arms around his neck and kissed him. He yielded and returned my kiss fiercely for a few seconds but then pulled away and pushed me back as something almost knocked him off his feet.

Watching Avery stagger backwards, I felt my insides turn to water as a slithery cackle punctuated the air. Maybe it was only my imagination, but I thought I saw long silvery wisps swimming through the gloom, caught glimpses of claws, long terrifying teeth, and a shimmer of cold merciless eyes. Avery was knocked back again as they descended on him, but then he steadied himself and seemed to concentrate on the air around him. I heard cries of frustration and anger as he used his dwindling power to push them back.

I ran toward Avery, deciding that if he was to die right now, then I would die with him, but he anticipated this and I found myself being pushed back as he focused his energy on getting me out of harm's way.

"*Nooo! Avery, no....*" I screamed, and then found that I couldn't speak. I was flung to my knees at the foot of a tree, my arms yanked up to cover my head so that anyone looking upon the scene would think that I was cowering away from what was happening. I fought to move or to at least speak to him, but I soon realised that it was futile. Worse, I realised that since he was using his dwindling strength to keep me out of the way, he was leaving himself defenceless against the attack. When they descended upon him again, he was knocked off his feet and thrown back against a tree with a horrific cracking sound. The force of that collision would have killed a man, and for a moment I thought I had lost Avery, until I heard him utter a low moan. He ground his teeth together as he was pinned to the tree and pummelled by the spirits, who tore at his clothes and drew bright spots of blood on his face and neck.

"She was right, there they are!" I heard someone shout out and my horror deepened as three white men with guns rounded the rock face. One of them had a heavy silver chain hung over one shoulder. They were joined by Master John with Mr Walker, Jupiter and Mama the last to appear.

When I saw Mama I stopped trying to fight my way out from under Avery's control and for a moment completely forgot about the danger he was in. She was so thin now that her face was all sharp angles with hardly any flesh to soften the protruding bones, and her arms were like twigs hanging out of her shirt. When Avery had told me about the evil spirit she had conjured up, a part of me had wanted to believe he had been exaggerating about the danger she was in, but I could see that it was literally eating her alive. She looked even older now and her eyebrows were peppered with grey. She was also extremely weak. Mr Walker and Jupiter were all but carrying her. But the worst thing about her, the thing that chilled me to the bone and made me think we were too late to save her, was the blankness I saw in her eyes, as if she was no longer present within her own body. Her expression was one of intense hate when her gaze fell on Avery, who had stopped struggling and was staring at Mama with his mouth open.

"Put the chains around it, now!" she shrieked. "I cannot control them for much longer."

At first no one moved. The three men seemed afraid, not only of Avery, but of the very air around him, which was alive with hateful, malicious, invisible things. Then two of them moved forward, the third keeping his gun on Avery as the heavy silver chain was wrapped around him. Avery seemed to weaken further and cried out in pain. I felt the hold he had on me give slightly as he sank to the ground.

Then, the air around him grew quieter as the spirits Mama had summoned were banished back to wherever they had come from, their groans of frustration and disappointment seeming to linger long after they were gone.

It was only then that Mama seemed to come back to herself a little bit. The blankness in her eyes slowly diminished and she even managed to regain strength enough to stand on her own.

"Jupiter," she cried. "Now! Do not give it a chance to get away."

Jupiter released the hold he had on her and moved toward Avery. Panic surged through me at the sight of the axe in his hand.

"No." Master John grabbed hold of Jupiter's shirt roughly as he passed him. "I'll do it!"

He took the axe out of Jupiter's hands and moved cautiously forward whilst Avery gazed at him with quiet hatred. Avery had blood on his chin and he bared his teeth, exposing his fangs. He hissed almost seductively, making fear leap into Master John's eyes.

Avery! I pleaded. *Let me go. Let me go!*

I struggled even harder against him as Master John loomed over Avery with the axe.

"Kill it!" Mama Akosua screamed. "Cut off its head! Kill it now!"

I realised then that it was no use trying to break free with my physical strength. I had to use my mind if I had any hope of escape. So I concentrated as Master John raised the axe above his head with both hands.

I think the panic and fear must have given my mind the sharp focus it needed because I felt the hold he had on me loosen and then fall away completely. I was on my feet and running in seconds, my gaze on the axe in Master John's hand as I ran to put myself between it and Avery.

"*Luna!*" Mama screamed, the word nearly lost in a

tangle of inarticulate pain and fear too deep to completely fathom as Master John brought the axe down with brute strength before he had time to register that I was directly in its path.

I stood paralysed with fear and everything seemed to slow down as I watched horror bloom in Master John's eyes at the realisation that he wouldn't be able to stay his hand in time to prevent the mortal blow.

The axe came down within inches of my shoulder but before it could connect and sever my flesh and bone, the killing instrument came to an abrupt stop as if it had connected with solid matter. Master John winced in pain as if his arm had connected with stone.

Avery, I thought as I reached up and pushed the axe away from me.

"Stop!" I cried. "You can't kill him."

Master John stared at me, wide-eyed and shaking slightly at the realisation of how close he had come to killing me. Then rage twisted his face.

"You dumb nigger! Get out of the way."

He struck me then, catching the side of my head with the back of his hand and I hit the ground hard. Avery lurched forward and up onto one knee with a snarl as Master John leapt back with a scream. I didn't give myself time to register the pain radiating along the side of my head as I scrambled to my feet.

Avery was weakening, and fast. I could see it in the way he fell back onto both knees and barely struggled against his chains.

"Jupiter, finish it off!" Mama Akosua commanded. "Now, before it is too late!"

"No," I cried and moved once more to stand in front of Avery.

"Luna, what are you...?" Avery began but I spun on him before he could finish.

"Hush, you... you devil!"

I didn't let my gaze linger on the look of utter

confusion on his face or focus too long on the fact that his mouth quivered with uncertainty at my words. I had to act fast if there was to be any chance of getting him out of here alive.

"Luna, stand aside," Mama said. "The demon has bewitched you. Stand aside so we can break the hold it has on you."

"No, Mama. You kill it now and it gonna come back."

I don't know what made me say that, but judging from the expression on Mama's face, it was true and I could only conclude that I had somehow plucked the knowledge from her thoughts because Avery looked as surprised as everyone else.

"You know that be true, don't you, Mama?"

"Yes," she said gazing thoughtfully at me. "They *can* come back to life but if we cut off its head, burn and scatter the remains, it should..."

"No," I said suppressing a shudder at the thought of Avery beheaded. "That ain't gonna work. We has to kill it when the sun goes down, so's the evil can go back to where it come from."

"You cannot know that. You..."

"I do, Mama," I insisted. "I spent weeks learning its secrets and letting it think it can trust me. I knowed you was coming for me, Mama. So I tricked it so it be here in the day for you to catch. But you can't kill it now. You has to take it back to the chapel. That where it be made so we has to kill it there at night."

"This is nonsense," Master John said as Mama watched me carefully, suspicion in her shrewd dark eyes. "Your mother told us it will regain its strength at night."

"Not... not with them chains on it. But you go on and kill him, Massa," I said and took a small step to the side even though everything within me screamed in protest at leaving Avery exposed to him. "But who you think he be looking to kill first when he come back?"

Master John gulped and sweat broke out on his brow at

the thought of being in Avery's grasp once more. After a few moments of silence, he gestured to the two men standing at either side of Avery and I breathed a sigh of relief.

"Pick it up. We can strap it to one of the horses and take it back to the plantation that way."

"But..."

"Do it!" he snapped.

I did what I was dreading then and faced Avery who was looking at me in bewilderment. All hope deserted him when he looked into my eyes and although it broke my heart to see this, I forced myself to meet his gaze with contempt.

"You'd better be sure about this," Master John said to me.

"I is," I said, my gaze never leaving Avery's. "He gonna suffer more this way and I never has to worry about him coming back." *Don't listen to my words, Avery, listen to my thoughts. I love you. Please, listen to my thoughts and know I'll find a way to get you out of this.*

But it seemed as if he was keeping his promise to never read my mind again because his face crumpled and he seemed to wilt as the two men picked him up and dragged him away.

I stayed where I was for a few moments, the raw pain that was binding itself to me like a living thing with a will of its own.

I planned to do everything in my power to try and save Avery but I was alone and faced with seemingly insurmountable odds. How *was* I going to get him out of this alive?

The only thing I knew for certain was that I would die trying.

Chapter Twenty

The ride back to the plantation was the worst two hours of my life. As the woodland around us grew denser, slowly creeping closer until it bullied us into riding single file, my sense of hopelessness grew stronger. This wasn't helped by the fact that Avery was now slumped unconscious over his horse, which was being led by one of the men with guns. The other two followed close behind on one mount, their guns in their laps and their nervous gazes trained on Avery's inert form.

Master John rode in front, his chest puffed out, making him look like a peacock in his green jacket and I was forced to endure the sound of his nauseating voice as he joked and bragged his way throughout the entire journey. I could only imagine the hideously exaggerated reports of Avery's capture that would make the rounds once he got back to the plantation.

And of course there was Mama, who rode with Mr Walker. If she wasn't watching me carefully then she was watching Avery. And that's probably the only thing that gave me hope that he was still alive.

She had made it perfectly clear as we walked through the woods back to the horses that she knew I was lying. And I suppose it hadn't been that hard to deduce because I hadn't been able to keep my gaze off Avery who no longer had the strength to resist as he was dragged away.

"What is that I keep hearing, my child?" she had asked softly.

I managed to tear my gaze away from Avery, whose eyes had begun to glaze over.

"What, Mama?"

"A word, I keep hearing it over and over again. *Avery*. Why do I keep hearing that, Luna?"

I felt my throat tighten but was able to force a smile. "I don't know, Mama. You the one who be knowing everything."

I quickly turned in case she saw more than I wanted her to see in my eyes.

"Yes, my dear. I know *everything*. My poor Luna. You look so sad. It must have been terrible to spend all those weeks in that house and have that beast force itself on you, again and again."

I rounded on her, my anger flaring.

"He ain't never laid a finger on me," I said sharply.

"He?"

I bit my lip. I had fallen into her little trap so easily. Then I leaned close and whispered softly in her ear.

"You has what you want now, Mama. So make it go away."

"What do you mean?"

She kept her voice low but I heard stirrings of uncertainty in her tone and her gaze slid guiltily away from mine.

"You know what I be talking about. I can feel it eating away at you still, so make it go away before it takes *you* away from *me*."

She stopped dead in her tracks and for a few seconds she looked like a child who had been caught harbouring a deep, dark secret.

I left her standing there in the morning sunlight and made sure I didn't look at Avery as I walked away.

And now it was as if she had completely shut herself off from me. Her gaze when it met mine was cold. I knew that shrewd mind of hers was working furiously behind her impassive expression. When I was a child, I thought that the bond we shared was unbreakable but when she was sold, it had broken as easily as an egg shell. I didn't know her at all now and I felt a profound loss because the three-year-old me would have known exactly what that look in her eye and the set of her shoulders meant. And Mama would have known to trust me, to trust my judgment in wanting to save a seemingly evil being.

I realised that I had never really recovered after she'd been taken away from me, and that strengthened my resolve. Regardless of what it cost, I would not lose Avery, ever.

But I couldn't ignore the fact that the odds were firmly stacked against me, especially when we left the woods and were thrust into the full glare of the sun. I grew to hate the sun that day as it beat down hatefully on my beleaguered Avery. A silent, golden king, it was the most cruel and pitiless nemesis.

The only thing that made the journey back to the plantation bearable was the feel of Jupiter's strong arms around me and the sound of his deep voice as he related all the changes that had taken place in my absence. It helped keep my mind from tumbling into the depths of despair as I tried to think about what to do. But the longer I thought about it, the less likely it seemed that I would be able to save Avery. I even wondered if maybe it would have been kinder to let them kill him. At least that way he would have died knowing I loved him instead of believing the vile lies I had told, which now seemed only to have delayed the inevitable.

At last we got to the plantation and went straight to the clearing where the chapel sat waiting in the mid morning sunlight. It appeared older, darker and more sinister; the evil presence that had plagued it for so long stronger than ever before. It was like walking into a wave of cold malice. Avery was dragged off the horse and dumped on the ground and when I saw his face, a sharp, clean fear came barrelling into me and my chest tightened.

He looked like a corpse. His skin was grey, his lips had turned blue, and his eyes had sunken into their sockets.

"He...he dead?" I couldn't conceal the tremor in my voice.

"No," Mama said coolly behind me.

It seemed as if I could breathe again, especially when I saw Avery's eyes flutter in response to my voice.

"Good," I said. But I was running out of time. "We has to get him in the chapel."

"But that's out of the sun."

This came from the biggest man, the one who had been the most nervous during the journey. He was staring at me in an accusatory manner and I noticed that his grip had tightened on his gun.

"Get him into the chapel, damn it!" Master John said.

The man glared at him for a few moments before reluctantly gesturing for the other two, and they began to drag Avery to the chapel. Master John followed, barking orders and generally making a nuisance of himself, as always.

"I am going back to the plantation to get some rest so I will be strong enough to keep the demon bound when night falls," Mama said.

I nodded slowly. Mama leaving had widened that narrow chance I had of getting Avery away from the plantation. But only by the smallest of margins.

"I has to let Mary know I's all right then I's gonna come and find you so's we can go home," I said to Jupiter, all the while thinking about how to get a hold on one of the horses.

"No, I need Jupiter to come with me," Mama said, eyeing him surreptitiously. He frowned and glanced from Mama to me. "I will need him to help me prepare."

"You should tell them mens to stay in the trees, as far away from the demon as they can get," I said. "In case he... it tries to control them. I's come to you later, Mama, if Massa Geoffrey be letting me, so's I can help you get ready."

She nodded and said no more.

I walked away, the weight of their suspicious gazes like a bull's eye on my back, and with every step I took from the chapel and Avery, it felt as if my heart was being torn to pieces.

I had almost reached the trees when I heard Avery cry out.

"*Luna! Luna*!"

A tremor surged through me and I stopped dead in my tracks. The urge to respond to that tortured cry was overwhelming, but Mama was still watching. So I walked on, even faster than before, and practically ran into the woods.

When I was far enough away from the chapel and any prying eyes, I stumbled to a stop and leant against a tree with my hand pressed to my chest. It took a few minutes but my breathing eventually slowed and the pain threatening to render me apart began to diminish.

Feeling in control again, I was about to move away when I saw Zila standing about five metres away, her eyes lit with cold, calculating fire as she watched me. Cursing myself for being careless enough to let anyone see me in that state, I glared at her before I walked away, knowing she had become yet another obstacle I would have to contend with before night fell.

When I left the woods, I glanced anxiously up at the sun, which seemed to have climbed even higher in the sky, before I ran down the hill toward the main house. A sense of urgency overtook me as I ran under the ever dominant glare of the sun. I sensed that death was on its way and, like the sun, it would be almost impossible to escape. I ran past the cotton fields, barely glancing at my fellow Negroes, and on toward the main house in search of Mary. I needed her to deliver a message. I also needed to say goodbye because I knew death was coming and when it did, I didn't want to leave this world without saying goodbye to the woman who had been like a mother to me.

I felt a prickle of apprehension when I reached the mansion, remembering all too well that only a month ago my whole life had amounted to little more than tending to this house and the every whim of its occupants. I shuddered in spite of the boiling heat.

I was almost at the kitchen door when I saw three of the other slaves. They stared at me with identical expressions of wary astonishment before they smiled brightly, although not brightly enough to dim the suspicion in their eyes. They stopped what they were doing and made their way over to me.

"Luna, you's alive. Praise Jesus," Natty, a short, earthy woman said as she beamed at me.

"It sure is good to see you, Luna. We's all praying for you," Sirus said. He was a tall, gaunt field hand.

"You is?" I said coolly. "It sure didn't look like that from where I's standing that night."

Their smiles slowly faded. It was probably the imperious disdain emanating from my gaze more than my words that had them peering at me fearfully.

"It...It wasn't like that, Luna."

"Get out my way," I snorted contemptuously before I barged past them, for I had seen Mary come rushing out of the kitchen.

She looked thinner and there were deep circles under her eyes. When she saw me she came to an abrupt stop and stared at me for a few seconds. Then, dropping the basket of vegetables she was holding she ran up to me with tears streaming down her face.

"Luna!" Her embrace nearly knocked me off my feet. "Luna! Oh Lord, Luna. It's true, you's alive."

She pulled away and held my face in her hands. "You all right, girl? What happened?"

I could see the other three eagerly straining to hear, so I

215

dropped my voice and pulled her with me away from them.

"I's fine, Mary. Really," I said glancing uneasily at the sun, which was like an hourglass slowly emptying me of hope.

"Oh, Luna. I thought you's dead. I's sure of it. But what happened? Why did it take you away?"

I found I couldn't answer. It was too difficult to talk about Avery and have to pretend to hate him when my heart was aching and I feared for his life. So I only shook my head.

"Look, Mary. I has to go. I only come to find you 'cause I wants you to know that... I... I missed you."

She stared at me in astonishment as if a dream she had given up on had finally come true. I realised in that moment that although she hadn't allowed me to keep her at arm's length as I had done with everyone else on the plantation, she had begun to believe that I didn't really care for her at all.

Then her face crumpled up and she began to cry again.

"Oh Lord, Luna. What happened to you? What it do to you?"

"You hush now, Mary," I said smiling sadly. "I's all right. It didn't do nothing to me. I just needs you to know, that's all. I has to go now. But can you find Massa John and tell him to come to my cabin?"

Now she looked bewildered. "He ain't here. He gone to see some lawyer man." Her voice fell to a whisper. "But why you wants him to come to your cabin? When has you ever wanted him in your cabin?"

"I needs to ask him something."

She placed her hands on her hips and fixed me with a no nonsense stare, and as always when faced with that look, I gave in.

"You know I's free now but he be trying to find a way to keep me here so I needs to speak to him."

Now she was glaring at me. "Girl, I think you done lost

216

your mind. You think you can talk him into giving you up by letting him have some of what he about to lose?"

"Mary, please. Just do it!"

"All right. But don't you be shocked none when you end up back here with the rest of us."

She went to move away but I grabbed her and hugged her again before I let her go. With tears filling her eyes again, she gave me a long questioning look before she left.

Ignoring the small group of Negroes that had gathered, I walked away. Once they were out of sight, I started to run, racing against the grains of sand that were slowly slipping through the hour glass.

I ran into the woods, where I slowed to a fast walk in order to catch my breath.

I had asked Mary to get Master John to come to my cabin because he had the keys to the gun cupboard. He had also been wearing one this morning. My plan was to get him alone and find a way to get the gun or keys off him, then get one of the horses from the stables. It was a feeble plan at best, complicated all the more by the fact that Master John wasn't here and I didn't know when he would be coming back. And time wasn't on my side.

Feeling as if there was a noose around my neck, tightening with every second that passed without my having done anything to get to Avery, I walked on, desperately racking my brain for a more feasible plan.

Then, with a gasp, I came to a stop in the woods.

Chapter Twenty One

Julia was standing in the dappled shadows cast by the trees. She snorted in an almost bored fashion and came ambling forward. I stood rooted to the spot in surprise, hope brightening my failed spirits like a full moon on a dark night.

"You sure is a clever, clever horse!" I exclaimed when it sank in that she wasn't an illusion.

I kissed and patted her on the neck. Then, in a rush of excitement I remembered the satchel I had hidden under her saddle. It was still there, along with the loaded gun.

Tears sprang to my eyes and I had to take a moment to steady myself.

Julia being here was like a miracle and in that moment I felt something I had never felt before in my life: self-belief. It was a beautiful feeling and it seemed as if all the events in my life had been leading up to this one perfect moment in which I would dare to brave the impossible and in doing so achieve something extraordinary.

I was going to save Avery. There was no doubt in my mind now about whether or not I could do it.

Exulted but still aware of the sun straining to reach me through the leaves above, I lead Julia through the woods toward one of the lesser known tracks to the clearing. Perhaps this newfound belief in myself had made me over-confident because I was so busy searching the trees to my left, where the men were likely to be keeping guard, that I didn't see Zila kneeling with her back to me, directly in my path until it was too late.

I stopped, feeling like a small animal that had been caught in a trap. Barely breathing, I started to back away with Julia when Zila turned around.

To my surprise, she wore a tense, anxious expression as if she too had been caught in a trap, but then it melted away and she breathed a sigh of relief. "It's just you."

She got to her feet and disappeared behind a large bush where she started thrashing around with something large and heavy, occasionally cursing in frustration. I was more curious than fearful of her presence at this stage but I reached for the gun anyway and held it against my side, hidden by my skirt. I didn't want to have to hurt anyone, but if she forced me to, I wouldn't hesitate to shoot her.

After a moment she poked her head out from behind the bush, her hair littered with leaves and twigs.

"Well, ain't you gonna help?" she asked curtly.

When she received no answer, she rolled her eyes and, with great effort, managed to pull a wheelbarrow partway out from behind the bush. The rest of it was obviously stuck.

"What you doing with that?" I asked.

"What you think I's doing with it? How else you reckon I's gonna get your demon out that chapel?" She let it go with a huff and wiped the sweat from her brow.

"How dumb do you think I is? You's hell bent on seeing me dead just a month ago and now you wants to help me?"

My voice was soft but there was no denying the menace in my tone. She chose to ignore it, however, and put her hands on her hips, her chin tilted up in defiance.

"Yes, and I's feeling bad about that all month, so quit going on about it. I has my reasons for helping so put that gun away. You know you ain't gonna use it."

"You sure about that now, Zila?"

She looked slightly taken aback at that and appraised me as if she were really seeing me for the first time. When she spoke again, her tone was slightly less belligerent than before.

"I says I's here to help."

I looked thoughtfully at her. My sixth sense was telling me I could trust Zila. In fact it was allowing me to see her as she really was, another lost soul grasping at love and the small moments of happiness that it could offer. Unfortunately for her, her heart would always be with Master John, and although I would never be able to fathom how she could love a man like him, I understood her for the first time that day too. Even so, could I really afford to trust her when there was so much at stake?

"I don't be needing your help, Zila."

"Oh, is that right?" She pulled a bolt cutter out of the wheelbarrow. "So how you reckon you gonna get them chains off it? You think you gonna bat your eyelashes and them chains just fall right off, huh?"

She dropped the bolt cutter back into the wheelbarrow.

She had a point. I hadn't really thought any of this through, but she obviously had. "All right. You can help. But I swear, you better not do nothing to–"

"Just stop your cussing and help me with this!"

"Why is you really helping me, Zila?" I asked as I joined her in tugging at the wheelbarrow.

"Let's just say that life be a whole lot better when you ain't here. So if I has to save that thing to get shot of you, then that's what I's gonna do."

We managed to free the wheelbarrow, and, after taking a few moments to catch her breath, Zila absentmindedly patted Julia, who had been nudging her playfully.

"There's something mighty unusual about this horse. Where you get it?" she asked as she took hold of Julia's reins.

"It his horse," I mumbled.

Zila grew still and she eyed Julia apprehensively before

220

taking a few steps away from her. "*His* horse? It drink blood too?"

"No! It be just a horse, Zila."

She didn't look as if she completely believed me but she took hold of Julia's reins again. "All right. We's going that way. I told Johnson to tell them mens guarding the demon that Master John be wanting them back up at the main house. So they be gone by the time we gets to the chapel. Now get the wheelbarrow."

Typical of her to leave me with the cumbersome wheelbarrow, I thought, but didn't complain as I followed her through the woods.

"Tell me something. How come you loves him?" I asked.

She quickly spun around and glared at me. "You a witch just like your mama if you know that."

"You know what kind of a man he be and what he can do," I continued. "So how come you loves him?"

"How come you loves that... that, whatever it is?"

"I loves him cause he be worthy. Can you say the same about Massa?"

"Just hurry up with that wheelbarrow," she flung back at me.

"You know he gonna kill you if he finds out what you done."

"He ain't!" she retorted, but she didn't sound so sure. After a few seconds of silence she spoke again. "Another reason I's helping is so's you'll make your demon leave him alone. Tell it not to kill him and make it stop hounding him with them dreams." She rounded on me when I didn't answer. "And don't tell me he ain't the one doing that cause who else can it be?"

"I can try," I replied.

We stopped close to the chapel and Zila went ahead to make sure that there was no one there. I hid with Julia and the wheelbarrow as far away from the trail as I could. It was midday now and I kept glancing up at the sun through

221

the leaves, feeling the noose tighten as I waited for Zila to return. I was beginning to think that something had gone wrong or that maybe she had deceived me, when I saw her hurrying back through the trees.

Looking around anxiously, she took Julia by the reins again.

"Come on, let's go. Hurry up and quit making so much damn noise with that thing. You want the whole plantation to know we's down here?"

I directed an icy stare at her back and chose not to point out that with the amount of noise she was making shouting at me, I wouldn't be surprised if she could be heard all the way over at the Marshall plantation.

At last we got to the clearing and although the aura of evil was even stronger now and stirring restlessly like a caged tiger, I barely noticed it in my haste to get to Avery. Zila led Julia around the back toward the stream whilst I entered the chapel with the wheelbarrow.

Suddenly infused with the strength and speed that Zila had obviously thought necessary in the woods, I raced down the aisle with the wheelbarrow.

He was lying on his back on the floor by the altar, the heavy silver chains still wrapped around his chest.

"Avery?"

He looked thinner somehow, as if he was shrinking inside his clothes and there was no colour to him at all or any sign that he was still alive.

Nearly choking on my fear, I grabbed the bolt cutter and started to try and cut the lock on the chain but my hands were shaking and I could barely hold onto it. Zila came in through the back door and grabbed the bolt cutter out of my hands.

"God, Luna! Don't you know how to do nothing?" she snapped as she pushed me aside.

I stood and took a step back, feeling as if all the air was being sucked out of me as she cut the padlock and pulled away the silver chains. I hoped he would wake up or at

222

least give some sign that he was still alive, but he only lay there looking like a week-old corpse.

I put my hand to my mouth and couldn't help the sob that escaped me. It was like I was caught in that never-ending fall again, plummeting lower and lower into despair, and there was nothing I could do to end this torment.

"We's too late, he dead."

"You stop that now!" Zila exclaimed. Her tone was sharp but when she looked up at me, her eyes were calm and sympathetic. "We ain't gonna know that till it gets dark. Now get the blanket. We needs to get him covered."

Her words cut through my panic and, wiping away my tears, I got the blanket out of the wheelbarrow along with the ropes she had brought along.

"My, he sure is handsome." She was gazing at him in awe and gently brushing the hair out of his face. "The devils is always the handsome ones."

I ignored the sharp pang of jealousy that touched my heart at the sight of another woman touching him so tenderly, and with her help, set to wrapping a cold, lifeless Avery up in the blanket.

I wept silently as we covered him, expecting a sharp retort from Zila at my tears, but she was strangely silent. I could sense absolutely nothing from Avery, not even a hint of the tantalising melody that had grasped my heart, and I lost all hope, for I was sure he was dead.

When it came for me to cover his face, I hesitated, feeling as if I were closing the lid on a casket. After a long agonising moment, I kissed him on the lips, noting how cold and hard they were now, and then covered his face securely with the blanket.

"I's gonna take his legs, you take his arms," Zila said, placing herself at his feet.

"You're not taking it anywhere!"

We both jumped up at the sound of that familiar voice. Mama.

She was blocking the chapel door with Jupiter. We had been so busy tending to Avery that we hadn't heard them enter. The battle I had feared ever since Avery told me that Mama was looking for us had finally arrived.

I wiped away my tears as she walked up the aisle toward us. Zila slunk away from Avery and tried to edge slowly to the back door.

"You!" Mama pointed to her. "Stay where you are. I am not finished with you."

"Stay out of this, Mama!" I said.

"I knew it!" She was furious.

Her face twisted itself into an ugly mask of raw rage. But I could sense that this was much more than just anger and I didn't like it.

It was the evil that resided here. Its presence in the chapel was like a noxious vapour invading my senses and intensifying the powerlessness I felt at seeing Avery in such a lifeless state.

"Did you think you could deceive me?" she continued, caught in the grip of its soulless hatred. "You! A puppet dangling from the strings it pulled. Stand aside, now!"

"You gonna have to kill me first before I lets you touch him!"

"Do you dare to challenge me? Foolish girl! I will slit your throat and wash the ground with your blood before I let you take that demon away!"

"Mama Akosua, please, stop this," Jupiter cried, as he came between us.

He had been wearing an expression of resigned dismay when he'd entered the chapel and saw us trying to rescue Avery, but now he was clearly frightened. He tried to pull Mama away by her arm but I closed the space between us so my face was only inches from hers, my own anger flaring like lightning ripping through the sky.

"I done told you to make it go away!" I hissed, taking hold of her chin. "Look at me, Mama. I know it ain't you talking, so make it go away."

At first her eyes were dark, blank holes, the rage slithering within their depths. But like a mist slowly lifting, I saw her true self begin to return and I released her chin.

"What... what... did I say?" She blinked uncertainly and looked to Jupiter, who exhaled in relief but was still tense, anxiety in his deep brown eyes.

"You says you'd kill me, Mama. But it be that spirit talking."

She gasped, disbelief tightening her face, but then comprehension and shame descended upon her.

"It is stronger here," she said and took a step back. She looked as if she wanted to run as far away from the chapel as she could. But then her gaze fell on Avery's body and she hardened again. "But I mean what I say. I will not let that demon have you."

"It ain't your choice to make, Mama."

"What lies has that thing been filling your mind with? It may have the face of an angel and it may pretend to be something else with those clothes. But it is evil. Evil, Luna. I will not let you give yourself over to evil, so step aside and let me finish this."

"He ain't evil, Mama, so don't be calling him that!"

"It kills to keep a life that no longer belongs to it. It *is* evil and I will not let it live!"

I was about to say more but found that I couldn't speak. I was standing here fighting a losing battle with Mama whilst Avery lay dying a few feet away, assuming that he was even still alive. The self-belief I had carried through the woods up to this point swiftly deserted me and I was left feeling helpless. It had been stupid of me to believe myself capable of doing something this daring. But I couldn't give up, even though I knew I could never win in a battle against Mama. She was too strong.

Then I thought about Avery and how easy it had been for him to get me to do anything he'd wanted, with just a single word or a look. He hadn't ever tried to meet my anger with fire. His way had always been one of love and tenderness, and I decided that might be the only chance I had of winning this battle.

"Please, Mama, listen. Just listen. He a slave too. He a man once and he had that took away from him just like us. And even then we remembers who we is cause we has each other. But he all by hisself and he forget who he be, but he knows now. He knows now cause I helped him remember, Mama. So please, you can't kill him."

"You do not know what you are talking about. It has filled your head with lies. Lies! I will not let you give your life to it!"

"So you gonna let them demons on this plantation has me instead? Cause you know Massa John ain't never gonna let me go."

She couldn't answer or even look at me.

"I's alone with what you calls a demon for a month, Mama. And I's safe. I's safe with him, Mama, safe. How many of these white mens could you leave me with and know that I's safe?"

She was floundering, weakening.

"But... but... If I let it have you, you will be lost to me forever. I cannot let that happen."

"Oh, Mama. I *was* lost to you. I done died on the inside when they took you from me. But I remembers now. I remember them years and everything you taught me. He helped me remember and I ain't never be lost to you again. But you has to let me do this cause I ain't gonna let him die. He need me, Mama. You has to let me help him."

I wept as I spoke and at first I thought I had failed and would never get through to Mama. But something within her seemed to stir at my last few words and she stared at me intently, as though some missing link in a long chain had finally been restored.

She was calm, almost serene when she spoke again. "You do not have to do anything to earn my devotion." I knew she was referring to my thoughts that night when I'd

226

ridden away from the plantation with Jupiter and Father Geoffrey, thinking I would never see her again. "It is your birthright, the only thing I can give to you and it will be yours always. In life and in death."

I felt like that little girl again, the one who had sensed her mother returning home and had run down the hill to wait by the trees until the love of her life appeared to bless her day with a smile. Leaning closer, I pressed my forehead against hers as we used to do when I was a child.

"In life and death," I repeated.

"Jupiter. Help them take him outside," Mama said when I pulled away.

At first he didn't move. Then, lowering his head, he walked over to Avery.

"It... *He* is not dead yet," Mama continued. "But you must hurry because Massa John will soon be here."

Chapter Twenty Two

Outside, the scorching noonday sun beat down on us as Jupiter, with our help, placed Avery on his stomach with his arms and legs dangling over the sides of the horse. He then tied him to it as securely as he could and fastened to the saddle the spade that Zila had brought.

When I made to mount the horse, he stopped me. "No, Sister Luna. I will take him away from here."

When I faced him he immediately lowered his gaze and on impulse, I reached up and kissed him softly on the lips. He looked up with a start, bewilderment in his deep, dark eyes, and a vulnerability you wouldn't expect to see at the core of such a strong, courageous man.

"Thank you, Dembi. But *I* has to do this."

He looked completely bewildered at the mention of his real name, as if he were a beggar who had been told he was actually a prince. He didn't speak as I got on the horse but looked as if he wanted to take my hand and tell me to stay.

Still apprehensive of Mama, Zila had been lurking in the background trying to draw as little attention to herself as possible. But she spoke up now, although timidly.

"Do this mean you ain't gonna put a curse on me or nothing?" She smiled nervously.

Mama merely regarded her coolly without uttering a word and Zila's smile disappeared as fast as a cold drink on a hot summer's day.

"Don't you worry none, Zila. Mama's forgiven you," I said.

Mama merely grunted. "I do not need to put a curse on this foolish girl. That Massa John is a curse of its own."

Zila blanched but didn't answer. I picked up the reins and faced them one last time. "If I can, I's gonna come back," I said straining to hold back tears.

"Will you just go already!" Zila said impatiently.

I ignored her tone. "Thank you for helping us, Zila. I ain't never gonna forget it."

She looked slightly ashamed for a few seconds but it didn't stop her calling after me as I rode away.

"Don't forget what I said about them dreams now. You hear?"

I rode as quickly as I could through the dappled sunlight and soon escaped the woods onto the main road.

I brought Julia to an abrupt stop when I spotted Master John with Master Peter and the two men who were supposed to be guarding Avery. One of the house slaves, Johnson, was with them, and as they walked up from the plantation house on their way to the woods, I saw him wringing his hands together. He appeared to be talking to Master John. Even though they were some distance away I could see that Master John's face was a hot shade of red, which meant that he was angry. Very Angry. And as I watched he stopped to bark something at Johnson before he struck him across the face with what I assumed was a gun. I felt a twinge of guilt as I watched Johnson fall heavily to the ground.

Master John was in the process of leaning over Johnson, no doubt to strike him again, when he saw me. He straightened, the colour draining from his face, his expression blank for a second as he processed what he was seeing. Me on a horse and the unmistakable form of a man wrapped in blankets lying across my lap. He stood gaping at me in shock for a few moments, as did the other men.

Even though it was the last thing I wanted to do considering Avery's plight, I forced a smile and blew Master John a kiss. His face turned the colour of a burst tomato as I turned Julia away. He began to shout, angrier than I had ever heard him. "*Get my horse! Get my horse!*" he screamed, but the sound of his voice was soon lost to the wind as I sped away.

I headed out to the grasslands, not thinking too much about where I was going only intent on getting as far away from the plantation, and Master John, as possible. Despite my depressed spirits, I could feel the same pull to let go that I'd always felt whenever I rode Julia and so, letting my worries fade into the background, I surrendered to the moment. I became at one with everything: the rhythm of the powerful horse beneath me, the wind sweeping past my face, the flock of birds cutting across the somnolent blue sky and the thunder of the horse's hooves as they hit the earth. My psychic sense was in tune with everything but the one thing that mattered to me most. Avery. I felt absolutely nothing from him and the sun, my silent nemesis, was still high above us, scorching the earth with her deadly gaze.

And there was more. I felt an ugly ripple curling toward me which forced me to bring Julia to a stop. I turned her around. At first I could only see a tiny cloud of dust on the road, but then four horses came into view, the rider of the horse in front dressed in green. It could only be Master John.

With Avery strapped to the horse, I couldn't ride as fast as I wanted, so I knew they would soon catch up.

I expected to feel a quiver of fear or apprehension, but there was only a dark, deadly calm as I watched them.

Let them come.

I turned Julia around and set off again. I tried to think of somewhere to take Avery where they wouldn't be able to get to him until after dark. Numerous images began to flash across my mind like petals on the surface of a fast moving stream, images of all the places where Avery had hidden provisions for me. One in particular stood out. A cave by the Mississippi River. The perfect place to hide him until nightfall and it wouldn't take me too long to get there.

But they were closing in on me fast. I didn't need to look behind me to see that, for they were clearly emblazoned in my mind's eye. Master John was in a frenzy, his whip coming down on his horse in savage strokes as he tore across the countryside, edging ever closer to his prey. They were sure to catch up to me before I could get to the caves, but a plan was already forming in my mind.

I turned left, choosing a circuitous path, which, although it would take longer, would also give me an opportunity to stop, or at the very least, slow down my pursuers.

Urging Julia on a little bit faster, we soon came to rocky ground, which was punctuated by a few thin, wraithlike trees. Here, the earth sloped gently upwards. It felt as if there was a hook puncturing my chest, and every time Avery was jostled by the jarring movement of the horse, it tugged painfully. But I had to hurry. They were close enough now for me to hear the faint sound of Master John's voice as he screamed my name.

The climb up the mountain seemed to take an age and for the first time during that ride I began to feel a tingle of fear. The horse's reins felt slick in my moist hands, and there was a twinge of pain in my forehead from concentrating not only on making the ascent, but from keeping my mind's eye trained on the men chasing me. They were probably no more than five metres behind but just as I began to think that they would surely catch up to me, I saw the ravine up ahead.

I pushed Julia faster and quietened my mind, sinking even deeper into the trancelike stillness as I raced toward the precipice and the sheer drop beyond.

Time seemed to slow down when I reached the edge, the three-metre gap yawning like a hungry mouth, and I became aware of everything in those seconds. My heartbeat and Julia's slowed down as I reached out and forced a solid calm on her, our minds as one, so that when I felt the fear crawling through her as the ravine drew closer, I was able to push it away. I was also able to sense Master John's disbelief when he saw what I was about to do and his rage and frustration was like a serpent's hiss at the back of my mind.

That dumb nigger.

Those words came through the clearest, along with his belief that I wouldn't be able to make the jump and he would have to watch me fall to a gruesome, bloody death. I pushed all thought of him aside and the world fell eerily quiet as we reached the edge and Julia jumped.

We flew through the air in one fluid motion, and as we soared over the ravine, I was aware of Master John and his men coming to a stop before they reached the edge, looking on in breathless disbelief as we landed with a brain-numbing jolt on the other side.

Everything sped up again in a rush of noise, the sharp clap of Julia's hooves, the harsh cry of a lone eagle, and the sound of my heart pounding. I didn't stop to look back at the four men on the other side of the ravine. I kept going. As we disappeared from sight, I heard Master John barking orders at the other men. He sounded desperate. "That way! We'll cut her off before she gets down to the other side."

I concentrated only on the task ahead as I guided Julia down the precarious slope, the hook in my heart tugged more often now that we were heading downhill. I also kept my senses honed in on my pursuers and timed my descent so that I would reach the bottom at exactly the right moment.

About fifteen metres from the bottom I saw the first man on the right making his way along the base of the mountain toward me with Master John close behind. The other two were on my left.

It was exactly as I had foreseen it. They were still far away and I could easily have swept down and past them before they could reach me, but my plan had been to stop them. And so, steadying myself, I held the reins in my left hand and took out the gun with my right.

Slowing down slightly, I aimed the gun at the first man on my right and fired. The gun cracked through the silence like a whip. His horse tumbled and went down in a screech of pain trapping him beneath it.

I aimed the gun again.

Master John was seconds behind the man I had just taken down but his quick reflexes had enabled him to steer out of the way when the horse fell. But, just as he moved directly beneath a large dead tree, I fired at one of the branches, bringing it crashing down. Master John was knocked off his horse and flung backward, head over heels, to the ground whilst his horse scrambled away.

Remembering the amount of times he had knocked me off my feet with a slap and the degradation I had suffered at his hands, I kept the gun trained on him, my finger tightening around the trigger.

I so desperately wanted to kill him, but I couldn't. I couldn't.

Too many slaves up and down Mississippi would suffer horribly if I shot a white man, so I lowered the gun. I reached the bottom of the mountain. The third man rode toward me on my left.

I swept past him easily, and, as he altered course to follow, I brought my right arm across my chest so that the gun was just below my left shoulder. Turning my head to the left only long enough to take aim, I fired, hitting his horse.

I didn't waste time watching him go down but stayed facing forward as I sped away. With my inner vision I knew Master Peter had stopped when he'd heard the first gunshot, so he wasn't going to be a problem. I rode on, only looking back when I had put enough space between us, and saw Master John slowly growing smaller as the distance between us grew. I watched him throw his riding whip down on the ground, and roar in rage, before he stamped on it like a spoilt child.

I didn't need my sixth sense to tell me that he wasn't about to give up, but hopefully he wouldn't be able to stop me.

Now that the exhilaration of the jump and defeating Master John was fading, misery came in swift nauseating waves. I felt drained and trapped by the sunlight as we rode over the green plains, but although I had lost hope, I rode on because I had to see this through to the end.

At last I spied the cave, its dark opening like the maw of death. I dismounted and led Julia into its murky depths, where I untied Avery, dimly aware of the fact that Master John and Master Peter were now on one horse and would soon be here. It didn't matter now, because they wouldn't reach us in time.

I tried, I tried so hard, but no matter how hard I concentrated, I couldn't pick up anything at all from Avery, not even a solitary spark to tell me he was still alive. I pulled him down off the horse, his weight knocking both of us to the ground. The blanket had come away from his head and tears sprang to my eyes when I saw his beautiful face blank, hard and white, a mere shell of the man I had fallen in love with. Crying openly, I eased myself out from under him and got to my feet. There wasn't much time left.

I led Julia out of the cave where she stood flicking her ears, her large brown eyes gazing at me in a bemused fashion.

"Go!" I said not wanting Avery's horse to fall into Master John's possession.

She took a step toward me.

"Go!" I screamed and moving forward, gave her a hard

slap on the flank.

It worked and she trotted away, but then stopped to stare back at me. When I advanced on her again she galloped away out of sight.

They would soon be here.

I went back into the dark, dank-smelling cave and knelt down in the dirt before Avery. Stroking his face, I kissed him one last time, his face blurred by my tears, then I stood up and returned to the mouth of the cave.

Master John and Master Peter were riding up toward the cave. Both of them spotted me at the same time and Master John leapt off the horse before it had even come to a stop. He dropped heavily to the ground before scrambling to his feet. He ran toward the cave.

"*Luna!*"

I aimed the gun at the roof of the cave.

The last thing I saw was Master John, his face writhing with the same fear I had seen earlier, when he thought he was about to kill me with the axe.

"*Luna!*" he screamed as he ran toward me. "*What are you doing? Luna, Please!*"

I pulled the trigger.

The gun blast was excruciatingly loud in the confines of the cave and I looked up in time to see a tide of chalky white rocks rain down on me. I crumpled like a sheet of paper under its might as the roof caved in and buried me in a tomb of stone. At first I didn't feel anything, but then white hot pain burst across my head and chest and I tasted blood in my mouth. The only part of my body that wasn't subjected to that searing pain were my legs, which were completely numb.

I realise now that I had never had any intention of making it through that journey. You see, I was certain that Avery was dead and I didn't want to live without him. So, selfish to the very end, I didn't think of those at the plantation who would be waiting for me to come back to them one day. I didn't even think of Avery and what he would think or feel if by some miracle he was still alive and woke up at dusk to find me dead.

I only thought of myself and of living in turmoil without him which would be worse than the pain of mangled flesh and bone. When oblivion finally came for me, I embraced it, my last thoughts of Avery as all pain, misery, and life faded away and I ceased to exist.

Chapter Twenty Three

The first thing I saw when I opened my eyes was a hazy surge of blood engulfed in yellow flames. Then my vision cleared and I realised I was looking up at a beautiful sunset. I sat up, surprised to find myself alone, for I was sure I had been lying in a man's arms. I'd even had the sensation that someone had kissed me on the forehead only moments before and my face was slightly damp, as if a tear-stained cheek had been pressed against mine. Caught still in the lazy snare of sleep, I looked around and saw that I was sitting in a field of saffron-coloured grass. And as the last of sleep pulled away, leaving me completely alert, I got to my feet and elation broke over me.

Sunset.

My nemesis had been forced to retreat and I smiled at that baleful fiery eye as it slowly sank beneath the trees. I looked down at my clothes, which were torn, dirty and soaked in blood, some of which had dried to dark brown crusts. There was also blood on my face and in my hair. But there wasn't a single wound on me. I felt as strong and vibrant as I had the day that Avery had bewitched my mind.

This could only mean one thing. He was alive.

But why was I alone?

I spun around, expecting to see him behind me or walking toward me lit in the glow of the setting sun, but saw only a house, the same farmhouse he had shown me that morning.

Knowing that something was horribly wrong, I ran up to the front door. It was open and I entered a large living room with comfortable, solid wooden furniture. My bible was on the table along with the gold cross he had tried to give me that morning.

I backed away from those items as that awful feeling of falling seized me again.

He was telling me goodbye.

"No," I whispered as hot tears rose.

I stumbled outside, the setting sun seeming to mock me now.

I had fought so hard, and for what? I wasn't going to let him do this to me. I ran, and for a moment I thought I saw him standing in the distance watching me but it must have been my imagination because he was gone the moment I laid eyes on him. But I ran toward where I had seen him anyway, stopping only when two figures on horseback rose slowly up from the horizon before me.

It was Jupiter and Father Geoffrey. When Jupiter saw me, a beautiful smile lit his face until he saw the blood on my clothes and it disappeared like a stone dropped into a lake. He jumped off his horse and ran toward me.

"Luna?" he cried, his terror increasing when he saw my tears.

"I ain't hurt," I said.

He stood watching me intently for a few moments and then slowly drew me into his arms.

Jupiter. Always there when I needed him the most.

I wept and wept.

Avery had left me. After all I'd said and done, he had left me anyway.

But why?

I wept in Jupiter's arms.

Chapter Twenty Four

I waited for a month.

I spent every day hopeful that when darkness drew the world under its comforting cloak, I would be with Avery. But always I found myself alone at the end of each night.

I knew he was nearby, I could feel it in my blood, but he didn't come for me and I was left in a deep dark hole, bewildered and utterly abandoned. And I couldn't understand why he had done this to me.

So after that month, I accepted Jupiter's hand in marriage.

And so began my long, slow death.

Over the years I did everything I could to forget Avery, but it was like trying to forget the sunrise. It wasn't that I didn't love Jupiter, because I did. He was my only reason for waking up in the morning. He eased the gaping hole in my heart, gave me love, joy and eventually a family. But whereas Jupiter was a man I could love and seek comfort from, Avery was a part of my soul.

The most agonising thing about those years was that I sometimes caught tantalising hints of Avery's presence. It happened mainly at dusk, or some nights I would be jolted from sleep, convinced that he was either in the house or somewhere outside. But the moment I tried to hone in on him and draw closer to that heartrending lullaby, it was gone and I was left again with that unbearable pull in the pit of my stomach, a pull which slowly turned into a gaping hole as the years wore on.

And he continued to look after me and everyone I cared for. If there was ever a threat of any kind, it would miraculously resolve itself. If money was needed, I would find a large amount in a coat pocket or left in a cupboard. And true to his promise, he gave me the greatest gift of all one sultry summer evening, a few months after the birth of my son Dembi.

I was leaving the house with the baby to call Jupiter inside for supper before it got dark when I saw three figures walking toward the house. Two men and a woman. I almost dropped the baby when my eyes fell on the woman. They weren't close enough for me to see them clearly, but my soul recognised hers immediately although I couldn't really call her a woman, for she was no more than a girl.

With a trembling hand to my mouth I called out to Jupiter, unable to tear my gaze away from the young woman.

"What is it?" he asked when he came bounding to my side.

I handed the baby to him and could only point to the three people moving toward the house.

"Should I get my gun?" he asked.

"No," I whispered. "It... it's..." I couldn't continue and a tear slipped down my cheek.

She was closer now and I was simply entranced by how beautiful she was. She was the same height as Mama Akosua, her complexion like butter, and she wore her dark wavy hair in two French plaits. At first Jupiter gazed suspiciously at the approaching trio as he held Dembi tightly to his chest, his body tensed for action in case they should prove to be a threat. But when the young woman came close enough for him to see clearly, he relaxed, realising who she was and why I had tears streaming down my face.

At last she was only a few feet away from me and although I longed to touch her I kept back, my hand tightly grasping Jupiter's free arm.

"Mama?" she said softly.

If I remembered correctly, she was no more than sixteen but she had the poise and self-assuredness of a much older woman. Her dark eyes were warm yet quick and searching, seeming to see and understand so much for someone of her years.

"You... you look nothing like him," I was able to say.

"No, silly. I look like you. Now I ain't gonna bite so give me a hug."

Love, pure and absolute, filled me when I moved into her embrace, and I realised that it had always been there beneath the trauma and the hatred I'd felt for Master Henry. And yet I had abandoned her.

"I... I don't even know what your name be," I whispered when I finally let her go.

"Why it's Lina. Same as yours."

A tiny line appeared on her brow when she saw my expression and for the first time, her confidence seemed to waver as she looked from me to Jupiter. "Your name *is* Lina, ain't it?"

"No, Luna," Jupiter answered, and placed a comforting hand on her arm.

"Our Mama always thought your name was Lina," one of the young men said with a quick glance at Lina who seemed to be completely at a loss for words now and was looking down at her feet. "I guess they heard wrong."

I brought my hand up to her face.

"Lina," I said and smiled. "A beautiful name for a beautiful girl."

She brightened immediately at those words, something that caused my shame and self-loathing to flare.

"Come inside. We... we has lots to talk about," I said.

I stayed at the door for a few moments as they all

241

entered the house. The sun would be setting in a little while. I looked around and wondered if Avery was somewhere nearby observing our little reunion. I sighed heavily.

I was so tired of this constant struggle whenever I thought about Avery, and I thought about him all the time. A few years had passed by then and although I was still furious with him, every time he did something to demonstrate how much he cared, I missed him so much that it felt as if my soul was drowning.

On the verge of tears, I turned around and entered the house to properly welcome the new additions to our family.

Despite the miracle of having the daughter I thought I had lost return to me, the years were still hard to bear, and I was often tormented by strange dreams of Avery, some of which were excruciatingly real.

In one of those dreams I was back at the mansion but Avery was nowhere to be found. Gripped by the same mindless panic that had consumed me the first time he went away, I ran out into the night in search of him, walking once more for hours through the woods to the lake where I was sure I would find him. But when I got there, the lake we had once sat beside in the sun had turned into a dark, dank swamp. And Avery wasn't there.

Distraught and feeling as if I were caught in that never-ending fall, I wept and called ceaselessly out to him, my cries a mantra of loss and pain. There were others there with me, though I barely took notice of them. One was a male who observed my distress with a mixture of sympathy and fascination as he tried to talk me into coming back to the mansion with him. But I wouldn't leave and instead sank to my knees by the swamp crying out for Avery.

I woke up with a start, drenched in sweat and shaking violently. The grief, the loss, was so raw and keen that I wasn't able to sleep again that night. I rose, wandered outside onto the porch, and searched the unwelcoming night.

"Where is you?" I asked in a faint echo of the dream. "Where is you?"

There was no answer, only the gaping hole his prolonged absence had left.

In another dream, I found myself in the dark, disconnected from my body and with no sense of where I was. I could make out hazy shapes and images but they disappeared the moment I focused on them. The only thing I could be sure of was that I was needed and I felt myself being drawn forward and down. That's when Avery blazed into view. He appeared to be caught in the darkness and was completely unaware of my presence, his handsome face frozen in terror as something, some cold, dark fury, descended on him. I felt a surge of rage and I rushed at this thing, sending it back, and then I was burning, caught in a circle of fire, my screams rising as the flames consumed me.

I woke up to find Jupiter gripping me by the shoulders, fear lining his face as he called my name. I was still caught in a whirlwind of fire and couldn't speak, only gasp for air. The pain melted away as Jupiter wrapped his arms around me, his hand shaking as he caressed my face. Unable to get the image of a trapped and terrified Avery out of my mind, I wept, barely aware that Lina was by the door, her expression hidden in the shadows. But if I had been able to see her face I was sure that it would have held reproach. We had never discussed Avery, but I knew that she was aware of him and what he meant to me. And I often caught her watching me at dusk when I felt his absence most. She never hid her resentment during those moments and I didn't know whether it was directed at Avery and what he was, or toward me and the fact that I couldn't stop loving him. That night, she left a few moments later and Jupiter held me all night as I cried inconsolably, for I was sure Avery was in some kind of mortal danger.

The rest of that week saw me descend to such severe depths of misery that Jupiter and Lina were afraid to leave me on my own. I merely went through the motions of wife and mother, and had it not been for Dembi and his younger sister Mary, it is unlikely I would have managed to get out of bed. Jupiter, the kind and patient man that he was, didn't try to force me to tell him what was wrong, though he was worried and on edge. Luckily, at the end of the week I was woken from a fitful sleep by the same melancholy symphony that had drawn me to the chapel the day I'd first laid eyes on Avery. It was gone the moment I tried to focus on it but it felt as if a steel ring around my heart had been loosened and I was able to go back to sleep that night with the knowledge that Avery was alive.

Those years were long and hard. And as they wore on I began to doubt that Avery loved me the way that I loved him, but I felt that he at least cared. However, that assumption was called into question when I made a startling discovery one mild, spring day.

I was in town with Lina that morning when I heard the news that something had happened to Zila during the night and now nobody knew where she was. Master John had been found alone in her cabin covered in blood and too drunk to remember what had happened.

The news left me shaken. I hadn't seen Zila since the day she had helped me get Avery to safety. We had never been friends, but she had helped me, helped Avery, and so I couldn't sit and do nothing when she could be hurt or in danger. So, forgetting about my errands, I left Lina in town and went straight to Mama's small home.

As always, her front door was open and she was preparing some kind of tea when I rushed in.

"I know," she said without turning.

"You know? Then why you sitting there? We has to find her."

She placed the tea on the table in the middle of the room and sat down. "Drink."

"Mama!" I cried. "There ain't time. She could be hurt. She... she could even be dead!"

"She is not dead. She is safe now. I know so. Besides, we used to be slaves and we are also women. So what do you think we can do?"

"God, Mama, you sure can be evil at times," I cried as I moved to the table. "This is 'cause she helped me that time. It's 'cause..."

The words died away and I was left rooted to the spot in shock. As I leant over to shout at her, my hand brushed the back of the chair and an image came to me. It was night time, the room lit by a single candle, and there was a game of Awore on the table that had been forgotten amidst the lively flow of conversation and laughter. It was all there in that fleeting vision, years of visits and the friendship that had slowly bloomed between these walls under the gentle benevolence of candlelight. A friendship between Mama and Avery. I was completely unprepared at what such a vivid glimpse of him after so many years would do to me. It was like I had been struck by lightning. He looked sad but was so much more beautiful than my feeble memories of him were able to yield. I can't explain how betrayed I felt. He had ignored me, completely ignored me for years, but had been visiting Mama the whole time. And she had kept it from me. It made sense now why she appeared to be so unconcerned about Zila's plight.

I straightened and gazed down at Mama, and although I was trembling slightly, I kept my face devoid of expression.

She sighed softly. She had, no doubt, anticipated this moment.

"Yes, Zila is fine. Massa John would have killed her if I hadn't foreseen the danger she was in and asked Avery to help her. But knowing that foolish girl, she will be running back to Massa John the moment she is healed."

Pulling my shawl around me, I walked to the door,

stopping only when she spoke again.

"He loves you. If you must hate someone, hate me. I was the one who summoned the evil at the chapel and that's what has kept him from you."

Without acknowledging her words in any way, I left the cabin.

That discovery sat between us like a putrid wound for many years. I was angry, more so at Avery than Mama, but he wasn't there and so Mama bore the full brunt of my rage. She didn't ever speak of it or acknowledge the small changes in the way I behaved toward her. But her eyes beheld it, her expression always that of the martyr who receives her punishment without complaint.

I am ashamed to say that the anger and bitterness stayed with me until the day she died. And on the day we laid her to rest, the pain and guilt that wracked me was almost enough to eclipse the taunting anguish of Avery's absence. I was inconsolable that day and I wanted nothing more than to go back in time so I could forgive her and ask for her forgiveness in turn.

But I should have known Mama would never fully leave me. *You will have my devotion in life and in death*, she had told me. And as always, she never failed me. She came back to me in dreams and continued to guide me for the rest of my life. She also urged me to never give up on Avery.

But despite Mama's reassurances, I had given up hope and was sure I would die without ever seeing Avery again. Time had robbed me of the young beautiful face he had fallen in love with and every year it continued to take more from me. Every line that marred my face was an affront, every streak of grey in my once dark locks, a violation. And my once lithe, toned body had long ago succumbed to the ravages of childbirth and the trappings of a comfortable life. I mourned those loses, for they were small deaths that I buried along with my hopes of one day being reunited with Avery.

Then, one night, when I was in my forties, something miraculous happened.

I was dreaming and, as was always the case whenever I dreamt in those days, I found myself at the chapel. But this time I was young again and kneeling at the altar with my bible clutched to my chest, praying as I had done that fateful evening so many years ago. But instead of being outside by the trees, Avery was standing a few feet away with his back to me. He was dressed in the clothing he must have worn when he was a reverend, but they were torn, ravaged with age, and soiled with clumps of earth. His hair was already past his shoulders.

He was upset and his emotional turmoil washed over me like a tsunami until I was drowning in his pain, and self-loathing. That's when I knew that this was more than just a dream. Needing to comfort him, I tried to stand but could only manage to raise my head and when I did, it felt as if I was being torn apart as I separated from the version of myself that was kneeling at the altar, a separation that was excruciatingly painful and left me feeling weak and dizzy.

Avery turned around and there was instant recognition in his eyes, which pushed back some of his inner turmoil. But it abated for only a moment before the shame broke over him again with renewed force. He hung his head and stepped away.

And I knew why. I knew what he had done.

It had been a few years since he had been turned into a vampire and out of disgust and self-loathing at what he had become, he had tried to refrain from drinking blood so that he wouldn't have to take anymore lives. He had managed to survive for a week and a half, getting steadily weaker and more delirious with pain as the demon within him raged for blood. That night, almost too weak to pull himself out of the earth, he knew he wouldn't be able to last another night without blood. So, overcome by that mortal need, he had stumbled and crawled through the woods in search of a victim, eventually finding a farmhouse. Unable to go any further, he had stayed on his knees in the woods and sought out the weakest mind within the house and summoned them to him.

At first he thought he had failed to entice them out of the house in his weakened state but then he heard the sound of bare feet treading carefully in the undergrowth. Invigorated by the scent of warm human blood slowly drifting through the air toward him, he managed to pull himself to his feet, the pulsing pain driving him forward in anticipation of the feast as his bloodlust consumed him. Almost completely lost in the savage, crimson trap that always descended in the seconds before a kill, his fangs were already elongated and ready to tear into human flesh. But then a little girl in a long white nightgown appeared out of the gloom. She was no more than nine years old and had red hair which was tied up in two bunches. She stood in the dark woodland gazing up at him and even though he was in control of her mind, she was still afraid.

Completely mortified, he had quickly sent her a command not to be afraid, telling her that she was safe. And although a part of him wanted to send her back home, he was completely overcome by his thirst, which was like fire thrilling through his veins, burning him alive.

It took all the will power he had to keep from attacking her long enough to search her thoughts for a pleasant memory, settling on one of her slave Cassie, a large mulatto Negro with a brutal scar cutting across what would otherwise have been a pretty face. The little girl, whose name was Amanda, smiled in her daze as he brought forth a memory of Cassie singing one of Amanda's favourite hymns whilst she cooked. Amanda loved Mammy Cassie, probably more than she loved her own mother, but the slave hated her. Amanda knew this even though Cassie was careful not to show it and it was a constant source of sadness for her.

"She does love you," Avery had said to her through the

flames of his anguish and she had smiled dreamily, her thoughts filled with Cassie singing softly to her.

Unable to hold off any longer, he had gathered her tiny body to him and, careful to ensure she felt no pain, he bit into her slender neck. At first she cried out as panic overrode the spell he'd placed on her, but then she fell silent.

He drank greedily, draining every last drop of her blood until he was left with the bloodless, rapidly cooling flesh of a cadaver. Then he wept bitterly at the monster he had become.

Eventually he gathered Amanda's limp body in his arms and took her back to the farmhouse, where he laid her outside the kitchen door. He knew that the first person to find her would probably be Cassie, the slave Amanda had been so sure hated her. But Avery knew Amanda had been wrong. Cassie did love her. Standing outside the farmhouse in the ethereal glow of the moonlight, he could sense Cassie's thoughts, and even in her sleep, those thoughts were filled with her love for her Master's child, the only thing she had to love and nurture after having all three of her own children sold. Knowing that Cassie would suffer terribly in the morning when she found out that Amanda had been taken from her, Avery turned his back on the farmhouse and disappeared into the woods.

But it seemed Cassie didn't have to wait until morning to discover what had happened to her darling Amanda. Perhaps woken by some sixth sense, she had ventured outside and found her beloved Mandy dead.

Avery had been fleeing through the woods when he heard her anguished cry, even though he was miles from the farmhouse. Impaled by that harrowing grief-stricken wail, he had dropped to his knees, consumed by remorse and hatred at what he had become. Moments later, he found himself standing in the chapel.

I felt my heart tearing as I observed his agony and torment. I wanted so much to comfort him and let him know that although I knew what he had done, I could never hate him for it. I had so much to say but I knew that my time with him was short as I was already wilting under the strain of looking up at him.

Hold on. I'm coming, Avery. Wait for me, I'm coming.

He glanced up at me, disbelief radiating from his soft blue eyes and then hope, hope like a lighthouse in the storm of his despair, lit up his beautiful face and then it was all gone.

The following morning it was as if every last vestige of strength had been drained out of me, replaced with a deep exhaustion that weighed down not only my body, but my mind. It was an effort just to raise my arm and I wasn't able to get out of bed that day. Having very rarely seen me sick during the course of our marriage, Jupiter spent most of the day hovering above my bed doing whatever he could to make me feel better. By evening I had begun to recover some of my strength and with it came a sense of peace because at last, the mystery of why Avery had sought me out had finally been solved.

I knew now that I had done it somehow. I had gone to him during his years of solitude and told him to wait. I didn't know how but I knew it was true. It was such a blissful discovery but one tempered with grief because Avery wasn't here with me to share it. The most exhilarating thing about this miracle was that it meant I was tied to him and that gave me hope that it wasn't the end for the two of us after all. Mama was right. I would see him again. If only for a moment, I would see him again.

All I had to do was wait. He had waited for me for fifty long, lonely years. I would wait for him until the end of time if that is what it took. And when I laid eyes on him again, I wouldn't stop telling him how much I loved him.

The years passed. My children grew up and began families of their own and old age found me. But even though the dreams of Avery had long since ceased, I never lost the conviction that I would see him again. When Jupiter died, I knew that my days on this earth would soon come to an end. My children were grown, happy and prosperous. Lina and Ebenezer were already expecting their third child. They no longer needed me. Jupiter had been the only one keeping me tethered to life and although he had been dead only a few days, I could already feel my strength leaving me. I knew I was giving up, allowing life to trickle through my fingers. But I felt no sorrow, only a sense of excitement at the prospect that this would all be over and I would be going on a journey. The anger I had harboured at Avery was still there, but it no longer suffocated me. I would never truly forgive him for leaving me, but I knew he loved me and had tried to act in my best interest. He had waited nearly half a century for me so I was prepared to wait for him until day and night ceased to exist if that's what it took for me to even catch a glimpse of him.

So I prepare and wait, knowing that my time will soon end and I will begin another journey. Part of my preparation involves writing down these experiences for you, my dear Lina, whether it will be to end this chapter or open a new one, only time will tell. But my sojourn in the sun is at an end and I will spend these last few days waiting for night to come with the hope that I will look out across the searing sunset and see Avery walking toward me as night closes softly in.

Chapter Twenty Five

At first I was only aware of the cold, an unforgiving chill deep within my bones, spreading outward to the very tips of my toes. Then, like a veil slowly lifting, I became aware of blinding whiteness and a pair of scuffed brown men's boots, *my* boots, immersed in soft snow. The boots were far too big, making my legs look like brown stalks. And no wonder I was so cold for I wore only a ragged blue dress that was too small and had only an old moth-eaten blanket around my shoulders.

Something else was different. No, not different, *changed*. And when I brought my hands up to my face I saw what it was. These were not the wrinkled hands of an old woman. These were the hands of a girl. Exalted, I touched the smooth, supple skin of my face and almost wept.

I was young again. But how? And where was I?

Teeth chattering, my feet feeling like chunks of ice, I turned around slowly, and when I saw the restored mansion, our mansion, looming before me, I felt an unrestrained joy that was wild, bold and mine. *Mine*.

And as the faint light of a wintery dawn bled into view, it all slowly began to come back to me. The weeks searching for the right herbs and then preparing them according to the instructions Mama had left for me. Watching a new day break over the oak trees as I tried to

252

gather the courage to begin a journey I wasn't sure I would have the strength to complete. And that horrifying moment when the last of the potion passed my lips and I felt myself being dragged into a sleep that locked tight around me like a vice.

When I woke up in the dark and began to scream and struggle against the wooden coffin, my cries muffled under six feet of earth, I thought I would go mad. And I would have succumbed to my terror had it not been for Mama's soothing presence reminding me of what I needed to say and do to call forth the spirit within the chapel. Gradually, I was able to rein in my panic for long enough to harness my power, the power of which I had only been vaguely aware my whole life, and then I was standing outside the chapel.

At last I came face to face with the evil that had sought possession of Mama's soul. It stood before me in a ghastly rendition of my younger form under a sky bleached of colour and substance. Everything in this place it inhabited was devoid of colour and light, only shadows seemed to flourish here, shadows and undulating cycles of its rage, loneliness and hatred for the living. But most of all, for Avery. I understood now that the vampire who had turned Avery had spent years conjuring up this entity with the blood of many, and had succeeding in bringing it to this place, a place which would eventually be its gateway into the world of the living. That vampire had been close to bringing it over into the body of a living being when Avery fought her and set the chapel alight, leaving the evil spirit trapped in this netherworld of shadow.

I fought to control my fear and revulsion as it slunk toward me, its laughter a piercing victory that stung and angered me.

It thought it had won. It thought it finally had what it had coveted for centuries: a body, and not just that of an ordinary woman, but the body of a powerful seer with which it could wreak unthinkable destruction. But like

Mama and Avery, this wretched evil had underestimated my strength. It would never take over my spirit, as I would always be too strong. My power, the power of a witch, lay in the ability to not only summon spirits and unseen forces, but to bend them to her will. This ancient evil was no different and I was able to easily subdue it and use its power to do my bidding.

Now I was here. Cold, weak, but here. And my years of pain and suffering would soon come to an end because he was coming.

I could barely contain my tears as I stood there waiting for him, those few minutes in the cold seeming longer and much harder to bear than the years I had spent pining for him. But finally I saw a dark shape standing motionless in the endless ocean of white snow.

As I looked at him my elation faded, and then crept away, because although he could see me clearly with his heightened supernatural senses, he didn't make a move toward me. He just stood there, tall, regal, and out of reach. For a moment, I was distraught and uncertain. My whole purpose for being here, all I had endured over the last forty years, and the hell I had gone through to bring myself to him was now being called into question. Had I made a mistake in thinking he wanted me to return to him?

I received no answer to that question, only the silence of a winter dawn and the being I loved standing motionless beneath a mournful winter sky.

After what seemed like an eternity of uncertainty, I reached out a trembling hand and took a step forward. Immediately, he appeared before me and grasped my outstretched hand, confusion and turmoil displayed across his face. I also saw hope, hesitant hope, but it was there in his soft blue eyes.

"Luna? Is it really you?"

"Yes," I said reaching up and touching his face. "Yes, Avery."

He was even more beautiful than I remembered and

now that I was once more under the light of his loving gaze, I couldn't for the life of me understand how I had survived the last four decades without him.

Overwhelmed with happiness and with tears sliding down my frozen cheeks, I folded myself into his arms and lay my head against his chest as he brought my hand up to his lips and kissed it. All my fears vanished and I wondered why I had ever doubted his love for me. It was in his eyes, in his voice, and the way he held onto my hand. He would never stop loving me.

"How? How is this possible?" he asked, his voice trembling with emotion.

"Magic. Powerful magic. Mine, Mama's and... and the spirit from the chapel."

I felt him stiffen and gently, he tilted my face up so he could peer into my eyes. "You summoned it? Was that wise?"

I pulled away from him sharply, the anger I had been harbouring against him for the past forty years rising up unbidden. "No, Avery. It ain't *wise*. But what else was I gonna do? You's able to walk away from me but I ain't never gonna give you up. Never! I thought I's gonna die without ever seeing you again but I still ain't give up on you."

"Please, don't be angry with me, Luna. I had to do it. In the chapel, when they had me bound and I thought I was going to die at sunset, the demon spoke to me. It said it would save my life, but in exchange it wanted you. It wanted me to make you into what I am because it knew that once the lust for blood became a part of you, it would be easier for the spirit to take over your soul. If I kept you with me I would have done the unthinkable and turned you into a vampire even though it would mean giving you up to evil. And I couldn't do that to you, Luna."

"I... I know. I know why you done it. But you shoulda had faith in me. I's stronger than that thing. I always was." I forced the anger from my voice. "With you by my side

I's strong enough for anything."

"I know that now," he said reaching for me, and I let myself be drawn back into his arms.

"You're freezing," he said. "Let me get you..."

"N...no," I said even though my teeth were chattering so hard that I was finding it difficult to speak.

"I don't know how much time I has but I wants the last thing I see to be this place so's I can remember them days waiting here for you at sundown. But... but there be another reason why I's come. I can't leave you, Avery so I has to ask something of you. Something I ain't sure you's gonna be able to do."

"Anything. Ask anything of me and I will do it."

"I wants you to make me into what you is, but there's something you needs to know first. The spirit in the chapel, it give me my youth but it hates us and so I don't be knowing if what it promised be the truth. If you trys to change me I... I might not live and if I does, I might be an old woman again. I wants you to choose and if you says no, I... I can accept it cause I at least got to lay my eyes on you one last time."

"Oh, Luna. Of course I will. I may have had the strength to walk away from you forty years ago but that strength has been broken by the pain of living without you. I cannot let you go a second time."

"But I mightn't stay like this."

The thought of losing my youth was a harrowing one, for how could he continue to love me if I were an old, wrinkled hag for all eternity?

"Your beauty never left you, Luna. I saw you change over the years and I loved all that I saw." As he spoke, he lightly traced his fingers along my face. "I loved the lines around your eyes from laughing, mostly at Mary. And these ones across your brow from worrying about little Dembi. I also loved watching your body grow softer and your bosom heavy from giving sustenance to your own children, no one else's. All these changes were signs of a full, happy life. It was the only thing that made it possible to stay away, the knowledge that if I hadn't let you go, you wouldn't have had a family. You are beautiful, Luna. Not even time can take that away from you."

I let the tears of relief flow freely and again, I wondered why I had ever doubted him and his love for me.

"There be just one other thing that I wants from you, Avery. I's doing this 'cause I wants to be with you forever. So you has to promise that you ain't never gonna leave me again. You has to promise, Avery, 'cause I ain't gonna let you do that to me a second time."

I knew there was an echo of that anger in my voice but it was hard to keep it hidden because the thought of being separated from him again tore too sharply at my wounded psyche.

"Nothing will ever keep us apart again."

So that is how I came back to him. But we still had one last hurdle and that was whether or not I would survive the change, and if I did, would I wake up a beautiful young girl or an old woman? But nothing could make me turn back now that a life with Avery was once more within my grasp.

So I lay in the newly redecorated red velvet bedroom in one of the gowns he had bought for me all those years ago, my face turned to the window as I bid the light of day a final farewell.

He made sure I felt no pain when he bit into my neck and the last of my strength began to fade away as the blood drained out of me. I felt a little of that strength return when I drank his blood but I was still weak and time was running out fast for me.

The final moment had come and when he looked down at me with traces of blood on his lips and placed both hands on the sides of my head, he hesitated.

I reached up and wiped away the tears that were trailing a silvery path down his cheek. He was hesitating because he had to kill me to begin the transformation and I started to panic slightly at the realisation that I had maybe asked for too much from him. But if he didn't go through with this, I would die anyway.

"Avery, you has to hurry," I said, my voice no more than a whisper.

He squeezed his eyes shut for a few moments and when he opened them again, he looked completely broken. "Just... just make sure you come back to me, Luna."

"Avery, even if this don't work, I... I's gonna find a way back to you. I always gonna find a way back to you."

He kissed me carefully on the forehead, his grip on the sides of my head tightening. The last thing I saw was the haunting agony in his eyes, and then nothing.

***

When I woke up I knew immediately that I must have died and gone to Heaven because although I was lying in the red velvet room at the mansion, it was filled with flowers. Everything around me looked and felt different. The dress I wore was so soft and luxurious against my skin; it was as if I could feel the caress of every individual strand of the fabric. The colour was the most intense red I had ever seen. It shimmered softly under the lamplight, which was no longer a soft amber but a vibrant yellow that made the room look as if it were awash with sunlight. Everything in the room seemed to have hidden layers I could unearth simply by looking hard enough. The only thing wrong was the pain, a burning ache radiating from my bones and unlike anything I had ever felt before. I was also plagued with a hunger and thirst that seemed to eat away at my very soul.

I got out of bed, marvelling at how light my body and movements were. When I went to the mirror, a shock awaited me. I expected for a moment to see myself as I had been before Mama's potion. Although I was young again, I had never seen myself like this before. My skin was completely breathtaking. If there was such a thing as brown gold, then I was looking at it. And my eyes were like a dark prism of so many different colours hidden within the deep brown. The longer I looked at myself in this new form, the more it dawned on me that my outer appearance hadn't actually changed. It was my vision that had changed, for I no longer had the vision of a human being, but that of a vampire. I tried to remember what I used to see whenever I looked in the mirror and the effect began to lessen even though it was all still slightly heightened. It seemed I could command what I saw, just as I could control the things that I could hear. The house, which had always been as silent as a church, was so *noisy*. Its creaks, groans and sighs were like an eternal lament and even the sound of a spider in the corner spinning its web had become a part of that mournful symphony. Outside I could hear the heartbeat of some woodland creature and the sounds it made as it foraged for food. I could also hear a million insects, their movements like that of a small army. It was all a beautiful chorus that I could amplify or dim with a mere thought.

I found myself drawn to another noise from outside, some distance from the house and realised that it was footsteps, a man's footsteps. They were like the sound of a heartbeat to me. My heart sang with joy and it was almost enough to drown out that awful ache and thirst. Those footsteps were Avery's and he was coming back home. I focused on him and miraculously, although I was still in my room, my mind was somewhere else entirely, in a vast domain of rooms and doorways and sometimes large stretches of unfilled space.

I knew I was in Avery's mind because everything I saw in those rooms invariably seemed to lead back to me. Even the memories of his life before he came to America were coloured with his impressions of what I would think and feel about the person he had been back then. But I couldn't help focusing on those years he had spent alone in the wilderness before he'd found me. There were so many of them, stretching forth like a dry, arid desert. Seeing those lonely years combined, along with the ones that had followed after he'd let me go eased some of the anger I had harboured for most of my life. He had suffered so much and so had I. But those days had finally come to an end for both of us.

He was on the way back to the mansion with gifts for me. My beautiful, thoughtful Avery. He was mine now until the end of time.

I left the room and hurried out of the house toward the sound of his footsteps.

One chapter of my life had come to an end and another was just beginning. I was a daughter of the moon now and I gladly cast off my old life along with its fears as I ran to the man I loved.

Chapter Twenty Six

Atlanta 2011

I put the journal down and sat staring at the wall for a few minutes. My mind was ablaze with images of Luna and Avery and I had no doubt that what I had read was real. Luna and Avery had existed and they were still out there somewhere.

But behind the exhilaration I felt at my extraordinary discovery lay a quiet anguish and a feeling of intense foreboding. Not wanting to acknowledge its existence, I jumped out of bed and ran downstairs to search the internet for information. It didn't take me long to find what I was looking for and for a few minutes I could only sit and stare at the computer screen in amazement, an icy chill running up my spine. By the time I shook myself from my awestruck reverie and printed out what I wanted, the sky had begun to lighten and I could already see the sun making its ascent over the horizon.

At the sight of the sunrise my thoughts turned briefly back to Luna alone in the crumbling mansion and her feelings of dismay at the coming of the sun and another day separated from Avery. I also saw her as the powerful vampire retreating from the dawn with her beloved, knowing that nothing would ever keep them apart again. I realised that in just one night, I had completely fallen in love with those two beings and I knew I wouldn't rest until I had found them.

Needing to share my life-changing discovery with someone, I ran upstairs to my aunt's room, even though I knew she wouldn't appreciate being woken up so early, especially after such a late night.

My hand was shaking as I gently shook her awake.

"Auntie," I said softly.

She woke with a start, her arms flailing as she looked around in sleepy alarm. When her gaze fell on me she sank back down onto the pillows, her dreadlocks creating a dark halo around her delicate heart-shaped face.

"Dallas?" she mumbled, her eyelids already beginning to close.

"I found Luna's journal. She's real and so is Avery."

"Luna's journal? What are you talking about?"

Her eyes were still closed and I knew she would be asleep in a few seconds if I let her so I sat down heavily on the bed. Her eyelids opened to thin slits.

"Luna. She was real. We're her descendents. We're even psychic like she was. Look. I found this online. It's the chapel."

I pulled out the photograph I had found and gave it to her. She yawned and put it on the bed without even looking at it. I noticed her eyelids beginning to droop again so I spoke quickly.

"I've seen the chapel before. I've been dreaming about it for years. And yesterday something odd happened with this girl. I didn't understand it at first but now I do. They were here. They were here in Atlanta."

She was wide awake all of a sudden and propped up on her elbows, her almond-shaped eyes fixed on mine in a penetrating stare.

"Forget about the journal, Dallas." It wasn't like her to be this serious. "And stay away from that chapel."

I looked down, upset by the fact that she couldn't see

how important all of this was to me, to all of us Marshalls. I was quiet for a few moments as I tried to steady the heavy swell of disappointment.

"But the chapel," I said finally. "It's the only way I can prove that this is true. If I go there, I know I'll be able..."

"Chapel? What chapel? Would you just get to bed and leave me alone?"

I looked up quickly. She was lying on the bed with her eyes half closed again. "The chapel in her journal. You mentioned it just now."

"I didn't say anything about any damn chapel. What I said was that you need to get out of my room and let me get some sleep."

She had already turned over and pulled the pillow over her head but I didn't care because I felt a tingling excitement. She didn't remember mentioning the chapel. She didn't remember because she wasn't the one who had ordered me to stay away from it.

They were real and they were still in Atlanta.

I ran out of the room and into the bathroom.

After a quick shower, I got dressed and packed a few things before leaving a note for my aunt letting her know that I was going to Mississippi and would be back tomorrow night at the latest.

I felt an apprehensive giddiness when I jumped in my aunt's car and drove to the airport. I was about to do something that would change everything, not only for me, but for all of us Marshalls. All I had to do was get to the chapel.

***

After a very long and tiring morning filled with too many frustrations and minor setbacks, I found myself at the Holbert plantation house. They weren't doing any tours that day but, armed with my sketchpad, I tried to charm my way onto the property by telling the housekeeper I was an artist doing a very important project on old church buildings. But in the end it took a very large bribe to get permission to visit the chapel. The housekeeper, having tucked all the money I had brought with me in her shirt pocket, became suddenly helpful and even offered to take me there. But there was no need. I left the house and ducked into the trees, knowing exactly where I was going as if I had taken this path many times before.

It was a much longer walk through the woods than I had been expecting but at last I broke out of the trees and into the clearing. It was a slightly overcast day and heavy grey clouds hung over the clearing, adding to the aura of wretchedness that clung to the place. The chapel loomed before me amidst a tangle of wild grass. Even though many years had passed, it still had a sinister and forbidding aspect to it and I shivered as I took it in.

I was scared now and cold, even though it was a warm, sticky day. But I hadn't come all this way just to turn back, so I approached and only hesitated for a second before I pushed against the wooden door. It gave grudgingly and I walked into a cool dark space that smelt of burnt wood and damp and spoke of years of decay. The oppressive energy I had felt in the clearing was even stronger inside and I clearly felt the presence of the hundreds, perhaps thousands of people for whom this chapel had been the last thing they had seen before dying in agony and terror.

I exhaled a shaky breath. I was surprised Luna had not sensed this on the many occasions she had sought sanctuary in the chapel because the evil here was like a dark cloak that had wrapped itself around me. Needing to find whatever proof still existed here and leave, I quickly walked down the aisle to what was left of the altar, constantly looking over my shoulder and expecting to find something behind me each and every time. When I got to the altar, I knelt down and felt around, trying to find a loose floorboard. To my astonishment, I felt one shift slightly under my probing fingers and I pried it open, breaking two fingernails in the process.

I was expecting to see the money and the map Avery had left for Luna in case of emergencies, but instead I found a package carefully wrapped in a red silk scarf. I removed the scarf and uncovered a very old and tattered green book. It was the bible Luna had hidden here so very long ago. I stroked it in awe and then wrapped it back up in the scarf and put it carefully into my bag. I thought about staying and having a proper look around for other clues that they had existed, but the atmosphere was so claustrophobic and foreboding that I headed back outside into the daylight. Besides, the bible was all the proof I needed.

Back outside, I rubbed away at the dirt on my trousers and tried to get the sooty black stains off my fingers as I walked to the back of the chapel where the stream was waiting for me. I stared at it for the longest time, imagining Luna leaning over it in her despair whilst Avery watched from his hiding place in the trees. Being in this place made them seem so close that I could almost see them.

Inspired, I sat down on the grass and took out my notepad. I began to sketch the images that came into my mind. I sketched many pictures of the chapel and the stream from as many angles as I could, always inserting an image of Luna or Avery as I imagined them to look in my head. When my hand began to ache, I finally put my pencil down and saw that the sun was beginning to set. It wasn't the sizzling blood red sky Luna had been looking at the first time she had unwittingly come across Avery, but a sultry mix of dusky oranges and golds blotted by smoky grey clouds. I got up, not wanting to get lost in the woods once the sun set and plunged everything into darkness. Apprehensive now that it was almost dark, and I was still here with the evil that had cloaked this clearing in malevolence for centuries, I hurriedly gathered up all the loose sheaves of paper and slung my bag over my shoulder, then walked quickly toward the trees. In my haste, the drawings flew out of my hand and large sheets of paper floated softly to the ground around me.

"Damn it!" I mumbled, feeling quite anxious now as I scooped down to pick them up. In my uneasy glances over my shoulder, the chapel was like a silent wraith in the fading light.

I gathered up all the drawings but found that there was one missing, the sketch of Luna kneeling at the stream.

"I should have known you would come here despite my warning this morning."

I froze, my mouth suddenly dry and my scalp tingling. Even if it hadn't been for that unmistakable English accent I would have known that smooth, deep voice. Slowly, I straightened, feeling a degree of fear, because even though he had spoken softly, there had been an unmistakable edge in his tone.

A tall muscular white male was standing in the gloom cast by the trees. When he moved out of the shadows into the burning gold light of the setting sun and I saw him properly, I felt my heart leap. His hair was short now, framing an impossibly handsome face, and he wore a white T-shirt, faded jeans and white runners. He glanced briefly at the drawing of Luna kneeling by the stream, which he was holding in his left hand.

"This is very good, Dallas," he continued.

I couldn't speak. Luna had described him in her journal as handsome, beautiful and perfect. But there was really only one word to accurately describe this man. He was *fine!*

He stood there watching me carefully as if waiting for something. No, not waiting. *Listening.* Realising too late that those were not the kind of thoughts I should be thinking around someone who could read minds, I quickly looked down at the ground.

"I'll stop if you like," he said politely.

266

"No," I said quickly, unnerved and embarrassed. "I know so much about you, it's only fair I let you get to know me a little."

I thought I saw relief pass over his features but I couldn't be sure, especially since he appeared to be so stern.

"This isn't a safe place to be. Luna's journal should have taught you that, if nothing else."

"I know. But I had to come. And... and... this isn't the first time I've met you, is it?"

"No, it isn't. And although I usually make you forget our encounters, you always remember the moment you lay eyes on me again."

He was right. I was remembering everything now. The time I got lost in the mall at age five, he had been there. He had bought me an ice cream and waited with me until my nanny found me. There were many memories of him flitting through my mind now, most of them merely brief glimpses of him over the years but it seemed he had always been there.

"You were there last night, and it was you at the Candy Room that time. You took me home when Omar went off with that girl."

I had been only fourteen at the time, drunk, and maybe even a little bit high on something. Omar was twenty-five, liked young girls and drugs. When Omar left that night I had fallen asleep (well, passed out) in the ladies toilets and the next thing I remembered was being held up in Avery's arms as he tried to flag down a cab. He had spent the entire journey home lecturing me about my reckless, irresponsible behaviour whilst I gazed up at him adoringly, wishing he would stop talking and...

"Yes, I remember exactly what you were thinking that night. I don't need reminding," he said.

I smiled sheepishly, glad that my dark skin hid the warm blush that was spreading across my face.

"I want you to leave here, Dallas, and never come

267

looking for me again."

My smile disappeared. Slightly stung by his words, I fought back tears and tried to keep the emotion out of my voice.

"You... you're different from how she described you."

His face darkened. "That was some two hundred years ago. I'm nothing like I was then so don't mistake me for some gentle puppy like some of your other relatives have made the mistake of doing in the past. Now, go. I don't want you anywhere near the chapel when it gets dark."

"Wait," I said. There was a slightly petulant tone in my voice and I had one hand on my hip. "I want to see Luna before I go. I'm not leaving until I see her."

He flinched at the mention of her name. But when his gaze met mine, the anger dancing in his eyes made my heart quicken. For the first time I was reminded of the fact that I wasn't dealing with a man. I was dealing with a powerful superhuman being.

"I'm not going to ask you again, Dallas," he said.

Scared, I nodded and he held out the drawing to me.

But my thoughts were still on Luna, my curiosity piqued by his reaction when I'd mentioned her name. I may have been frightened but I considered these two beings my family now and it wasn't going to be easy for me to walk away from them. So when he held out the drawing a thought occurred to me. Something I had read in Luna's narrative. He had once described his body as living marble, so maybe, just maybe...

I moved toward him but instead of reaching for the drawing I quickly stepped past his outstretched hand and, closing the space between us, placed both hands on the side of his head.

He could have easily evaded my grasp but he merely stiffened slightly when my warm soft hands met his cool skin.

Images, *so many* images, came rushing at me in a furious whirl. It felt like I was at the heart of a tornado and

I almost released the hold I had on him, the intensity of the onslaught like a lump of hot coal in the middle of my brain.

There were too many for me to be able to decipher but most of the ones that I could make out were of Luna. Luna in the drawing room of their mansion, at times laughing or angry but mainly sitting quietly reading or writing in her journal. There was one of Avery at her side, the two of them the only thing standing between a large crowd of white males armed with guns and a household of blacks. Another powerful image was of Avery running through dark woodland, materialising behind Luna just in time to see her snap the neck of a dog before throwing it to the ground. Her laughter pierced the night as she used her telekinetic power to hoist a screaming white male up in the air whilst a group of runaways slowly backed away from the sight, not knowing of whom to be more afraid, the slave catcher or the demon that had saved them from torture or death. Another scene showed Avery looking through a shop window at a wedding dress and then that same wedding dress lying crumpled on the floor of a large, stately house.

The sharpest image, the one that had the strongest emotional attachment, emotions that were almost violent in their intensity, was of Avery standing on the wind – and rain – swept roof of a cathedral in London looking out into the night. Finally his gaze fell on someone who had taken something precious from him, a being who had hurt him more than he thought possible and whom he hated with a passion that went beyond life and death. He stood up, the long sword in his hand glinting in the moonlight and he gave chase.

I wanted to see more, I wanted to see who or what had caused him so much pain but the images were too numerous, too intense, the pain in my head growing until it felt as if I might buckle under the strain. Then I felt his hands on mine, pulling them away. The images receded, taking the pain along with them.

"Have you seen enough, Dallas?"

There was an undercurrent of anger in his tone but I noticed that he held onto my hands a few seconds longer than he needed to before he let them go.

My head was still swimming with all that I had seen and I was deeply shaken, not only by the intensity of those images, but the answers that had come with them.

Breathing heavily and with tears in my eyes, I gazed sadly up at him.

"She's dead?"

Again he looked down, struggling with it even now, although she had been dead for over forty years.

"Yes, she's dead." His voice was completely toneless but there was no denying the turmoil in his eyes.

I let the silence settle as the light faded around us, the hulking sinister presence of the chapel deepening the sadness that hung between us. At last he was able to meet my gaze again, a weary smile on his lips.

"You were so much easier to deal with when you were a child."

"Really?" I asked, surprised because I had been a little nightmare who had terrified both parents and the nannies they'd hired to care for me. Only Grandma had been able to cope with me.

His smile broadened, almost touching his eyes.

"Yes, you were a nightmare. But you were adorable. And you couldn't come looking for me then." He sighed heavily and the smile faded. "Go home, Dallas," he said gently. "Being near me has its price, something Luna came to see too late. So go home."

I blinked back the tears, struggling with my anger at being turned away but feeling an overwhelming compassion for him. He was in so much pain and I could see it was hard for him to even look at me, to look at anything connected to Luna. And he would live forever with this pain.

"Can I ask how you knew, yesterday, that I would be in trouble?"

He smiled again.

"Mama. We became friends in the years that followed. Even after her death, her spirit lingered and she tells me whenever I am needed by either my family or hers."

He held the drawing out to me again but I shook my head.

"It's yours."

He nodded. Unable to prolong the moment any longer, I said goodbye and although it was hard to do, I walked away from him.

Feeling his gaze on me as I walked into the woods, I decided that this wasn't over.

I'm going, Avery, I thought to myself, knowing full well that he could hear every word. I could even feel him reaching into my mind. *But I'm not leaving Mississippi. I'll be back and it won't be so easy for you to turn me away next time. So get ready, Avery. Get...*

Ready... ready?

Already...

It was already so late but I had no intention of staying in Mississippi overnight. Even if I had to spend most of the night at the airport, I was going to make sure I was on a flight back to Atlanta before morning.

Feeling a degree of relief now that I had made that decision, I hurried through the woods to my rental car. I couldn't explain why I felt so torn up or why I was clutching my drawings of the chapel. A part of me wanted to throw them away but the thought of doing so horrified me. When I got to the car I noticed that there were tears drying on my cheeks and I felt a sudden desperate urge to run back through the woods to the chapel. But, for what? I quickly got into the car. The sooner I was on a flight out of Mississippi, the better.

But before I drove off I took a moment to admire the setting sun and was momentarily filled with longing and an immense feeling of loss.

I shook it off as I pulled away from the plantation and made my way to the main road, barely noticing the heavens as night slowly pushed the day back and took over the sky once more.

Also by A. D. Koboah

PEACE

Peace Osei is young, beautiful – and addicted to heroin; the only thing that can keep painful past memories at bay. But when Mohamed, a past love, re-enters her life demanding answers to questions she is not ready to face, it threatens to send Peace swimming deeper into self-destructive waters. Having spent so long drifting away from the real world, can Peace find the strength to face the past and banish her demons?

Out September 2012.

Visit the author at www.adkoboah.co.uk

Made in the USA
San Bernardino, CA
01 April 2013